The Ex-Wives

The Ex-Wives

DEBORAH MOGGACH

HEINEMANN : LONDON

First published in Great Britain 1993
by William Heinemann Ltd
an imprint of Reed Consumer Books Ltd
Michelin House, 81 Fulham Road, London sw3 6rb
and Auckland, Melbourne, Singapore and Toronto

A CIP catalogue record for this book
is available at the British Library
isbn 0 434 47351 0 (Hardback)
isbn 0 434 47352 9 (Paperback)

Phototypeset by Intype, London
Printed in Great Britain
by Clays Ltd, St. Ives PLC

'I don't think I'll get married again.
I'll just find a woman I don't like
and give her a house.'

Lewis Grizzard

For Max Eilenberg, Mike Shaw and Rochelle Stevens

One

Buffy was sitting in what he still insisted on calling the saloon bar of his local, The Three Fiddlers. The racing commentary was drowned by the noise of a drill. Outside, as usual, they were digging up the road. This time, according to one of those self-congratulatory *Bringing It To Your Community* placards, they were laying down cable TV. The noise of the drilling was joined by the hooting of cars, stuck in the inevitable traffic jam this caused at the junction with the Edgware Road. He was feeling mulish and dyspeptic. Despite his post-breakfast sachet of Fybogel his bowels had failed to move that morning; nor had his first Senior Service, inhaled vigorously into his lungs, had its usual, prompt effect.

He gazed into his foam-laced, empty glass. He was feeling his age, whatever that meant. Depending on his mood, *sixty-one* shifted both ways – *only sixty-one* and *my God, sixty-one*. Today it was *my God*. Events had conspired to irritate him, an elderly reaction he knew, but still. First there was the bowel business, or non-business. Then, when he had gone out on this glorious summer's day he had had another undeniably elderly reaction: how did young girls manage to wear such indescribably hideous clothes? Once he had looked forward to hot weather, revealing, as it did, achingly tender shoulders, slim legs and promising hints of cleavage. Now girls cropped their hair and wore those awful, awful boots. Those with the most monumental buttocks wore luminous shorts; the slim ones, on the other hand, enveloped themselves in drooping layers of black, like Greek grannies. And

1

he himself, of course, was entirely invisible. Not a flicker from them. Nothing.

It was then, when he was looking at the only recognisably female woman, that he had tripped up on an upturned paving stone, outside his block of flats, and almost taken a header. Blasted TV cables. Testily, he reflected upon choice. Nowadays, choice had been removed in the things that mattered, like saloon and public bars. Once harmlessly divided into two sections, two pungent little microcosms of society which one could visit at will, depending upon one's finances and the presence of a female companion, pubs had now been knocked-through and neutered – Tony Blackburned into a mid-Atlantic no man's land of bleeping machines and androgynous creatures probably working in PR. On the other hand, there seemed to be a proliferation of choice in what one already had too much of anyway. Take lager. Nowadays there were about a million different brands, the more obscure the better – he should know, he'd done the voice-over for one from East Senegal or somewhere – who needed them? Though of course the repeat fees were welcome.

And then there were all these TV channels, cable and things, popping up when it was flustering enough keeping up with the four one already had, especially now they had a video and Penny kept recording *The Clothes Show* over his *Palm Beach Story*. And then self-righteously blaming *him* because he apparently hadn't labelled it.

'I don't see why you make such a fuss' she said, 'you never get around to watching all those boring old films anyway. It's so anal, darling, to hoard.'

'I just like to know they're there. It's like church.'

'But you never go to church.'

'Exactly. But I know I could, if I wanted. It's *there*.'

She had tossed her shiny hair and clipped shut her brief-case. Then paused. She had stood still, like a fox, scenting a rabbit a long way off, through the undergrowth. Her nostrils flared. *Maybe she could write a piece on it*. That's what she was thinking. He knew her so well. Maybe one of her cuddly,

2

tabloid *Aren't Men the End?* pieces, with blush-making references to himself; maybe something for a woman's glossy, *Cosmopolitan* or something, *Ten New Grounds for Divorce*. An amused, middle-class think-piece for *The Times*. She spread her talents widely. My God, she even wrote for *High Life* – one of the ten grounds for divorce, in his opinion.

But Penny was in Positano, writing a travel piece for somebody or other. She was writing a lot of travel pieces lately. This, of course, was the real reason for his irritability. It was lonely, shuffling along to Marks and Sparks to buy a *Serves One* meal. By now he knew them by heart. *Cumberland Fish Pie* – disappointing, too much potato; *Lasagne* – a bit ersatz but okay. They reminded him of periods in his life he preferred to forget. Besides, there was never quite enough in a *Serves One* so he usually bought a *Serves Two*, which was just too much, of course, but being greedy he always ate the lot, scraping out the foil dish, and then fell heavily asleep, waking in the middle of the night with heartburn. Then there was the wine problem. A half-bottle wasn't nearly enough, of course, not nearly. But a whole bottle was marginally too much, with the same results except when he woke it was with a flaming throat and palpitations. When Penny was there it was fine; she was a light drinker which meant he could polish off practically the whole bottle but not quite.

Besides, he liked to chat. He liked her breezing in from the outside world, tut-tutting at the mess and half-listening to the events of his afternoon. She was invigorating, in a vaguely abstracted way. She had breeding – her father was a brigadier – and a Home Counties gloss to her, she sorted things out and got things done. She could be good company – amusing, full of gossip – especially when there were other people present; when they were alone she was inclined to boss him about. She was at her best with workmen – good-natured but firm and authoritative; rather the way she handled him, in fact. Otherwise she treated him the way she treated the dog – with brisk testiness, especially when he got under her feet or stood in front of the fridge.

3

He wasn't good at being alone. He got bored. He missed the bickering, the sulks, even the hours she spent on the phone when he was trying to watch the TV. Scents in the bathroom – perfumes she got as promotional freebies – lingered for days after her departures. Actually, they didn't exactly remind him of her; they reminded him of some idealized female presence, the sort of woman he had never met, and certainly never married. The sort of woman who cooked him dinner unresentfully and laughed at his anecdotes even though she had heard them before; who didn't record over his videos. Who didn't call him 'darling' with an edge to it; why did women only use endearments when they were particularly irritated, or trying to make some sort of point?

He got to his feet. George's tail thumped; he got up, with difficulty, and gazed up at Buffy, his eyes moist with devotion. Why had no woman, in all these years, ever looked at him quite like that?

Buffy bought another pint from the landlord. He was new, an impossibly tanned, athletic type. God knew why he had decided to run a pub. The world was becoming filled with handsome, vigorous young men. They sprang up from nowhere, or sometimes from Australia, and ran the sort of enterprises that seemed vaguely beneath them; the sort of businesses which used to be run by boring old geezers you could rely on to be there year in year out, for ever. These new ones all looked as if they had just dropped in to do you a favour. This particular one was called Curtis, he had heard the name, but the moment had passed when he could have called him Curtis, casually, and now it was too late.

Buffy sat down; George sank to the floor. Penny seemed to have been away for ages; in fact she had only been gone for two days. The trouble with these absences was that you had to be particularly nice to the person before they departed, and particularly nice to them for quite a while after they returned; it gave a marriage an unnatural glaze, a stagey feel. Also, because they had been abroad it made everything you had done seem even more petty and trivial than usual. If

4

that was possible. She always returned tanned and somehow taller – he forgot how tall she was until he saw her again. Radiant, too, but full of complaints to make him feel better. 'Christ, the hotel . . . more like a building site . . . bull-dozers, mud . . . We had to watch a fashion display, three hours, would you believe it they all wore *flares* . . . almost as bad as folk dancing, no, not quite, nothing's as bad as that . . . then we had this nightmarish rum'n'rhumba evening . . . Shirley got totally paralytic, you know, she's the one from *Family Circle* . . . and everyone had the most appalling hangovers the next day . . .'

She brought him back things to eat – obscure Greek sweet-meats wrapped in foil, Sicilian anchovies, things that leaked in her suitcase. He was touched by this, of course, but it made him feel like a housewife whose husband was returning home. This in turn let to the inevitable operational hitches once they had gone to bed. The longer she had been away, the more honour-bound he felt to attempt some sort of sexual congress on her return. After some dampish fiddling around they both knew they would never get any sleep this way, it could go on for hours. 'Don't worry,' she'd whisper, 'I'm totally zonked, anyway.'

Two

Celeste. Charming name, charming girl. Celeste, handing round chicken sandwiches. It was a hot day in July; the day of her mother's funeral.

Celeste lived in Melton Mowbray. She was twenty-three, an only child, now orphaned by her mother's final shuddering breath. She had an only child's tended look, and indeed had been dearly loved. She smelt of soap. Her hair was cropped short, and there were small gold studs in her ears. Her fragile grace and inky eyes gave her the look of an antelope, startled by an intruder, but like all impressions this was partially misleading. In fact she had a stubborn streak, and was very good at maths. Her nimble fingers had made her Cats Cradle Champion at her primary school. She was logical. Columns of figures were to be one of her few reassurances in the tumultuous year that lay ahead. Buffy was deeply impressed, when he first saw her, by the way she cupped a phone to her ear, wedging it with her shoulder, whilst with her free hands she wrapped his numerous pharmaceutical purchases in plastic bags and rang them up at the till. He was hopeless at that sort of thing.

In those days Celeste wore angora sweaters in pastel colours. Sometimes, when she cycled, she wore a track suit. Fashion, that collusion of narcissists, did not engage her interest for she was a solitary person and her pleasures were solitary ones – swimming in the local baths, her stinging eyes blind to the gaze of the lifeguard; bicycling; biting the bits of skin around each of her fingernails, one by one. If she had

6

neuroses she was unaware of them, for her family had no words for stuff like that, nor sought them because they were nothing but trouble. They led a quiet life. She wore a gold crucifix around her neck but the reason for this, the fathoms of faith it crystalized, were so far largely unexamined too. She was an innocent, something still possible in Leicestershire.

The lounge was crowded with mourners. *Mourners*. She had to fit this unfamiliar word to the faces. Some of them were relatives she had never seen before, and would never see again. Amongst the people there were several large men from Ray-Bees Plumbing Services. They fingered the mantle-piece ornaments that from now onwards, for ever, it would be her job to dust. Though chronically unreliable – 'Don't get rabies!' was a cry that had once confused her – they had turned up *en masse* for the funeral, probably as a skive. Her mum used to clean their offices.

Celeste went into the kitchen to fetch the stuffed eggs. She unpeeled the cling film; it shrivelled, and stuck to the down on her arm. She wanted to ask her mother the names of the relatives in the other room, but simultaneously she knew this was impossible. Post still arrived for her mother, wasn't this strange? Envelopes addressed to Mrs Constance Smith, one of them offering her the exciting chance of winning a Vauxhall Astra. There was a burst of laughter from the next room; funerals can be surprisingly jovial affairs. She longed for them all to go, and yet she dreaded the moment when they would leave.

She carried the stuffed eggs into the lounge. The noise changed; under the voices she could hear the low murmur of condolence, like another instrument, a cello, being added to an orchestra. 'Let me take those.' 'Why don't you sit down?' 'Budge up, Dennis!' She was Connie's little girl and what was she going to do with herself now? *Orphan* was like mourner, a new word she had to fit to herself. A word she had to be fitted up with, like a surgical implant, for life.

The air thickened with cigarette smoke. 'Little mole on his cheek,' she heard. 'Brand new candelabra.' There was a stirring. 'What time did you order that minicab, Irene?' Upstairs, in the wardrobe, hung her mother's clothes. They would remain there, hanging. Each time she visited they would remain in exactly the same order. If, that is, she could bring herself to open the door. She had no idea it would be like this; that death would change all her mother's possessions – transform each one of them into something charged and motionless. Objects that were meaningless and yet impossible to touch, as if a spell had been put on them.

In the end, of course, she had to do something about it all. She took a week off work, to sort things out. Shoes were the saddest, with their dear, empty bunion bumps. Scrawled recipe cards were the worst, in her mother's handwriting. So was anything her mother had repaired doggedly, with bits of sellotape. So was everything. Celeste felt frail and elderly; she did it slowly, and had to sit down a lot. Outside there was the blast from a radio as Stan next door repaired his car; she didn't even know what day of the week it was. She emerged like an invalid, blinking in the sunshine. She was numb but surprisingly enough she still noticed things, as if she had a secretary beside her, taking notes. What was this new cereal called Cinnamon Toasts? Why did the scratchy beat of Walkmen always sound the same, as if everyone was listening to exactly the same pop song, all over Britain? Who could answer her questions now?

She was basically a cheerful sort of person and grief was like a foreign and alarming country, visited by other people but never by herself. The death of her father didn't really count because she was only six at the time. She must be in that country now, though it didn't affect her as she had imagined, the landscape didn't look like the brochures, and she couldn't recollect the exact moment when she had crossed the frontier. In some ways she felt exactly the same, though Wanda, who lived opposite, said she looked awful and how about coming over for a spot of supper, they were having Turkey Thighs Honolulu? Douggie was cooking it, with tinned pineapples not fresh, but what else could you expect in a dump like this?

Celeste ate heartily. She had always had a good appetite and it seemed to persist through everything, like traffic lights still working when a city has been evacuated. Wanda wore a purple leotard; below her freckled cleavage her breasts looked as tight and glossy as plums. She was a bit of a goer; her husband Douggie had had a vasectomy.

'Why don't you go to London?' she asked.

'Why?' asked Celeste.

'Why not? Want to be stuck *here* all your life? God, I'd do anything to get away.' She sighed. People confided in Celeste nowadays, more than they used to do. Her bereavement had made them readier to pour out their own complaints, maybe to keep her company. She had learnt a lot about other people's troubles these past few weeks. 'Sub-let the maisonette' said Wanda.

Celeste felt nauseous. 'I can't decide things like that.' She couldn't decide what *clothes* to wear in the mornings. Such an effort. Tonight she felt stupid and sluggish, like an amoeba; like some lowly, spongey form of life that only flinched when prodded. She felt sleepy all the time. Was this grief?

She walked home, across the street. Behind her it darkened; the porch light was switched off, in Wanda and Douggie's house. She let herself into the empty hallway. Silence. This was the worst part; coming home. If she had switched on the radio she would have heard Buffy's voice reading the Book at Bedtime ('Ivanhoe') but she never listened to Radio 4. She went upstairs, past the closed door of her mother's bedroom, and brushed her teeth. Wanda was right; she was alone in the world now, she could do anything. She could give in her notice at Kwik-Fit Exhausts. The overall'd men there, joshing around, seemed big and oily and threatening now; the word 'fuck' made her flinch.

Suddenly she felt dizzy. She sat down, abruptly, on the lavatory seat. This panic, it had struck her several times in the past few days. It resembled the panic she felt when she repeated the same word – 'basin', say, or 'sausages' – over and over until it became meaningless, except it applied to every word in her head. It was as if knitting had been unravelled and she couldn't work out how to bundle it together again and push it back into some kind of shape. Oh, for those safe days of cats' cradles! She gazed at the tiles her Dad had plastered around the bath. Every third, and sometimes fifth, tile had a shell printed on it. As a child she had tried to work out the inexplicable, adult reason for this but she had never asked him; the minute she had left the bathroom she had forgotten all about it and now it was too late. Her own name, Celeste, seemed strange to her. *Celeste*. So utterly unlikely.

It was a stifling night. Across England, people slept fitfully. Buffy grunted, exhaling a rubbery snore. He was dreaming of toppling columns. Children had kicked off their duvets; they lay, breathing hoarsely, their damp hair painted onto their foreheads. Dogs lay on downstairs rugs, their legs twitching with the voltage of their hunts. Celeste lay, dewy between her chaste white sheets, unaware of the clock that was already ticking, that would transform both her past and her future, and take the decision about going to London out of her hands.

The next morning, two days after the funeral, she knew she could put it off no longer. She had to tackle the stuff in the sideboard drawer. Shoeboxes and envelopes and tins full of paperwork. She lifted them out and spread them over the floor – old bills and letters, yellowing guarantees for long-vanished appliances. Careful, biro'd sums in her mother's writing. Now she knew why she had been so reluctant to start this. It made her mother so completely dead.

She opened a biscuit tin – Crawford's Teatime Assortment. Inside it were some old post office books, Spanish pesetas, odds and ends. And an envelope. *Celeste*.

Later, she would remember the moment when she picked up the envelope. The ache in her thighs from kneeling on the floor; the sunlight on the carpet. The thud, thud of a ball in the street outside; it was a Saturday, she was only aware of it then. The different, ringing thud when the football bounced on a car.

She opened the envelope. Inside it was a letter in her mother's handwriting. And a small gold fish.

Three

None of the usual doddery old regulars was in the pub that day – the four or five men who made even Buffy feel sprightly. He drained his glass and walked out, blinking, into the sunshine. Penny was due back from Positano the next day, flying into Heathrow at some time or other. Eight years ago, that was how they met. They had both been what was coyly called 'between relationships' at the time – i.e., in his case, bloody lonely. He had been in L.A., the loneliest place on earth, working on a pilot for a TV series that in fact never got made.

He noticed her on the plane: shiny chestnut hair, cut in a bob; it swung when she moved. Silk blouse. Her head bent over one of those portable computer things hardly anybody had then. A look of high-powered, total absorption in what she was doing that posed a challenge to a chap. Very attractive.

After the meal he had made his way to the loo, and got pinioned against her seat by the duty-free trolley; even in those days he was by no means slim enough to squeeze past. He had bent down to her and whispered: 'Why is it, when the duty-free trolley comes round, is it pushed by a steward you've *never seen before*. And *never see again*? During the entire flight?' She had laughed and whispered 'They keep them in a special storage compartment.'

The plane landed and they bumped into each other in the terminal. He was trying to smuggle in some particularly fine bottles of Napa Valley claret and, approaching the *Nothing to*

Declare part of customs with his clanking carrier bags, he had tapped her on the shoulder. 'Be a sport, and bring these through.' She was a sport, she did. For all she knew the bags could have been full of IRA guns. Full marks to her; she carried them through with that upper-class confidence, that stop-me-if-you-dare, little man look which he had always found impressive in a woman, especially when directed at someone else.

Once safely through he had introduced himself. 'Russell Buffery,' he said, shaking her hand.

Her face lit up. 'I thought I recognized the voice! Golly, you don't look like I expected.'

People were always saying that. What did they mean? What on earth were they expecting? He had never liked to ask.

'You were such a marvellous Mr Pickwick,' she said. 'I was in bed with glandular fever, I heard all the episodes. Glandular fever takes that long.'

So they shared a cab into London. She said she was a journalist and she wanted to do him for one of those *My Room* things in one of the colour supplements. He gave her his address: a mansion block in Little Venice. Well, Maida Vale.

On the appointed day she turned up, with a photographer. She wore a white linen suit; she looked as brisk and business-like as a staff nurse. He adored nurses. On the threshold of the living room she stopped and stared. 'My God, what a pigsty!' She wandered around the room, stepping over the various items strewn on the carpet. Her eyes were wide with wonder – admiration, almost. 'People usually clean up for days before we arrive.'

It looked perfectly all right to him – in fact, he *had* tidied it up a bit – but he sensed he was onto something here. Something powerful. *Pity*. It was here to be tapped.

'My ex-wife threw me out, you see. I ended up in this place. Blomfield Mansions is full of redundant husbands, a human scrap heap.' His voice rose, his rich brown voice.

Molasses, tawny port, liqueur chocolate dripped through honeycomb – all these comparisons had been made. His voice-box had brought pleasure to thousands, seen and unseen – millions, maybe. It was without a doubt his most reliable organ, where women were concerned. 'They fester here, crippled by alimony,' he throbbed. 'They sit alone in the pub, gazing at polaroid photographs of their childrens' birthday parties they've been banished from attending. They sit in the launderama watching, through the cyclops eye of the washing machine, their single, bachelor bedsheet turning, entwined with their pair of Y-fronts, a parody of the embraces they had once known . . .' He stopped. Maybe this was a bit over the top. But no; her face had become softer, blunter somehow. Even the photographer had sat down heavily in the one good armchair and was fumbling for his cigarettes.

'At night they wander the streets, watching young men buying bunches of flowers at the Top Price Late Nite Store; young men, clutching a bottle of wine, eagerly springing up front steps and pressing the bell of their beloved. They pass pubs whose windows, nowadays tactlessly unfrosted, display tableaux of loving couples who, between kisses, argue playfully about what film they're going to see that night, ringing their choices with biro in their outspread copies of *Time Out*.'

Her eyes were moist; so were his. When she switched on her tape recorder, her fingers trembled. 'Tell me about your little room,' she said.

It wasn't little, actually; it was quite large. But she was obviously deeply affected. He had her now; he was an actor, after all. George Kaufman had said: if you hook your audience in the first ten minutes, you've got them for the play. And dammit, this story was true. He himself was quite over-whelmed.

'Of course, she kept most of the furniture,' he said, kicking aside some takeaway containers as he crossed the room. 'Except one or two family heirlooms even *she* didn't have the

gall to nick, mostly because they're so hideous.' He pointed
to the sideboard. 'That was my granny's. The door's broken,
where she kicked it in.'

'Your granny?'

'No no. Jacquetta. My ex-wife. We were having a row.' He
pointed to the wall. 'This is the only picture she let me keep.
An incredibly dull lithograph of my old Oxford college.'

Penny nodded. 'It is dull, isn't it.' She picked up a piece
of pizza crust. 'Shall I throw this away?'

He nodded. 'I always leave the edge, don't you?' He
pointed out the curious china object that the cast had given
him when he had played *Lear* in Hartlepool; could she make
out what it was? She couldn't.

He went to the mantlepiece, moved aside a bottle of Bells,
and pointed to a photo. 'These are my sons, Bruno and
Tobias.'

'Aren't they sweet!'

'I've got some more, somewhere.'

'More what?'

'Children. Older than this, though.'

She looked at the two smiling faces in the tarnished frame.
'When do you see them?'

'Weekends. When she lets me.'

She pointed to a glass tank. 'What's this?'

'Their stick insects.'

She peered into the wilting foliage. 'Where are they?'

'Difficult to spot them. You see, they keep quite still and
they look just like sticks. Sometimes I look in there and think:
maybe that's the way to go through life – in camouflage, not
moving. The only way to avoid the pain.'

That did it. She was his. And within a month she had
moved in.

Pulling George behind him, Buffy made his way along the
parade of shops. Eight years had passed since then. Abercorn
Hardware had become the Video Palace. There were Arabic
newspapers at the newsagents, and kiwi fruit, each with

a little 50p sticker on it, outside what was once a proper greengrocers but was now Europa Food and Wine. 50p each! Schoolboys sauntered, sucking ice lollies; they seemed to be let out at all hours of the day, now. One of them said: 'It was him what stole it. I was well gutted.'

What did he mean by that? *Well gutted*. Buffy had to keep in the swim, for the sake of his sons. Bruno and Tobias were teenagers now; they had put stick insects behind them. They mustn't think of him as an old fuddy-duddy. He had a suspicion they found him vaguely dated and irrelevant, like an ionizer.

It was hot. The workmen had gone, leaving paving stones stacked like dominoes and treacherous pits of sand. George suddenly stopped, pulling Buffy back; he lifted his leg and relieved himself against a length of plastic piping. The sign above him said: *Sorry for Any Inconvenience*.

Buffy chuckled. He must remember to tell Penny that. She would be home soon, and everything would be all right. He was hopeless at being alone. Without her invigorating company he felt rudderless and bereft . . . Had any of his wives ever felt the same way about him?

For some reason this made him feel irritable again. He glared at a car, double-parked outside the dry cleaners. It was empty; its engine was running, filling the air with exhaust fumes. There was a baby seat inside. On the back window was a sticker saying: *Keep Your Distance! Give My Child a Chance!*

Buffy stood, transfixed. He read it again. Car stickers in general irritated him, of course – from the leery *Honk If You Had It Last Night* to the prissy *I'm Lead-Free, Are You?* But this one, for some reason, filled him with an almost apoplectic rage. It was so bloody self-righteous, that was why.

A woman came out of the dry cleaners, carrying a plastic bag. She stopped, and stared at him. 'Can I help you?' She looked him up and down. He looked down. It was only then that he realized he was still wearing his bedroom slippers.

Four

Penny wasn't in Positano. She was in a flat in Soho, three miles up the road, lying spreadeagled over a man called Colin. He was asleep. Sun glowed through the blinds; the room was bathed in that soupy twilight known only to invalids and adulterers. She wasn't the sort of person who usually went to bed in the afternoon. The street sounds below – a car door slamming, the idling mutter of a taxi cab, waiting for somebody – they had a sharp, tinny echo. Guilt did that. The sounds could come from another country. In fact, she was supposed to *be* in another country. She had spread out her guide books, fanwise, on the rush matting of Colin's floor. Berlitz, Baedeker, Penguin. Glancing at them, she wrote in her notebook.

Positano, the haunt of sybarites and sun-worshippers, is still the Med's best-kept secret. Its winding, cobbled streets offer breathtaking vistas of the wine-dark ocean . . . Down below a car alarm sounded, *hee-haw . . . Braying donkeys tippety-tap down the lanes, carrying picturesque panniers of local produce . . .* Lazily, she ran her finger over Colin's hard, broad shoulder. *Towering, majestic cliffs . . .* she wrote, *terraced with vineyards and olive groves, and charming pink dwellings . . .* She ran her finger down his back . . . *dropping to a rocky shore far below . . .* She slid her hand between his legs. *. . . where boulders nestle between the luxuriant foliage of the bougainvillea . . .*

Colin grunted, and shifted. She moved, her skin unsticking from his. It was very hot; the Pentel was slippery in her hand. She had arrived at Naples now, *bustling and cosmopolitan, home*

17

to superb museums and 499 churches, a city that bestows its favours generously but that only opens its heart to the cognoscenti . . . She sipped her tea; it was stewed. *Sitting at a bustling pavement café in the Palazzo Reale I treated myself to a welcome glass of their refreshing local wine, Lacryma Christi del Vesuvio . . .*

She thought: *Penny Warren took a mid-week bargain break, departing Gatwick and flying to Soho, still London's best-kept secret, where she travelled from the bedroom to the bathroom, returning from the bathroom to the bedroom courtesy of Sunspot Holidays Ltd . . .*

Colin mumbled into the pillow: 'Your elbow's digging.'

'Sorry.' She removed her arm. She was so apologetic with him; despite her hard elbows she felt softer, more yielding.

'Where've you got to?'

'Sorrento.'

She lay slumped across his hard buttocks, her Pentel poised. The sheer *thisness* of what was happening made her stomach contract. Until she met Colin she hadn't committed adultery; she hadn't had time. She had written lots of pieces about it, of course: *Infidelity, Do's and Don'ts. Lipstick on his Collar,* God, how corny. *It's Your Affair – the Cosmo Guide to Extra-Marital Manners.* But then she had written pieces about everything. She mostly wrote for women's magazines and the women's pages of newspapers, cunningly disguised as *You* or *Living* though everyone knew that only women read them. She had been doing it for twenty years now. She was brisk and reliable, or she had been until recently. She knew where to lunch, and what sort of mineral water to order. She knew the difference between collagen and silicone. She thought she knew everything. She ruthlessly plundered her friends' lives for copy and cross-questioned their adolescent children about the latest trends. Despite her Sloaney shoes and Conran suits she knew what 'well gutted' meant. She knew all the fashion designers by their first names and went to the memorial services for their boyfriends. She held the fort in editorial offices when somebody took time off briefly – very briefly – to have a baby, or when they took a bit

18

longer off to write a sex-and-shopping novel they got their colleagues to plug. This was what she was like, this Penny who took the tube to work and taxis at lunchtime, who breezed through London unaware, who juggled a demanding husband and a busy freelance career, who thought she knew everything.

Until now. She didn't know about this. She had no idea it would feel like this. The simple fact of another man's hands on her skin, the smell of him. The pole-axing body of him. His breath in her ear. His damp balls beneath her tenderly kneading fingers. All this. The other Penny he awakened, who was always there but she didn't know it, who surrendered herself up to him – softer, more yielding, nicer. Who charted his moles between her outstretched forefinger and thumb, wondering at anything so humdrum, but not humdrum to her. Who rubbed her chin against his stubble. What was this, pheremones? Had she written a piece about them yet? It was exhilarating to be so lost, and yet discovered. It was terrifying.

This simply wouldn't do, she knew that. Her mother would be appalled; she would advance on Colin with her secateurs. Buffy would be – she mustn't think of Buffy. Even calling him a demanding husband made her feel guilty. Demanding was much too simple a word, even she knew that; marriage was more complicated than that. But you tried to make your husband simple, the equation an understandable one. When Colin called Buffy a boozy old fraud she bristled with hastily-assembled loyalty, but she was grateful, too. It made her position clearer, as if it were printed in one of her magazines. *P. W. – let us call her that – is a successful career woman and has been married eight years to a man fifteen years her senior. Once a well-known Shakespearean actor, his career had suffered a decline, due to domestic complications and a reputation for drink, and he was now known mainly for his mellow tones extolling the benefits of Rot-Away Damp Proof Courses. Was his a huge talent tragically squandered or a very small talent ruthlessly exploited? Time alone*

19

will tell. All P. W. discovered was that as her career prospered, his stagnated, that while she changed and grew, becoming a strong, independent woman in charge of her own life, etc etc, how many times had she written this, *he needed more from her than she was prepared to give. Like many men, a seemingly strong exterior* (in his case, pretty fat) *concealed inner insecurities and a man out of touch with his feelings. As the years passed she realized that instead of marrying a father-figure she had in fact married a child.*

Oh, God, this made her feel even more guilty. It was a wholly new sensation, like the first twinges of shingles. She wasn't used to having a conscience. She was a *journalist*. Journalists are born without a conscience, like certain car engines are constructed without a fan belt. She was tough, wasn't she? From strangers, she had extracted humiliating personal confessions; from public figures she had dug out revelations of bisexual encounters. One of her best friends hadn't spoken to her since being featured in one of her most successful series, *Me and My Depression*. That's what journalists *did*. They fiddled their expenses; they never paid for a holiday in their lives. It was part of their job description. She had had the country cottage totally redecorated, and a large Victorian conservatory added, for a feature that she had never got round to writing at all.

Poor Buffy. She was really very fond of him. Like communism in Eastern Europe, her marriage was suddenly crumbling so fast that she couldn't keep up with it. She was betraying her husband with chilling efficiency. She had been away on six trips now, packing her suitcase with suitable clothes for the South of France or the Norwegian fjords, ostentatiously – probably too ostentatiously – hunting for her passport, casually dropping the names of the imaginary hacks whose drunken exploits she would catalogue upon her return. Kissing Buffy goodbye, with Judas lips, and hailing a cab in the Edgware Road.

She travelled straight here, of course, to her other life. If it was an early morning flight Colin would still be in bed. Dumping her luggage on the floor she would tear off the clothes she had just put on and joyfully join him on his futon. For the three or four days of her trip she didn't dare leave the flat, in case somebody saw her. It was Colin who went out for supplies, and to buy the relevant guide books for her to crib. She had once written a piece about a man with two families, neither of which knew about the other's existence. She had called it *The Man who Ate Two Christmas Dinners*. In fact, he had to eat so many meals twice that he put on three stone and both women finally fell out of love with him and ran away with other men. But she had learnt some valuable tips about the mechanics of the whole operation. The alibis. Well, lies. The construction, in her head, of a whole scenario she came to half-believe in herself, with its own cast of colourful characters. She felt like Trollope, or someone. There was Shirley from *Family Circle*, and Coral from *Chat* who always went down with migraine. Then there was Hamish Dimchurch – God knows how she had thought up the name but she felt she knew him quite well by now. Hamish Dimchurch was a sozzled old freeloader who worked for *Catering Today* and who cropped up in all her stories simply because Buffy always asked about him – maybe he recognized a kindred spirit. 'Was that old rogue Hamish there?' he would ask eagerly.

Something wet was running down her face. It was tears. Surprised, she wiped her nose and sat up. She hardly ever cried. She looked at Colin's prone, naked body, the new pattern of hairs she was only just getting used to – thick on his legs and a little trail down his lower back. He was still asleep. Her husband liked chatting but Colin hardly talked at all; that was one of the things that had attracted her to him in the first place. Buffy was like the dog; he followed her around the flat, telling her the plot of some old movie he had been watching that afternoon on the TV – Gene Tierney in *The Razor's Edge*, stuff like that. He adored old films and knew the names of everybody; he had even worked with some of them. She should never have married an actor, everybody said they were impossible – egocentric, childish.

21

She was crying properly now; loud, dry sobs. She got up and took her tea mug into the kitchen. Her legs were bendy from lovemaking; her hipbones felt sore from Colin's incredibly hard futon. He was too young to mind about things like comfort. Buffy, on the other hand, was a martyr to his back. When he had tried to seduce her, that first time, he had said: 'You've just got to try out my new orthopaedic mattress.'

She pulled off a piece of kitchen roll and blew her nose. She mustn't wonder what he was doing, and how he was managing without her. That way madness lay. After all, she had slipped from him and he hadn't even noticed. What sort of marriage was that? It was the most peculiar sensation, falling in love with somebody else. She felt nauseous all the time. Her rib-cage ached. She felt as if her spirit had moved out of Blomfield Mansions and only a husk remained there, like a pupa whose butterfly had flown. She probably looked all right to Buffy, from the outside. But if he prodded her, she would collapse.

In the next room, Colin got up. Hurriedly she wiped her eyes. He wandered in and levered open a bottle of lager. His body looked damp; his cock hung red and raw. He looked well-used.

'Why are photographers so hairy?' she asked. 'I've often wondered.'

'Hey, how many've you seen like this?'

'None, I told you. But they all wear Paul Smith jackets with the sleeves rolled up, and you can tell by their wrists.'

He crooked his arm around her neck. 'Come and live with me, or I'll do my karate chop.'

'Oh, what's going to happen to us?'

He didn't reply. She looked at her watch; the adulterer's reflex gesture.

It was convenient, Colin living in Soho. Despite the ravages of redevelopment there were still some of the old speciality shops left. On the last day of her trip she would go out and buy stuff to bring home – *kephtédés* and *hummus* if she had been to Greece; salt cod, from a place near Brewer Street, if she had been to Portugal. It was risky, of course, because she might be spotted by somebody coming out of the Groucho Club, but she couldn't bear to let Colin do it – not this. Making love to him was bad enough, but sending him out to buy food for Buffy seemed in even poorer taste.

On Thursday she went out to Camisas and bought some Neopolitan specialities – buffalo mozzarella, *prosciutto* and tiny, ethnic-looking olives. She packed them in her suitcase. Then she rubbed some Sudden Tan cream onto her face, and typed up her copy on her portable 'Tosh. She didn't feel guilty about this – who cared if she actually went to Italy or not? Most of her fellow hacks spent their entire time in the hotel bar anyway, and cribbed it up on the flight home. Besides, her copy would probably be subbed down to 300 words, or maybe cut altogether if there was a last-minute ad. No, this part of the operation just gave her the pleasant, prickly sensation of petty lawlessness, like feeding foreign coins into a parking meter. Nothing more than that.

She closed her laptop with a click. She was dressed in her travelling outfit, ready to leave. In the other room, Colin was watching TV. There was an advertising jingle, then Buffy's voice boomed out, loud and clear: 'Baileys Babywipes. Big absorbency, for little bottoms.'

'Turn it off!' she yelled.

She dragged her luggage down the stairs. Colin kissed her goodbye, in the hallway. She nuzzled the gold hoop in his ear.

'Come on, Pen,' he said, 'make up your mind.'

'How'll he manage without me? He'd be lost.'

'Don't listen to that helpless crap. He's a ruthless old bugger. He'll survive.'

She held him, tightly. It still surprised her, to embrace such a slim man. She was forty-six. Was it fashionable, at her age, to have a toy boy? She had written pieces about it. On the other hand she had written just às many pieces on the advantages of an older man. He ran his lips over her face.

'Don't!' she said. 'My tan'll come off.'

She sat in the cab as it crawled up Regent Street. When did *having an affair* become *leaving your husband*? They were two such different things. She hadn't realized this until now. It was like sexual intercourse and childbirth; one might lead to the other but need they? The prospect of moving from the first experience to the second felt utterly terrifying, like stepping out of an open window into thin air. Could she really make it happen? Did she dare?

In fact, it happened without any decision on her part at all. And sooner than she thought.

Five

Blomfield Mansions wasn't full of ex-husbands. Years earlier Buffy had told Penny that it was full of lonely men crippled by alimony but that was just a sob story. In fact, the residents of the grimy old Edwardian building consisted of the usual mix found in this part of London: Arabs – though not really wealthy ones or they wouldn't be living there – whose wives hid their faces from Buffy when they found themselves squashed next to him in the lift but whose children stared up at him with the usual candid interest. Old couples who had lived in the place all their lives. A pallid doctor called Lever who Buffy was convinced was an abortionist. Some bland and pleasant Americans who never stayed long. And a large proportion of what Penny called Anita Brookner women – spinsterly or widowed, of an indeterminate age and usually engaged in some dowdy job, probably of a clerical nature. Buffy had lived in the building for ten years and knew a lot of the inmates; he was also a loud and active member of the Residents' Committee – a sure sign of his own lack of outside employment, but still, he enjoyed the cut and thrust of the meetings.

His long-term enemy was an elderly Hungarian called Mrs Zamiski. She lived in the next flat and for many years had waged a war against his dog – one of those rumbling campaigns that have gone on for so long that everyone has forgotten about them, like events in Namibia. Her windows faced the front. They overlooked the main road and the so-called gardens. These consisted of a strip of balding lawn and a dense, dusty shrubbery. Several times a day Buffy took George out, and it was amongst these bushes that he (the dog) relieved himself – or, as one American child shrilly pointed out, *went to the bathroom*. Mrs Zamiski, who seemed to keep a perpetual vigil behind her net curtains, always timed it perfectly. She waited until George was in a squatting position, then she flung open her window and yelled, 'Feel-thy animal– I call the porter!' So Buffy had devised an ingeni-ous plan, whereby he and George crept along the edge of the lawn, close to the building and out of her line of vision. From there it was a brisk trot straight into the middle of the shrubbery, where nobody could see them at all.

It was a shame, really, that he couldn't just let George off the lead and disclaim responsibility, sauntering past the bushes and letting the dog get on with it. But George had become unpredictable in his old age. Most of the time he was as lazy as Buffy – even lazier, if that was possible – and needed to be dragged along on his walks, sometimes in a sitting position. Lately, however, he had been seized with sudden and unprovoked rages. Off he would dash, barking wildly, and fling himself at the person who had unknowingly offended him. This was usually a cyclist. Seeing some pleasant, Friends of the Earth type pedalling along sent him into paroxysms of fury. But then sometimes so did a perfectly normal person walking along the pavement. This mostly hap-pened, embarrassingly, when the person was black. 'He's turning into the most awful old fascist,' said Penny. 'It'll be homosexuals next.' She had always loathed the dog.

This particular afternoon Buffy left the flat to buy his *Evening Standard*. It was one of his rituals. He didn't like the paper much, but on the other hand he couldn't bear not to read it in case he missed something. He felt like this about a lot of things. He was looking forward to seeing Penny; she was due back at any time now, and she always took a cab straight home from the airport. She had promised to bring back something nice for supper; he adored Italian food.

He shared the lift with an unknown businessman, possibly

Lebanese. George growled at him. Powerful aftershave filled the air as they descended wordlessly together. Not for the first time, Buffy speculated whether one of the Anita Brookner women was in fact a high-class call girl. He often encountered strange men in the lift, who never said hello, and Miss Bevins two floors up wore surprisingly high heels. It was a fun thought, anyway.

Buffy walked out into the sunshine. It was one of those blazing July days that made even the Edgware Road look picturesque. Shiny red buses trundled by. A nanny pushed a pram; above it floated a silver balloon. Passers-by had a shiny, hometown innocence, like extras in a Frank Capra film. His spirits lifted. It reminded him of the old days when he had emerged from the Colony Room, blinking, into the middle of a staggeringly normal weekday afternoon.

He edged along the side of the building and pulled George into the shrubbery. It was just then that a taxi arrived, though he didn't hear it, the traffic was too loud. Penny stepped out of the cab and unloaded her luggage.

At the same moment a courier, wearing arousingly shiny cycling shorts, came out of the front door. Chattering into his walkie-talkie, he mounted his bike and sped away.

George's lead jerked from Buffy's hand. The dog shot out of the bushes, barking hoarsely, and raced after the departing cyclist. Penny saw him. 'George!' she yelled, and ran after him.

Buffy emerged from the bushes and stared at Penny's departing figure, running down the pavement. She always caught the dog, in the end; she ran much faster than he did.

He walked to the taxi. Its engine was throbbing; the driver was obviously waiting. Later, Buffy remembered what he was thinking, just at that moment. That in the old, Colony Room days the driver would have unloaded her bloody suitcases himself and probably chased the dog too. Buffy also tried to remember if he had done the washing up for the past few days and collected Penny's clothes from the cleaners, as per instructions. He remembered thinking all this, the moment before he spoke.

'She paid you?' he asked the driver.

The man shook his head. Buffy looked down the road. Penny had disappeared. He took out his wallet; after all, she could pay him back from her expenses. He drew out a couple of twenty pound notes.

'So what's the damage?' he asked.

The driver flicked his cigarette out of the window and pointed to the fare, illuminated in its little box.

'Three pounds fifty' he said.

Six

Autumn, in London. The wind whipped the leaves off the trees and slewed them into the gutters. Black plastic sacks fattened in the public parks; it looked as if somebody had dropped them there from a great height. City brokers – even city brokers – were caught off-guard by a brooding melancholy they didn't have time to name. Restaurateurs dragged in their pavement tables; assistants in Selfridges discussed their Christmas plans, though they had been discussing them since the spring. Swallows departed; the first frost arrived, by stealth, one night. People sat in their cars, warming up their engines. Women searched for their one lost glove.

Celeste, who had lost her mother, moved to London in October. She rented a flat just off the Kilburn High Road. It was two rooms above a mental health charity shop. She tried to keep herself safe but oh, the noise, the fumes, the jostling crowds! The drilling in the streets, the skips full of rubble! Buses roared past her windows; beneath her, tubes rumbled along the Jubilee Line, making her house plants shiver. In the streets people bumped into her; they threw back their heads, draining Pepsi from cans. They stuffed their faces with handfuls of crisps. London assaulted her; she had been tenderly nurtured in the sleepy provinces, she wasn't used to this. Her London was picture postcards and Monopoly. Where was Vine Street, with its big red hotel? She was lost; she had lost everything. When she stepped out, in the mornings, she had to look down quickly to make sure she was dressed.

She had always been a slip of a thing but now she looked transparent. Shock had done that. The shock of the death was disorientating enough, but then she had been companioned in her grief. Not entirely, because grief removes the grief-stricken, nobody can reach them in their separate exiles where they have to suffer it out alone. But at least other people have been there too; they can describe the location and some of its features are familiar. This was different; she was totally alone in this. Nobody knew about the contents of the envelope, she had kept it a secret. And starting a new life, in a new city, sent her spinning into the bright October air, lost in space.

She knew where to go, and she often walked there. The streets were deafening, how did people bear it? On either side, houses were being gutted and refurbished. In Melton Mowbray everything stayed the same but here lives were being dismantled, nothing was certain. Rooms collapsed while workmen whistled; empty windows, like dragons' nostrils, breathed out smoke. From upper storeys long, jointed tubes of buckets dangled into skips; they looked like elephants' trunks. As she walked past they vomited noisily, disgorging dust. Nobody else seemed to notice. She passed a bakery; its buns were split open, like mouths, frothing cream at her. She flinched at everything, she felt so raw. The high street was jammed with traffic. How could there be so much, and where was it going? It was never-ending, like scarves pulled from a conjuror's pocket. Even the bicyclists were alarming, bumping on and off the pavement, glaring at people over their gas masks.

She went there and she stayed for a while, just looking, just telling herself she had come to the right place. She hid in a bus shelter on the opposite side of the road. She looked up at the windows of the building. Her heart thumped. Which windows were the right ones? Soon, somehow, she would find out. She would find a way.

She walked back in the dusk, down Kilburn High Road, the street of shoes. So many shoe shops, Saxone, Dolcis, their racks on the pavement, their wire baskets filled with ladies shoes, the sort her mother used to wear, *Final Clearance Sale!* Rows of single shoes, unbunioned as yet. She stood there, trying to cry, but she was beyond tears now. *To the best Mum in the world!* she used to write. She made her Mum birthday cards, they used to take hours. She remembered the weight of her mother's hand in hers. Grown-ups were baffling, but you thought you could rely on them. They worried about stupid things but that was what they were supposed to do. It made you feel superior. Adults never realize how superior children feel, how much of the time.

Celeste went back to her flat. She felt both very old, wearily so, and at the same time infantile and bereft. Somewhere in the middle should be herself, bringing home a Birds Eye Fisherman's Pie for supper, just arrived in London and looking for a job. She must learn to be this woman, a step at a time. And she must learn how to lie.

Beside the doorbell was a note. *Waxie, I'm at Lynns.* Who was Waxie? She didn't know any of the people in the flats yet, they were just thumps and muffled music. Opposite was a building with barred windows called Reliance House. It always looked closed, but today some men were going in and out, unloading cardboard boxes. What was everyone up to? The key to it all had been taken away from her. One letter, in a biscuit tin, had done it.

Celeste went upstairs and unloaded her shopping. Her skull ached; her insides felt heated and swollen. But it wasn't the beginnings of flu. It was anger.

Seven

'*Madam, I would like a shampoo and set!*'

'Hang on.' Archie fiddled with the volume controls. 'Okay. Once more, from the top. A bit louder.'

'*Madam,*' boomed Buffy, '*I would like a shampoo and set!*'

Archie rewound the tape – *tesdnaoopmahsaekildluowi, gabble gabble* – listened and nodded. 'Carry on.'

'*Fill her up please, top grade,*' said Buffy, into the mike. '*Show me to a table where I can see the pianist's hands.*'

'A bit more feeling on the *hands*,' said Archie.

'What is this, the blooming Old Vic?'

It was suffocating in the little booth. The air was thick with smoke from Archie's cheroot, and the walls were scribbled with multi-lingual graffiti, probably of an obscene or homesick nature.

'*This wine is corked!*' said Buffy. '*Take it back to the cellar!*'

The St Reginald College of English was situated above a massage parlour in Balham. Archie ran it, together with a couple of seedy ex-teachers who looked as if they had been sacked for paedophilia. The embossed crest above the door fooled nobody except foreigners; Archie had copied it from a jar of marmalade. Reginald was the name of his uncle.

'*I am a stranger to this town. Please direct me to your nearest building society!*'

The tape they were recording was compiled for East Europeans, newly-liberated fodder for Archie's language school. He called them 'the Great Stonewashed' after he had seen newsreels of them clambering over the Berlin Wall – clambering not to freedom but to enrolment at his establishment. These tapes were a bona fide money-spinner, that was what he thought – think of the market openings! – and were peppered with queries about mortgage rates and venture capitalism.

'May I make a down-payment on this appliance?' asked Buffy, choking in the smoke. 'For God's sake, Archie, put that thing out!' He squinted at his sheet of paper and leant towards the mike. *'Does this cellphone come with a written guarantee?'*

Why am I here? he wondered. To what depths have I sunk? I, who like Tiresias, have seen it all. What am I doing, stuck in a suffocating booth in Balham, teaching a lot of Lithuanians how to order shares in British Telecom? The chair was hard; his backside ached. No wonder his haemorrhoids were playing up again.

'Madam, kindly sell me a suppository!'

'What?' Archie squinted at him through the smoke.

He was doing it for the money, of course. The fee was really quite decent. Archie must be making a bomb from this place, in addition to – as he felicitously put it – dipping his wick into some fairly acceptable Commie crumpet. Ex-Commie crumpet.

But then Archie had always been a bit of a spiv. They had met during National Service when they had both been stationed in an arctic base camp near Kettering. Even then Archie had been involved in some complex manoeuvres involving petrol and bulk-order baked beans; no fool, he had been in cahoots with Warrant Officer Pickering, a key figure at the time and the springboard to a lifetime's racketeering. Bored and freezing, Buffy had loathed the entire two years and spent his time being as inconspicuous as possible, listening to Fats Waller records on his bunk and creeping out at night to meet girls from the local chicken-gutting factory. Despite his public school education he had failed to rise above the rank of sergeant, a tribute to the good sense of those in charge. Whilst he languished, Archie thrived and left the Army a fully-fledged entrepreneur. First it was reconditioned fridges, then snooker halls and the leisure industry. 'I got into gravel pits,' he said. 'The genesis of the theme park should, by rights, be credited to yours truly.' Buffy hadn't seen him for decades; they had happened to bump into each other recently in the Charing Cross Road, where Buffy had been browsing in a second-hand bookshop – another sure sign of his excess leisure, like knowing the names of all the waitresses at his local patisserie.

'It's a wrap!' said Archie in an irritating American accent. He disconnected the mike and they went into a small, leprous office. On the wall hung a framed certificate, testifying to Archie's qualifications as a senior EFL instructor. The Tippex beneath the name *Archibald Bingham* was clearly visible. Archie scratched his balls, coughed, and unlocked a drawer. From it he produced a wad of soiled banknotes and counted them out, one by one.

'Know how to say *You're a horny tomato* in Japanese?' he asked.

'No,' said Buffy. He took the notes. 'Shouldn't there be another ten?'

'My mistake, squire.' Archie reopened the drawer and passed it over.

It was lunchtime. Now he had no wife to go home to, Buffy had an impulse to ask Archie – even Archie – out for a drink. He felt this about the most unlikely people. But Archie shook his head and squirted some breath freshener into his mouth.

'Got a date with a promising little Czech.' He grinned. 'Play my cards right and it'll soon be Czech-mate.'

A wave of desolation swept over Buffy. Not that he was excluded from this twosome, but that he was desperate enough to have issued such an invitation to Archie in the first place. He had noticed this before, with a sinking sense of recognition. Once divorced, your standards plummetted. You rang up acquaintances you hadn't seen for years; you endured whole evenings in Dollis Hill with your accountant and his wife, drinking microscopic scotches and watching videos of their Kenyan safari. You sat in a pub for hours while some near-stranger told you about all the amazing things you could do with computer graphics. It was like suddenly having no money and going back to eating tinned macaroni. Anything to delay the return to that darkened flat.

He took the bus home. In the seat behind him an inebriated Irishman sang 'Loveboat, loveboat' all the way to Victoria, until the word lost all meaning – if, that is, it had any in the first place. Buffy didn't have the energy to shut him up. Was this all there was? Was this all he could expect, now? He thought of Prospero. His maturity fitted him for this role, he had grown into it – the noble forehead, the experience. My God, the experience. Why, now he had arrived at this bus-stop in life's journey, did nobody recognize it? Surely his past should lend him gravitas, but nowadays it was all producers half his age, drinking mineral water and getting phone-calls from their children.

All his old mates, the real characters, had gone; they had died from cirrhosis of the liver or retired to cottages in France. This young lot was sort of odourless, no patina to them. Even in its heyday the BBC didn't lend itself to dissipation but there was a certain style to things then, a Fitzrovian camaraderie, men with no discernible home life, women producers called Muriel, gruff and reckless, who were built like shire-horses and who could drink you under the table, and who knew who you might discover the next morning, snoring peacefully on your floor while the gas fire still blazed?

Buffy got off the bus at Maida Vale. The wind whipped his face; it was November and already freezing – why did November always seem colder than any other month? An illegally-parked car was being towed away; *weeee-weeee* wailed its alarm. How helpless it looked. He felt just like that himself. What a humiliating morning!

He tried to cheer himself up. At least there was no Penny waiting, with her hoots of mirth. *Honestly, Buffy, how could you?* It was undeniably lonely, that she wasn't there to listen to his exploits at the language school, which by now he would have worked up into one of his anecdotes. On the other hand it was a relief, that she wasn't there to be all superior about it. He must remember that. She had been insufferably superior. Her greatest feat, her most awesomely mind-boggling one, was that she managed to be superior *even when it was revealed she had been double-crossing him. For months.* He, Russell Buffery, had been the totally innocent party. She had been lying and cheating, packing and unpacking, and all the time shagging herself senseless with some under-aged photographer in Soho. *And yet she had managed to still be hoity-toity about it.* The whole thing was breathtaking.

Looking back over those final explosive weeks, he couldn't remember how she did it, probably some sort of conjuring trick. But she had managed, in some appallingly female way, to make *him* feel to blame. It was all, obviously, his fault . . .' Your infantile egocentricity . . . your drinking . . . your hypochondria . . . And another thing . . .' All his ex-wives said that, *and another thing.* You never helped with the children, you never helped with the washing-up . . . you were never supportive with my career . . . *and another thing* . . . you dropped ash on the duvet . . . you laughed at your own jokes . . . at that dinner party at the Robinsons', remember, you fell asleep in the soup, *the soup,* remember, we hadn't even started the main course, I could've *died* . . . a blizzard of *another things,* a smokescreen of them . . .

He remembered that mockingly sunny day, three months earlier. How he had unzipped her suitcase with feverish hands.

'I told you, I changed taxis!' she had cried. 'The cabbie from the airport, he was going on about darkies and what's the country coming to and I simply couldn't stand it. Racism is so repellent, especially when one's paying for it. So I got into another one!'

The self-righteousness of her voice, barely faltering even when she saw him taking out the bottle of Sudden Tan!

'That's for my legs. They always take the longest to get brown, not that *you'd* notice.'

See! She had managed to put him in the wrong, even then.

'Where's your plane ticket?' he had demanded. 'Where's your lira?'

'Don't be so paranoid, darling. It's bad for your blood pressure.'

Just then she stopped. He had pulled out a newspaper – *La Stampa*. It still had its sticker on: *Pat's News and Smokes, Wardour St. W.1*.

'Oh shit' she said.

Buffy paused outside Blomfield Mansions and looked up at the porch. Two cupids, carved in stone, were entwined above the doorway. They were portly and sooty; the private parts of one of them had chipped off. He knew how they felt. With what hopes, years before, had he once carried Penny across the threshold – well, not carried, because of his bad back, but he had lifted her, with a little hop, over the rubber doormat. How those cupids mocked him now! My God he was feeling maudlin, and he hadn't even had a drink.

He let himself into the flat, stumbling first over the dog and then over a plastic bag of empties. There was a funny smell coming from somewhere. Once he had been in the place for a bit he got used to it, but it always hit him on entering. The answerphone showed '1'. Briefly, but unconvincingly, he had an image of Penny, sobbing on the other end of the line and begging to come home. Asking him to forgive her. Grovellingly telling him that for once it was her mistake and she would always love him.

He replayed the message.

'Granada TV here, could you call back as soon as possible and ask for Gwenda.'

Granada TV! His spirits rose. He dialled the number. Maybe it was a cameo role – a fatherly family doctor, say, or a charismatic local MP. About time he was on the TV again. Maybe it was a major costume drama set in the Caribbean! They wanted him to play a plantation owner with a doting young native mistress.

By the time Gwenda's voice answered he was already making his acceptance speech at the BAFTA awards. 'Mr Buffery?' she said. 'Just to remind you, we don't seem to have received last month's rental on your video recorder. Would you like to pop in, or pop a cheque in the post?'

It was that sort of day. Well, year. Gloomily, he put George on his lead and left the flat. He stopped at The Three Fiddlers for a pint. His piles were so painful that he didn't sit down; he stood at the bar. In this position the weight on his feet made his corns throb but this was marginally preferable to the other thing. He had wedged cotton wool as well as corn plasters against his toes but they still pressed against the sides of his espadrilles, the thinking man's bedroom slippers.

None of his ex-wives had understood a simple fact: he didn't want to be a hypochondriac – nobody did – he just happened to have a lot of things wrong with him, mostly of a vaguely undignified but not life-threatening nature. He didn't seek the bloody things out. He didn't *want* them. Bitterly, he remembered Penny's shrill giggle when she first opened his bathroom cabinet. 'What're they all *for*? No, don't tell me!' Strong and vigorous, she had no patience with any sort of infirmity, and less so as their marriage progressed. Erotic back-rubs became brisk ones; brisk ones became progressively brusquer until they ceased altogether. 'Well they don't do much good, darling, do they? Why don't you go to your funny little osteopath?' When he was bedridden, the approaching rattle of the supper-tray took on an accusatory clatter, a *still-in-bed?* clatter, and she started forgetting the pepper mill.

It was a shame she wasn't ill herself more often because he was wonderful with ill women. Like many so-called hypochondriacs he was as interested in other people's symptoms as his own. In fact some of the most tender moments of his previous marriage to Jacquetta had come each month when she suffered her crippling period pains. She had had migraines too, an affliction Penny had airily dismissed as neurotic. 'Christ,' she'd said, 'you must've been a right couple of crocks.' That was long ago, when she was still interested enough in his past to be jealous.

It was late. The pub was empty except for Buffy, the bitter aftertaste of his various marriages and a couple of old girls called Una and Kitty, who always bagged the seats near the fire. They had men's voices and the compacted, pressed-meat complexions of serious boozers. Buffy was fond of them, but their wrecked faces always made him uneasy – did he look like that, or would he soon? Besides, he didn't feel like any sort of conversation today, even the amiable but minimal kind he would have with them.

He walked up the street, pausing briefly to enter the smokey inferno of Ladbrokes to see if his horse, Genie Boy, had won. It hadn't.

In the months to come he tried to recollect his state of mind that Friday afternoon. Bitter and gloomy, oh, yes. Vaguely cosmic too. His company had been spurned by Archie Bingham, and you couldn't get lower than that. His exes were living with other men, more harmoniously than they had ever lived with him, they made that perfectly plain, and his children were growing up without the benefits of his jovial good nature and panoramic breadth of experience. Did none of them realize what they were missing? He nearly tripped; the blithering pavement had been dug up, yet again. This time it was something to do with British Telecom. A pit was revealed; within it hung a knotted tangle of wires. You opened up somebody, and look at the mess inside! Divorce did that; surely it was a better idea to keep the lid on? Women were always prodding around inside him, tut-tutting like workmen, shaking their heads sorrowfully, sucking through their teeth and occasionally bursting into hysterical giggles. What was so bloody funny?

That was how he was feeling towards women in general, towards life itself, when he stopped outside the chemist's. He was, of course, a regular and valued customer at this shop. The same with Victoria Wine, opposite. He sometimes wondered what might happen if he ever moved away; how either establishment could possibly carry on.

He went in; *ping*. A blast of warm air caressed his face; perfume filled his nostrils. He paused on the threshold. A mysterious sense of well-being flooded through him.

Did it? Did it already? Even before he saw her? Yes!

Or was he just a corny old romantic, a silly old fool?

He felt it – warmth, happiness. He crossed the shop, past the racks of flowery spongebags and the cards of sparkling hairclips. Mr Singh, the pharmacist, didn't seem to be around, and the usual assistant was busy with a customer.

'It has its own tingle scrub,' she was saying, 'to tighten the pores.'

Then he heard a voice. 'Can I help you?'

He turned. A young woman got to her feet. She had been kneeling on the floor, stocking some shelves, that was why he hadn't seen her.

'Hello!' His voice sounded ridiculously hearty. He felt himself blushing. At his age! 'You're new,' he said stupidly, just for something to say.

She nodded. She was enchanting. Utterly, entirely enchanting. Slender, shy, beautiful; halo'ed, somehow, in innocence. She wore the usual pink overalls; above it her face was delicate and translucent. Limpid brown eyes, pointed chin, achingly stem-like neck. My God! She was like a sapling, a silver birch. She was like a single daffodil, surrounded by coarse plastic blooms. How on earth was he going to ask her for a packet of suppositories?

'Er, is Mr Singh around?'

She shook her head. 'He's just popped out to the post office.'

How could he discuss his piles with this radiant creature? If only it were the other assistant, the big motherly one, but she was still busy. It was the old French letters syndrome: why, when one wanted to buy something embarrassing, was one faced with the prettiest salesgirl? If only he could ask for

40

something impressive – special pills, say, to curb his incredibly powerful sexual drive.

'Anusol Suppositories, please,' he said. 'Oh, what a bag of infirmities is man!'

'Anusol? What's it for?'

'Haemorrhoids. Humiliating, I know.'

'It's all right, I won't tell anybody.' She smiled at him. 'Where are they?'

He paused. 'Er. The usual place.'

'No – I mean do you know where they're kept? The suppositories?'

'Ah. Up there.' He pointed to the cabinet behind her. She reached up. Her sleeve fell back, exposing a slim bare arm and a shadowy armpit.

'I'm going to the cinema tonight' he said, suddenly reckless, 'and it's agony sitting down.' *Come with me. Come out tonight. Like all ruins, I look best by moonlight.*

'What's on?'

'About six different films. Have you noticed how lovely, big things like cinemas have been divided into little cupboards, yet lovely little cupboards, like grocery shops, have been made into enormous big Waitroses? All the wrong way round, in my opinion. Still, you're too young to remember.'

'We only had a tiny cinema anyway, where I come from.'

'Where's that?'

'Melton Mowbray. Me and pork pies.' She fetched down a packet. 'Twelve or twenty-four?'

'Twenty-four. And I need some Algipan and some Multivite . . .' He fished in his pocket. 'And I've got some repeat prescriptions here . . .'

'Mr Singh will be back in a tick.' She took the bits of paper. 'Simvastatin,' she read.

'That's for my heart.'

'Fibogel,' she read.

'That's for my bowels.'

She gazed at him. He felt her tender curiosity bathing his internal organs. His embarrassment disappeared; he surrendered to her. He was all hers – his body, and all it was still capable of.

'What I really need is a complete set of new parts,' he said. 'Trouble is, the guarantee's expired.'

She laughed. 'I know about Algipan,' she said, fetching the bottle. 'My Mum was prescribed it.'

'Did it work?'

'Well, she's dead now.' Suddenly, her eyes filled with tears.

'Oh, Lord.' He fumbled in his pocket but all he brought out was a sort of compost – a sediment of disintegrated bus tickets and so on.

'I'm sorry,' she sniffed. 'Don't know why I said that.'

'Are you all right?'

She nodded. She wiped her nose, like a child, on the back of her hand, and bent her head to look at the prescriptions.

There was silence. Something had happened. When she looked up, her face was drained.

'Russell Buffery,' she whispered.

'That's me.' He gazed at her. 'What's the matter?'

She didn't reply. At that moment the other assistant strolled over, smiling.

'Hello.' She turned to the girl. 'This is one of my favourite customers. Isn't he nice? Remember Uncle Buffy, on *Children's Hour*?'

The girl stared at him. Then she slowly nodded.

'Uncle Buffy and his Talking Hamster.'

'Hammy,' said the girl.

'I didn't make up the name,' said Buffy. 'They did.'

The girl said: 'I used to listen to you, with my milk. That was *you*?'

Buffy nodded. 'Both of me.'

'Go on,' said the other assistant, 'do Hammy for her!'

'Why not Buffy?' He had always felt hurt, that Hammy used to get more fan mail than he did. He had grown to loathe his little sidekick. 'I can do other animals, you know.

Hens. Grasshoppers.' He made a small, scraping sound with his teeth. 'I can do a marvellous W C Fields.'

'Do Hammy!'

He sighed. Oh, well, at least he was famous for *something*. And it was delightful, that he had spoken to this girl when she was little, even if it had been through a radio. He raised his voice to a squeak. *'Well bless my cotton socks! Who's that coming through the dell? That rough little fellow with the twinkle in his eye?'*

'That was Voley,' said the girl. 'The rough little fellow with the twinkle in his eye.'

'You remember?'

She nodded. 'The vole. He was a burglar. He stole all the squirrels' nuts. Once I tried to open the radio, to see if you were all inside.'

'Never a good idea,' said Buffy, thinking of the knotted British Telecom wires.

'You were famous,' she said.

'Except all my fans were under five.'

'I used to wonder what you looked like.' Tilting her head, she inspected him. 'You're not like I thought.'

'Why? My ears aren't all furry?'

'Oh, I don't know,' she said, and sighed. When she looked up her eyes were glistening with tears again. Why? 'What happened, anyway?'

'The writer had a nervous breakdown. Couldn't handle all the sex and violence in the stories. So they got rid of us and brought in – '

'Timmy McTingle and his Little Red Choo-Choo Train.'

'Bit Freudian, I always thought.'

'I never liked him as much.' Her face cleared; she smiled again. It was extraordinary, watching the weather-changes on her face. Suddenly the shop was flooded with sunlight. *Ping.* Some customers came in. Just then the music started and they all broke into song, *Pennies from Heaven*, the bottles dancing on their shelves, lights chasing around L'Oreal and *Dispensary*. The spongebags, bellows-like, grunted the rhythm; on their display cards, the golden hairclips clattered their applause.

They did, in his middle-aged, susceptible heart. She had stepped into him, like a deer into a thicket, turning round and round until she had made herself the warmest of nests. He felt her there, lodged in him, even as she answered the phone, cupping it against her shoulder, and another customer came in and asked for something or other. It was the strangest sensation.

He walked down the street. There was a lift in the air, a quickening of London's pulse. Cars hooted, buses were crammed, the sodium lights flickered on, one by one, down the Edgware Road. For the first time in months he didn't feel excluded; he felt he had rejoined the bright, sliding stream of the city. She probably thought he was a boring old fart. Maybe she was a dream. Next time she wouldn't be there. But just now he was so utterly undone he had even forgotten to buy the *Standard*.

Eight

Things aren't as they appear. Celeste was learning this. Take Kilburn High Road; the shops in it. You thought they were selling one thing and they turned out to be selling something totally different as well. The florist's shop sold discount videos. The window of the post office was heaped with porcelain shepherdesses and packets of chamois leathers. She was surrounded by tricks and illusions. Some of the shops lied outright. Matthews Greengrocers was full of office equipment; a shop that said it sold office equipment was full of saris and canteens of cutlery. She walked past them on her way to work, past men holding cans of lager in front of them like votive offerings, at 8.30 in the morning! When she came home the shops had mysteriously been replaced, like stage props; windows were barred and new stalls had appeared on the pavement selling bin liners and Irish leprechauns. She couldn't get a grip on the place. The neighbourhood seemed like a pack of cards being shuffled behind her back. *Got you!* it sniggered.

She didn't like the way men looked at her, either. In the evenings they still carried cans of lager, but they were more pressing. It didn't do, to dawdle. She walked briskly even when she had nowhere to go. Sometimes she had to dodge into shops, the hot breath of them blowing onto her face, the *can I help you*'s. She felt sickly and bewildered. Even her body was something she had to re-learn. Men fixed their eyes on it but it was not quite her own, not yet. Her arms hung from her shoulders, her toenails were there, okay, but she felt she

45

had been taken apart and reassembled. She had to check that everything was in place.

Nesta helped her; Nesta at work. 'It's one thing to be pale and interesting,' she said, 'but honestly, Celly, you look as if you've seen a ghost.' She sat her down. 'You've got a bone structure to die for,' she said. 'Build on it.' Nesta had worked in the shop for a year and she was familiar with all the new products. 'I'd give my right arm for your eyes,' she sighed. In the mid-afternoons, when the place was quiet, she held a mirror up to Celeste's face and gave her make-up lessons. It was soothing. At work, Celeste became reacquainted with her skin and dusted powder onto it. 'Cleanse, tone, nourish,' chanted Nesta, like a prayer. 'They'll be around you like bees round a honeypot.' Her voice was wistful; she herself was plain and plump, though she had a devoted boyfriend who arrived each day at six o'clock prompt and loaded her onto his Honda.

Celeste had been working in the shop for a week before Buffy came in. It had been so simple; she had walked by, seen a *Salesperson Wanted* sign in the window, gone in and got the job. By the second day she had felt part of the fixtures and fittings. There was a lot to learn but it was only bottles and packets and things you could grasp. She was a whizz at the till; after all, she had done the accounts at Kwik-Fit, she was over-qualified for this. She liked stocking the shelves and pricing things, *pzzz, pzzz*, with her pricing gun. She liked the photos of lustrous women on the display cases, their pouting beauty invited her to accompany them to a place of which she was only dimly aware. She wasn't ready, yet. The outside world confused her but Mr Singh ran a tight ship and his shop was an oasis of perfumed confidentiality.

Alpha Pharmacy was in a parade of shops just off the Edgware Road. Blocks of mansion flats rose up behind it; down the road stretched the creamy crescents of what she discovered was Little Venice. She could walk to work each day; it was only a mile from the chaos of Kilburn but it was like stepping into another world. She felt stabilized; a hand steadied her on the playground swing. The shops sold exactly what they said they did, and she was working in one of them. She was in a middle-class neighbourhood where people knew what they wanted. She hadn't met Buffy yet, and she didn't know what he wanted, but she sensed a certain thrust and confidence in the air. Things didn't shift, and disappear over-night. The wine merchants opposite said *Est. 1953* on its sign and there they were every day, the same bottles in the window. Buffy, she was to discover, bemoaned the changes in their locality but she only noticed the reassuring con-tinuity; such is the seeking magnet of our needs. Even the drilling in the street outside didn't impinge, not while she was punching the numbers on her bleeping till. She liked it when the shop was busy and she didn't have time to think.

That day. What was special about that day? A Friday, and by lunchtime the city was quickening. She had felt this each week since she had arrived. In schoolrooms, unknown children fidgeted at their desks. Out in the hinterlands, in the factories, people listened restlessly for the hooter. Down the road, still unknown to her, Buffy was sipping his late scotch in The Three Fiddlers.

'Malcolm's taking me bowling,' said Nesta, 'after we've had a snack. You ever been bowling?'

Celeste shook her head.

'Got to find you a boyfriend, preferably with wheels,' said Nesta.

Celeste was standing on a chair, stocking a shelf with nasal sprays. She was remembering her dream, from the night before. She had pricked her mother with a pin, *hssssss* . . . The body deflated into a folded packet of plastic. She mustn't think of these things. Dreams were like those shops in Kil-burn; their displays were so jumbled up it gave you a jolt, to look.

'Be good, girls,' said Mr Singh, 'I'm popping out to the post office.'

He left. An elderly lady called Mrs Klein came in. Celeste was becoming familiar with customers' bodily disorders.

47

When people passed by the window she felt intimate with their hidden organs, like a plumber looking at a bathroom he had worked on and knowing the layout of the pipes. She was getting to know the regulars. Underneath Mrs Klein's musquash-clad exterior there lurked an irritable colon. The man in the wine merchants opposite had, beneath his polished brogues, a chronic attack of athlete's foot. In this city full of strangers women were emerging whose contraceptive methods were to become more familiar to Celeste than to their own nearest and dearest. Already she knew that the check-out girl at Cullens was on the Pill, and that the big, disordered-looking blonde at the framer's shop used an Ortho-Diaphragm size 75, plus jelly.

'You going out tonight?' asked Nesta.

Celeste shook her head; she always seemed to be shaking her head. She never went out; she didn't know anybody, she only knew what ointments they used. She wrapped Mrs Klein's purchases, then she sank to her knees and started to refill a shelf with Clairol Hair Tones. Another customer had arrived; she was talking to Nesta about rejuvenating face packs.

'My problem's a greasy panel,' said the woman, 'so I need two types in combination.'

Ping. Someone else came in.

' . . . it has its own tingle scrub . . .' Nesta was saying.

Celeste climbed to her feet. 'Can I help you?'

He was a large, florid, bearded man, well muffled up in a checkered scarf. He wore a beret. The first things she noticed were his eyebrows: thick black caterpillars with a life of their own. He was accompanied by a small dog. It was flat and matted, as if it had been run over at some point in the past.

She thought, at first, he might be an artist. Some local character, anyway. Bit of an eccentric. He had twinkly eyes and, when he spoke, a really beautiful voice – deep and resonant.

'Anusol Suppositories, please.'

48

For a moment she thought he was talking in some foreign language – he did look vaguely continental. Then he explained himself.

Looking back, she tried to remember what they said. He made her laugh, she remembered that. *Uncle Buffy*. It was him, how incredible! The voice inside her radio, inside her head. He had told her so many stories already. The musty scent of the armchair where she had curled up, picking at the bits of skin around her fingernails . . . The faint pop-pop of the gas fire. Her hands, smudgy from school. Hammy's squeaky falsetto, *''pon my soul!*, as she fiddled with her plaits, pulling at the elastic bands. He was a whole company of furry creatures, her friends; squeaks and grunts from her lost past.

Her throat closed. She felt dizzy, momentarily. But she was chatting quite normally, though there was a roaring in her ears. She wrapped up his parcels; she told him her name, Celeste. And now there was another man standing in front of her.

'Got any disclosing fluid?' he asked.

'Disclosing?'

'For these.' He opened his mouth and tapped his teeth.

Nine

Love, ah love. Warm sap rising through his wintry branches. What a miracle! Who would believe, at sixty-one, that such a miracle was possible? An old has-been like him, a discontinued model consigned to the scrap-heap. A man, spurned and cuckolded. A man who had seen his ex-wives, wearing their familiar clothes, in the company of unfamiliar men. He was an old pit pony, put out to grass. A noble monument, vandalized and corroded, fallen to ruin. All these, and more, if he could think of them.

Celeste had flung open the doors to his heart, dazzling him with her sunlight. A slip of a thing in a pink nylon overall. Looking back over his life, he wondered if he had ever felt like this before and decided he hadn't. Not like this, for love makes amnesiacs of us all. Besides, the break-ups of his marriages had spreadingly infected the past, like poisonous chemicals leaking from a shattered container, and even his early months with the various women he thought he had loved, when things should have been all right, were already tainted with something he should have recognized spelt danger ahead.

Take Jacquetta's moody, I'm-so-spiritual behaviour in Venice, on their honeymoon. The way she had stood for hours in front of that Titian painting, oblivious to his fidgety glances at his watch and longings for lunch. At the time he had been impressed by her rapt stillness, by the way other people washed over her but she remained, like a rock each time the waves receded. She had also looked very fetching

in her velvet cape. But already there was something osten-
tatious in her solitude; she was making him feel lowly and
coarse, preoccupied with his stomach and excluded from the
higher plane inhabited only by the Venetian painters and
herself. She had a knack of doing this, a knack which
developed as the years passed. When she started sleeping
with her shrink she actually managed to make him feel
excluded from a twosome too sensitive for him, a twosome
which alone breathed the rarified air of her psyche. It was
Titian all over again. Worse, of course, but the same sort of
thing.

Then there was Popsi's behaviour in John Lewis, when
they were buying curtains. Popsi, his first wife. Years and
years ago, this was, back in the sixties. They were both
hopelessly undomesticated but they had just moved into two
rooms in Bloomsbury and were making an effort. Popsi was
a cheerful, accommodating girl; she was usually cast in walk-
on parts as a country wench, bursting out of her bodice. That
day she had failed an audition and had sunk a few on the
way to the store. First she had stilled the department with
her rendering of 'There was a young lady from Bristol.' Then,
in an abrupt mood-switch, tears streaming down her cheeks,
she had told the elderly salesman about her abortion, how
his cutting scissors reminded her, how she was only sixteen
at the time and how it would have been a strapping boy by
now. Taking her arm and steering her towards the fabric
rolls, Buffy had realized that even if there wasn't going to
be trouble ahead, there was bound to be a fair amount of
embarrassment.

Celeste wasn't like any of them. In fact, she wasn't like
any girl he had ever met. She was fresh and unused. She
was like a shiny new exercise book in which he would begin
writing his most entertaining thoughts in his best italics. Her
youth made him feel wise and experienced, and about time
too. Where women were concerned he had always been susceptible; well, foolish sometimes. But she really was enchanting, the way she gazed at him in her forthright way and

asked him questions. It was the next day and he had brought in a roll of film to be developed. She really seemed pleased to see him.

'What are these then?' she asked. 'Holiday snaps?'

'Photos of the pavement.'

'The pavement?'

'The dug-up bits,' he said.

'Why've you taken photos of the pavement?'

'I'm going to send them off with a letter of complaint. Nearly broke my neck again this morning.' He handed her the film. 'It was already in my camera. Must've been there for ages, God knows what else is on it.'

'What do you think is?' She looked at him, frowning.

'Something embarrassing, probably. Something that's better left there undeveloped, like a thought you don't put into words.'

Yesterday she had been some blurred vision, as radiant and featureless as an angel. Today he saw her more clearly. Cropped hair, brown eyes, thick eyebrows – a delicate face but also a face of character and determination. There was a small pimple on her chin; her forehead was shiny, it was hot and stuffy in the shop. These minor imperfections made her human – more intimate and dear to him. He felt ridiculously familiar with her already.

'The past is mostly embarrassing,' he said. 'You haven't had enough of it yet to find out. It's there, ready to put out its foot and trip you up from behind.'

She paused. 'You're right, actually,' she said. 'I didn't realize that till lately. You think you know everything, that it's all what you think it is, then – whoosh!'

'What do you mean?'

She didn't reply. She looked at the order form in her hand. 'Matt or glossy?'

'I don't know. My wife was the camera expert.'

'Wife?'

'Ex-wife.'

They weren't divorced yet but to all extents and purposes she was an ex. Soon would be, anyway.

'What's happened to her?'

'She ran away last summer. With a photographer, appropriately enough. A gorilla called Colin. Christ knows what they find to talk about. Exposures or something.'

'Where do they live?'

'Above a pasta restaurant in Soho.' He snorted. 'Hope she's putting on weight.'

'You look terrible,' said Celeste. 'Here, sit down.' She indicated the chair which was set aside for old dears waiting for their prescriptions.

'When's your tea break?'

They sat in the patisserie down the road. From time to time she bent down and fed George pieces of buttered bun. 'He's the most slobbery dog I've ever met,' she said, fascinated. She wiped her hand on the tablecloth.

'What I don't understand about dogs,' he said, 'is why, when they only eat meat, does their breath smell of fish?'

'I know. Funny, isn't it. How're the piles?'

'Better.'

'Did you go to the pictures?'

He nodded. 'Have you noticed something? How, when they show a huge list of songs at the end of a film, Brahms and Diana Ross and the Beatles, there's always much more of them than you actually heard in the film itself?'

She paused, considering. There was a crumb on her lip. He leant across and wiped it off with his napkin, as if she were one of his children. How many times – hundreds, thousands – had he sat with his children in teashops, through marriage and separation, wiping their faces and trying to answer those totally unanswerable yet vaguely cosmic questions children ask, like *How many people in the world have the same birthday as me?* Now some of them shaved, his children and his step-children, and had driving licences, and still their questions hadn't been answered.

53

'Tell me things,' she said. 'I don't know anything.'

'Ask me a question.'

'Tell me about your wife.'

'Ex-wife.' He paused. He didn't really want to talk about Penny. She was like a room full of disgusting clutter one kept from the visitors. Nor did he want to do that throbbing, poor-me number that had once, all those years before, proved so effective with Penny herself. Celeste deserved better. He looked at her, fondly. Extraordinary thing, love. A miracle, after all he had been through, that he could feel the first stirrings of it, like the first stirrings of hunger after an appalling attack of food poisoning.

'What does she look like?'

'Not like you,' he said. 'Glossy and thoroughbred, in an impervious sort of way. As if water would run off her. She's a journalist, you see.'

'I've never met a journalist. Never met an actor, either. Back home, the high spot of the week was having our meter read.'

He laughed. Under her coat she wore a white fluffy jumper. There was a tiny gold crucifix around her neck. She was soft and feminine – the way girls should look, but never did anymore. Sort of absorbent. The opposite of Penny. He pictured a working-class home, factory hooters, a headscarved mother. Celeste, fragrant and solitary amongst the back-to-backs. She was too young to have seen *A Kind of Loving*. Oh, there was so much to tell her!

'Do you still see her?'

'Who?'

'Your ex-wife.'

'Not if I can help it. She has breakfast at Bertaux's every morning, I bumped into her there once, so now *that's* out of bounds. One of my favourite places too.' Bitterly, he lit a cigarette. 'They don't just steal your money and your furniture and your house, oh, no. They even steal your favourite tea shop, that *you* introduced them to in the first place.' He started coughing; his eyes watered.

54

Actually, Penny hadn't been so rapacious as some people he could mention. They had put the country cottage on the market but when it was sold she was only going to claim half. So decent of her, considering he had bought it in the first place. The Blomfield Mansions flat was rented so she couldn't get her claws on that. No, she had simply moved out, taking her designer clothes and her cookery books. Not even all of those. This was even more of a snub, of course. She was obviously far too preoccupied, too blithely happy, to bother about mere possessions. Too sexually sated to argue. Once the rows were over and the decision taken she had been rather kind, actually – more considerate and generous than she had ever been before. Nauseatingly condescending, in fact. Once she had actually asked: 'You sure you're going to be all right?' Like a torturer bringing you a cup of tea after they had just been pulling out your toenails.

He couldn't involve Celeste in all this; it was far too sordid for her. Look at her now, munching her second Viennese slice! The resilience, the appetite! The miraculous possibility of renewal! His past was a ditch clogged with half-submerged debris and broken prams. She was a lotus flower, rising out of it, unfolding her petals one by one.

'Have I got cream on my chin?' she asked anxiously.

He shook his head; he couldn't speak.

'What're you looking at?' she asked.

'Just you.'

Ten

The next day, her day off, Celeste took the bus down to Soho. In their woollen gloves, her hands were clammy. *She lives above a pasta restaurant*. She felt nauseous yet excited, as if she were about to step onto a stage. She also felt furtive – a new sensation, this; one of the many new sensations that were assaulting her nowadays. This one wasn't unpleasant, however; it was like a feather duster stroking her insides, heating her face and tingling her eardrums. As she neared her destination the buildings changed. They became pregnant with meaning; they almost bulged with it. *She*, Penny, had seen them. Maybe *she* walked past them each day.

Celeste got off in the Charing Cross Road. Thank goodness Buffy couldn't see her. He would think it really odd. They hardly knew each other and yet here she was, tracking down his ex-wife! Somebody pointed her in the right direction. Soho. She pictured strip clubs and scantily-clad women lounging in doorways. *Want a good time?* For a mad moment she pictured Buffy's ex-wife in a suspender belt and patent leather boots, blowing cigarette smoke at passing men. Soho was such a wicked word that her parents would only have spoken of it in lowered voices. If, that is, it had ever come up. The naughtiest thing in their street was Wanda's lurex leggings.

It was ten in the morning and a light drizzle was falling. Celeste stood, undecided, in Old Compton Street. Men approached her, one by one. They didn't want her body, however, they wanted her money. 'Got fifty pence?' A hand stretched out. 'Got some change for a cup of tea?' A purple face loomed close. 'A quid, God bless you, miss?' She couldn't see any women at all; maybe they emerged at dusk, like slugs. The only person she could see in a doorway was so bundled up she couldn't tell what sex it was; it sat there, surrounded by carrier bags.

She walked past boutiques selling clothes so unwearable-looking they must be fashionable. A lot of shops were closed, with *To Let* signs on them. On a corner, some Japanese tourists were standing around looking pinched. It was a chilly day. In the doorway of the Prince Edward theatre there was a large cardboard box with *Sony* on it; inside it, somebody was stirring. Soho wasn't how she imagined, but then none of London was how she imagined. There weren't any strip clubs, as far as she could see. None at all. Only pasta restaurants.

Lots and lots of pasta restaurants. *Pasta Fina. Fasta Pasta. Pasta'N'Pizza. Fatso's Pasta Palace.* Above them were rooms, she could see that all right. Lots of rooms, lots of flats. Windows with blinds on them, windows with curtains.

Which one was Penny's? How on earth could she hope to spot her? She couldn't possibly hang around outside every pasta restaurant in Soho waiting for somebody to emerge from the flat above. She didn't even know what this Penny looked like. She was probably out at work anyway.

Celeste walked into Soho Square. She sat down heavily on a bench. A one-legged pigeon hopped away. It was hopeless. She should have realized that.

Back home there was another note to Waxie, sellotaped to the door. *'See you at Bim's at 5.'* In this huge city, so huge she could never glimpse the edge of it, people were connecting up. Unknown people called Waxie and Bim, even with names like that they were finding each other. In the flat upstairs, music was playing. Footsteps thudded across the ceiling. Through the walls they laughed their loud Waxie laughs and left notes for each other.

57

She wasn't lost; she mustn't panic. She had stepped out of the past into this windy city, she had woken up from the long, false sleep of her youth. She had sub-let the maisonette back in Willow Drive, she had finished with all that, and finally she had found Buffy. He had embraced her outside the patisserie, holding her in a bear hug. His girth, his warm tobacco breath . . . He seemed to need her. He had mumbled into her hair 'I want to dissolve you in water and drink you up.' At least that's what it had sounded like. Did he really say that? Was it possible?

It was all so confusing. She had never felt like this before. Oh, she had felt desire – the flush and moistness of it, the dryness and the dizzy spells, the whooping clarity of the streets. She had kissed men in cars and she had even been to bed with one or two of them, but nobody had really entered her. With Buffy it was different. She didn't know what she was feeling, she didn't dare to think, but the next day, at work, there she was watching the door and waiting for him to come in. She borrowed a tester and rubbed blusher into her cheeks; she applied more lipstick. Still he didn't come. She stayed in at lunchtime; she just ate a sandwich in the back room, pausing when she heard the *ping* of the door and casually leaning forward to look into the shop.

No time passes more slowly than an afternoon in an empty shop. Nesta didn't notice anything, but then Nesta never did. Her friend from Nautilus Fitness down the road came in – business was slow there too – and took out her wedding photos. Nesta spent a long time over each one, sighing. It was four o'clock now. Celeste made up little ploys. If she went out to the lavatory he would come in . . . If she closed her eyes and counted to ten . . . Suddenly, ridiculously, she needed him. Maybe he had forgotten all about her. Maybe that tea had meant nothing.

'Shame his little face is out of focus,' said Nesta. Celeste turned. For the first time, she looked at what they held in their hands. Photos.

The package from the photographic lab was delivered at

4.30. It was her job to take out the individual wallets of photos and put them into the desk drawer, ready to be collected by the customers.

At six o'clock Nesta cashed up. Mr Singh opened the door to let the last customer out. In the street, the Honda puttered to a halt. Celeste slipped behind the counter, opened the big beige envelope and took something out.

She walked home along Kilburn High Road, past closed shops with their ghostly displays of shoes, past the illuminated pavement stalls selling jewellery. The bracelets winked at her confidingly. She felt like a criminal with a bomb in her pocket. She felt guilty, and deeply embarrassed, that she had borrowed Buffy's photos. It seemed such an intrusion into his life. She hadn't looked at them yet; she was putting it off, almost luxuriously, until she got into her flat. She passed *Afro-Caribbean Hair Beauty*, a big, busy place advertising *100% Human Hair Sold Here*. It was still open; within the shop, veils of hair hung from the ceiling like seaweed. She crossed the road, clutching her coat to her chest. In her pocket lay pieces of Buffy's life. It was amazing that nobody guessed what she had in there. Not amazing really, but *she* felt that. She paused at her doorway, fumbling for her keys. The charity shop was dark. Behind the window the mannequin leant towards her; today it was wearing a pillbox hat, set crooked on its bald head.

Upstairs she took out the wallet of photos and spread them over the table. The photos of the pavement hadn't been developed. He was either such a hopeless photographer that they hadn't come out or the lab had presumed they were a mistake, and too boring to print. She leant on her elbows, staring at the others. A train passed, way below. The table shook, as if there was a séance going on.

There were several photos of a country cottage; it had a conservatory, with a blurred figure inside it. In other photos various people lay around on rugs in the garden; Buffy was amongst them, fast asleep. He wore a red shirt and baggy blue trousers. Her throat tightened; looking at old snapshots always made her want to cry. Buffy, on some golden afternoon, raising his wine glass at the camera. Probably his wife was taking the photo. He looked younger, but then people in photos always did. Some teenagers, looking sullen. She couldn't spot a family resemblance but maybe they weren't his, she didn't even know if he had any children.

And one photo of Buffy, standing in a vegetable garden holding up a bunch of carrots. A bunch of carrots! How unlikely. He wore a panama hat and a floppy cravat; there was a broad smile on his face. His arm around a woman with shiny chestnut hair.

Celeste sat there for a long time, looking at the photo. The sun on the two faces; the woman's half in shadow, but distinct enough. His wife; you could tell, by the way they stood together. Chestnut hair, cut in a bob; jeans, white blouse.

Celeste sat there for a long time, gazing at this lost summer's afternoon, fixed forever. A whole life she knew nothing about. Buffy, holding up the carrots like a trophy. His hand on his wife's shoulder. The woman's lips were parted. What was she saying? Something even they had long ago forgotten. A moment between them, frozen. From time to time a tube train passed beneath the house; Celeste shook, the table shook, her teeth chattered. She gazed at Penny. Now she knew what she looked like. She could memorize the face, now. And she was going to find her.

Eleven

The hour before dawn, damp and dark outside, blackness pressing at the windows. In homes all over Britain nothing stirred except the glowing flip of digital clocks, keeping vigil in slumbering rooms. Couples slept back to back, dreaming their separate dreams whose wacky stories would dissolve in the morning like Alka-Seltzer in water. Children's noses were cold. A click, in a bedroom, as a light was switched on. A click, in a kitchen, as a boiler hummed into life. Lorna was getting ready for work. The floorboards creaked as she crossed the room; behind the plasterwork, pipes hissed as she turned on the taps in the bathroom.

She lived alone, deep in the countryside. As the sky lightened her cottage grew solid, detaching itself from its surroundings as if it were stepping forward. Behind it rose the shoulder of a hill. This was dotted with grey rocks which, as the light grew, revealed themselves as sheep. Below it lay a wood; tangled trees and the inkier clots of conifers. A fox slipped from it and crossed the lawn. Birds pecked at the swinging gibbets of bacon rind; they flew off when she emerged and reappeared when she left. She had lived here for years but she had always felt like a transient, tolerated by the animals who were the real inhabitants of the place. She didn't mind this; in fact she found it reassuring.

She bundled herself into her overcoat and scarf, pulled on her gumboots and set off through the wood. She was only middle-aged but from a distance she looked like an ancient crone in a fairy story. An old tramp, even. Who cared? She didn't.

Spiders' webs wreathed the bushes. She knew every inch of this path – the bleached, flattened grass; the rotting plank over the ditch. Above her the bare branches rose imploringly to the sky. It wasn't a large wood; she was familiar with most of the trees, as a teacher might be with her pupils. Some more than others, of course, one couldn't help having favourites. They had grown older, just as she had, but in their case they had grown taller too. Brambles choked their ankles and some had fallen, slantingly, and come to rest against their neighbours. She passed the dark, hushed fir trees; between their trunks the silence was thick enough to touch. The air there held its breath; nothing stirred.

She emerged from the wood and walked along the edge of a ploughed field. Peewits rose and wheeled around her, crying. They did this every morning; you'd think they would have got used to her by now. A few rosehips still clung to the hedge. The earth in the field was so freshly-turned, so sharply-cut that it gleamed like flesh. The sun was still low. Why, she wondered, did the clouds lie motionless on the horizon yet race at the top of the sky? There was nobody to reply to this but she didn't mind. Usually she didn't. She had always been a solitary person and was accustomed to making up conversations in her head. It was like cooking for one – at least you knew what you were going to get.

She wriggled through the barbed wire and crossed the next field: a sheep meadow with a puddled, rushy pond in the middle. In the spring she found frogspawn in it. Each year, when she discovered the grey tapioca knobbling the surface, she felt the same electric jolt she had felt as a child; it was one of the few surprises that never wore off. The low sun cast a pearly pink light on the trunk of an ash tree. Below her lay the valley, sunk in mist. It was a lost, secret valley. Nothing disturbed it, not even the hum of the main road beyond the gate. Far away, a dog barked.

She crossed the next field and climbed over the gate – she

preferred climbing gates to opening them. A container lorry thundered past. She had emerged onto the A2 dual carriageway. Each morning she felt shy, suddenly coming into the public like this. She smoothed down her coat, and walked along the verge.

The Happy Eater stood a hundred yards up the road: a brightly-lit cube against the brightening sky. It stood alone on the windy ridge – it, and its large plastic elephant slide. The sun shone on the dome of the elephant's head. A few cars were already parked outside. She made her way round them, and pushed open the *Staff Only* door. Inside, dazzling strip light; the Forest Pine fragrance of the rest rooms. She unwound her scarf and pulled off her gumboots.

Sixty miles away, in London, Celeste was nibbling a croissant. She was sitting in Maison Bertaux. *Penny has breakfast there each morning.* Each time the door opened, with a rush of cold air, Celeste's heart thumped. She looked up – not at the door but at the mirrored wall that reflected it. Each time she saw a mirrored stranger. Nobody she recognized, anyway, from the photo. She saw her own face – blank, peaky, glistening with sweat.

She fingered the chain around her neck. She had removed the crucifix, now; in its place she had threaded the tiny, gold fish. The fish she had found in the envelope.

'Two portions of toast, one Farmhouse Breakfast, one Yankie Do . . .'

Lorna carried the plates through the steamy kitchen. She spoke to Klaus, his face glistening under his paper cap. She worked automatically; her hands had a life of their own. She could do this in her sleep.

'One sausage and french fries, one hash browns . . .'

She was a dreamer; she dreamed up stories about people. They were like the birds in her veranda, flying in, swinging on the string as they pecked at the bacon rind, flying off. Each day it awed her, that there were so many unknown people in the world. For half an hour they warmed their plastic seat and then they were off again. Fuelled by a fry-up they disappeared from her life for ever, on their way to London one direction or Dover the other, to points beyond, to points anywhere, leaving a scraping of ketchup and a scrumpled paper napkin. Some of them were foreigners. She had to explain the menu to them; they counted out the strange coins, laboriously, for her tip. There were men in business suits who wolfed down the sort of breakfasts nobody's wives made anymore. Where were they driving, in their company cars? They left behind book matches from the Orion Hotel, Bridlington, and copies of the *Daily Express* with pencilled sums in the margin. They called her 'love' but this time tomorrow they'd be in Humberside. How many times, between then and now, would she have wiped this table clean? Even the waitresses came and went, girls called Peg and Gwen; they drifted through, their faces vague above their black bow ties. She was forever getting new name badges printed.

Meanwhile the rising sun was warming her garden; the mist was dispersing in the frogspawn meadow. She had worked here for two years but it never failed to surprise her, that she could step out of the countryside into this seasonless box whose Muzak played the same tunes all the year round, tunes she almost recognized but never quite.

She squirted a table and wiped it down; she laid out the cutlery. It was half past eleven but breakfast and lunch were all the same here. Customers ate the Traditional English Breakfast at two in the afternoon and the Gammon Steak at teatime. When people stepped in here time was suspended, as if they were in a plane. In fact a burly businessman was sitting down right now and ordering Scampi Tails. He had a sheaf of papers with him. Outside, his Ford Granada was spattered with mud, though she couldn't see that. He was muttering into a portable phone but she didn't catch the words. In fact she didn't notice because she was ringing up the till and it was Audrey who was serving him.

Besides, she was day-dreaming. As she re-stocked the lollipop jar she was thinking *it's only a matter of time*. As she tidied the courtesy newspapers she was thinking *someone I recognize, they'll come through the door*. A blast of cold air, a face puzzlingly familiar, like the familiar chords in the Muzak. Surely, if you stayed in one place long enough, by the law of averages it must occur? There must have been countless people already who had touched her life at some point, if only she knew it, somewhere along the way. In fact, only the day before a man who had buggered Buffy at public school had stopped here for a Danish pastry but she wasn't to know that.

All her life things had slipped through her fingers. Men; other things. Things she thought about in the middle of the night. Jobs, too. At her age she should be doing something more demanding than this but she had never got the hang of how people did it – the planning, the known destination. When she was younger she hadn't listened to anybody's advice, she was wild and wayward, and now she was in her forties nobody gave her any advice at all. People didn't, at her age.

Business was slow. The scampi eater had long since gone, unnoticed by her. She re-stocked the wall holders with leaflets. They listed Happy Eater Restaurants. All of them seemed to be situated on roundabouts and motorways – *Ripley By-Pass. M50 Junction 5 (Northbound). A55 Interchange, Clwyd*. Bit like her, really. People thundering past, knowing exactly where they were going, nobody stopping for long. *Got to get back to the wife*.

She went off-duty at three, clomping away in her gum-boots. Outside the sun cast a golden light on the Happy Eater logo: a fat red face pointing to its open mouth. A man and a woman were arriving in separate cars; rural trysts took place here because there was bound to be nobody local around. At weekends other couples converged here; divorced couples who sat in the smoking section, they always smoked, while their child played listlessly with the complimentary Lego. At the end of the meal the child would be passed from one to the other, like a baton in a relay race; on the Sunday they would reappear and the child would be passed back.

Don't think of it.

She walked along the verge. Traffic rushed past. She was heading for some farm buildings half a mile away, to do some photocopying.

Sprockett's Farm had been converted into retail units. It was called The Sprockett's Farm Country Mall. Conveniently sited on the A2, within easy access of the M2, it was in a prime position to draw in customers from a fifty-mile radius. The canny farmer had realized this, when he sold the land to the developers, and he had now retired to the Canary Islands. The orchard had been tarmacked over to provide parking for four hundred cars. Various outbuildings, picturesquely lopsided, housed various business concerns – the Threshing Barn Travel Agency, the Old Piggeries Video Rental. There was even a food store, of sorts. In the local village the shop had long since disappeared, killed by the megastores, so when Lorna needed some marmalade she had to walk here, to Quality Country Fayre, and buy a ludicrously expensive pot topped with a gingham mob cap and really made in a factory in Southall.

The Rank Xerox Copy Shop was housed in the old hen house. Beneath the ancient beams machines hummed – fax, photocopiers, printers. On the wall were clocks displaying the time in Tokyo and New York. Lorna went in. When she had first lived here there had been real chickens pecking around but now the floor was covered with beige carpet tiles.

Keith, the manager, was on the phone; he was always on the phone. His family had once owned a smallholding, across the valley, but it had been turned into a dry-ski slope and he had become a wheeler-dealer. He nodded at the photocopier and Lorna opened it. She had some staff documents to copy.

The last piece of paper, from the preceding customer, was

still under the lid. She took it out. The scampi-eater had been the last customer but she didn't know this. She just glanced at the sheet of paper, automatically, as one glances at a postcard on someone else's doormat.

She read it once. Then she read it again. Keith was still on the phone. 'Bring Barry along on Tuesday,' he muttered, 'we'll have that pow-wow about the hot-dog franchise.' He had seen nothing.

She stared at the piece of paper. It was the last page of a memo concerning a planning application. She stared at it, her heart knocking against her ribs. Then she bundled the piece of paper into her pocket.

Twelve

The flat was so damned small; that was the trouble. As a love-nest in Soho it had been deliciously romantic, how did that John Donne thing go, *and make our little room an everywhere* . . . Penny had to admit it; she had been hoist with her own petard. It was fine when she and Colin were grappling on the bed, but once they started walking about and doing normal things they kept bumping into each other. It was a trendy conversion, all uplighters and granite work-tops, but it was far too trendy to have any storage space and she and Colin kept tripping over each other's stuff. That was why she had jettisoned most of her possessions back in Blomfield Mansions. The bathroom here was so tiny that whoever was sitting on the lavatory found themselves jammed into a foetal position. Colin had suggested cutting two cat flaps in the door, so the person's knees could poke through, but he hadn't got a saw to do it with because there was nowhere to keep it.

At least Colin didn't read, so there were no books cluttering up the place. Maybe he couldn't read. She realized, with surprise, that despite their intimacy she had never seen what his handwriting looked like. He did everything on the phone, or else he punched in messages on his personal organizer. He was a child of the microchip era, and entirely visual. This, however, brought problems. His kitchen was a style statement and he didn't like Nescafé jars and things cluttering it up and blocking the view of his Phillipe Starck lemon-squeezer, which stood alone, spotlit like a museum specimen. Sometimes, when she wanted a laugh, she tried to imagine what this flat would be like if Buffy lived in it.

How weird, how totally absorbing it was, stepping from one life into another, from one man's arms to another's! The difference between their bodies was the big shock at first, the big, guilty thrill, but she had got used to this by now. She had surrendered herself entirely to Colin – his stubble, the scent of his breath, his limbs slippery with sweat during their vigorous and ever-more-inventive lovemaking. He was such a stylist in this, too. An animal and a stylist. He had changed her, she became different creatures for him. Sometimes she was an eel, sliding all over him insinuatingly, her own boneless gymnastics astonishing and impressing her. Sometimes she became a boy for him, juddering and perverse. Oh, and more, more. Their bodies went on such adventures together in the dark; the next morning she blushed to think of it. Of course, she remembered Buffy but she felt disloyal to compare them – Buffy's frequently fruitless huffings and puffings, the things he said that suddenly made her giggle, the companionability and occasional joint success. The sudden freeze when he got a twinge in his back. She was a different woman now, drugged with sex, smiling at shopkeepers. Maybe she was like this during the early years of her marriage but she could no longer remember that, she didn't want to. Life with Buffy in the big, peeling flat was in the past, and she was slowly getting used to another man. His domestic habits and routines were becoming familiar to her. She readjusted to him without thinking now, as if she had gone to France and had learnt to drive on the right side of the road.

But the flat stayed small. That was why she liked to go out for breakfast. Besides, it made her feel continental. Buffy had introduced her to Bertaux's. He had gone on about Soho being a village, the good old days, Bohemia and all that, actors and their floozies. However, she herself hardly ever met anyone she knew; the only salutations she received were the Triple X cans waved at her from the doorway of a defunct boutique. A row of men sat there and whooped at her when she passed.

She usually breakfasted alone. Colin either got up early to go out on a shoot or else he slept late, obliterated like a teenager, his face buried in the pillow and his shoulders criss-crossed with the marks of her fingernails. She bought her usual pile of newspapers, went into Bertaux's and sat down. Like most journalists she speed-read all the papers and never remembered a word of them afterwards.

She was just dipping her croissant into her coffee when she heard a voice.

'Excuse me, are you Penny Buffery?'

'Penny Warren, actually.' Buffy had recently asked her, sourly, why all his exes, the moment they left him, dropped his name with such unseemly haste and reverted to their old ones. She had told him she had always worked, as a journalist, under her maiden name. Besides, who wouldn't drop *Buffery* if they had the chance. 'It's ancient Huguenot!' he had said. 'It's terribly distinguished.' A lie, of course.

'Do you mind me butting in?'

'Of course not. Sit down.'

It was a pale young woman with a pointed chin and thick, surprised eyebrows that needed plucking. Pretty enough but, oh, Lord the clothes! So terribly anodyne. She was wearing a fluffy pastel sweater, the type of thing somebody would wear if they sung in a provincial choir. That complexion cried out for strong colours.

'How amazing, seeing you here!' said the girl. 'You're the journalist, aren't you?'

Penny nodded modestly.

'Gosh! How wonderful. You see, I've read a lot of your things. Articles and things.'

Later, Penny would wonder how she knew she was a journalist if she had got her name wrong. Later, much later, she realized that the whole meeting had been engineered. At the time, however, she just felt ridiculously flattered.

'They're really great,' said the girl.

'How nice.' She laughed. 'You probably remember them better than I do.'

'Have you got any tips?'

Penny looked at her. Boxy shoulders would set off the neck; emphasise the *gamine*.

'You know, tips on writing,' said the girl.

'Don't tell me you want to be a journalist.'

The girl nodded. She didn't seem more than a girl, though she was probably in her twenties. There was a dateless, fashionless air about her that made her look young and . . . Penny searched for the word. *Innocent*. It took her a moment to find it because it had been so long since she had met anybody to whom it could be applied. How sweet! She felt a warm rush of motherliness – a new sensation.

'You sure?' she asked. 'Karl Kraus said *journalists write because they have nothing to say, and they have nothing to say because they write*.'

'Is that true?'

'I've never had time to work it out.' She laughed. 'The thing is, do you believe what you read in the papers?'

'I used to. I don't know what I believe in now.'

'Ah! The first qualification for a journalist. That's a good start.'

'What do you mean?'

'What you have to do is believe in it while you're writing it. Like a man murmuring nonsense to a woman while he's in bed with her. Each piece you write, it's a little seduction.'

The girl looked shocked. 'That's ever so cynical.'

'I find it rather bracing,' said Penny. 'Still want to do it?'

The girl nodded. She was looking at her with a fixed intensity that Penny found gratifying. She seemed to be devouring every detail of her. In her Kenzo jacket Penny felt chiselled and experienced, a woman of the world with this young Candide.

They talked for a while. Penny told her how she herself had started. The girl seemed refreshingly eager to learn about

71

the business. She also looked biddable. What a stroke of luck, to have bumped into her! Or was it the other way round?

Beckoning for the bill, she asked: 'Want to start right now? Want to do a job for me?'

She took Celeste back to the flat; she had learnt her name by now. Celeste wore track-suit bottoms and pink trainers, dear oh dear. The sort of thing a children's TV presenter would wear on a Fun Run. Penny would have to sort her out. She felt like a mother, taking her daughter in hand. Motherhood was another thing she had been too busy writing about to ever get round to doing herself.

'It all started with my column *Penny for Them*. Ever read it? It's in *Mine*.'

'*Mine*?'

'The magazine. You read it?'

'Oh, yes,' said Celeste. 'Yes, of course.'

She certainly looked like a typical *Mine* reader. C/D Socio-economic group. *Mine* was a reasonably downmarket women's weekly, created to rival *Best* and *Chat*. Recipes, showbiz gossip and for God's sake nothing longer than 1.5 column inches. *Mine* readers had the attention-span of gnats. *Penny for Them* was a nice little earner because all Penny had to do was to reply to readers' tips. These were suggestions like: *To make that casserole stretch, mix the stewing steak with tinned macaroni for a family supper Italian style!* Or Buffy's favourite, *To make wet concrete more workable, add a little wash-ing-up liquid when mixing it*. For this, readers received a £5 postal order and all Penny had to do was write: *Great idea, Mrs B of Bolton!* or *I agree, but for a low-cal treat try substituting yoghurt*. Buffy, of course, had found the whole thing hysteri-cal and made up his own, like: 'Wondering what to do with those worn-out diaphragms? Try using them as handy kneel-ing pads when gardening!'

They walked up the stairs and Penny unlocked the front door. 'I thought I'd tap my readers' ingenuity. Recycling's the thing nowadays but it's so terribly dowdy, isn't it? So I thought that they could send in suggestions and Colin and I would do a book on it. *Recycle with Style*, something like that. Colin's going to take the pics. He's a super photographer.'

'Recycling what?'

'Anything.'

'What sort of things?'

'Things you don't need anymore.' Penny laughed. 'Like old husbands. I know! *100 Uses for an Ex-Husband*. Lay him on the floor, he makes a great draught excluder! Put him on all fours, to create a super bedside table!'

Celeste was staring at her. 'Really?'

'Only joking.' Penny laughed. 'No, it's things like how to grow avocados in your old Ford Escort.' She led her into the bedroom. The door wouldn't open properly. 'You see, I asked readers to send in their ideas and they did. We're being absolutely inundated.' The door was blocked by a large pile of packages. 'We can't move. Colin's kicking up such a stink. Have you got somewhere with a bit of room?'

Celeste nodded. 'I live in Kilburn.'

'Well somebody has to, I suppose.' She paused, and looked at her. 'Do you want to do a job for me?'

'What?'

'Take the stuff home and sort it into categories. I'll pay you, of course.'

Celeste stared at her. Slowly, she nodded.

'Done.' Penny shook her hand; it was small and surprisingly cold. What a relief! She needed to get this book finished quickly. A lot of her freelance work had dried up since the discovery of last summer's bogus travel pieces and she needed the money. Besides, it was supposed to be a fun thing to do with Colin. But what had started out as a sure fire money-spinner, and a bit of a hoot to boot, was rapidly turning into a source of friction between them because of those damn parcels cluttering up the place.

'I'll call you a cab. Could you take them right now?'

She was just lifting the phone when Celeste cleared her throat and asked: 'What was your ex-husband like?'

73

How did she know she had an ex? Maybe from the inventive nature of her uses for one. Penny sat down. 'I'm rather fond of him, actually. He's called Russell. Colin calls him a boozy old fraud but Colin can talk. He makes his living squirting washing up liquid into beer so it all froths up for the photograph.'

'What's he like?'

'Colin?'

'Your ex.'

'Why on earth are you interested?' asked Penny.

'I just am.'

The girl had a flat, Midlands accent. *I just um*. Despite the delicate appearance there was something forthright about her. Perhaps they were all like that up there, in the wilds of wherever – forthright, curious. Her colleagues weren't curious about anything unless they were going to write a piece about it. This candid interest was rather flattering.

'I'll tell you his all-time favourite scene in a film. It's a Truffaut film, you know Truffaut?'

Celeste shook her head.

'A babysitter arrives at an apartment one evening. She's a young girl, very pretty. A middle-aged man opens the door and welcomes her in. He shows no sign of leaving, nor does he show her the child she's supposed to be looking after. Finally she asks him, *Where's the baby?* He smiles and replies: *L'enfant, c'est moi*. That's Buffy for you.'

Celeste had sat down on the Eames chair. She was listening intently. What an odd little thing she was, with that direct gaze! Penny was starting to enjoy this. Colin never asked about Buffy. He was either too painfully jealous of her past, or else totally uninterested. She hoped it was the former, of course, but she had her suspicions. It was nice to talk to such an eager listener. She missed the rambling, chatty conversations of her previous life.

She settled into the sofa, remembering the first time she had met Buffy. It had been on that flight from L.A. She had been interviewing a particularly moronic film starlet and was feeling homesick for England. Californians, she had decided, all had irony bypasses. Then along came this big, twinkly man who had made her laugh.

'He's older than me,' she said. 'Our first date was going to the opticians to get a new prescription for his glasses.' She remembered the dinner afterwards, followed by the invitation to try out his Rest Assured Support Mattress – such an unusual seduction line that she had gone along with it. The experience had been quite erotic actually, in a cosy sort of way. 'I thought older meant wiser, ho ho. Just because he'd seen the original production of *French Without Tears*. Probably *been* in it, for all I know. He moved in a different world to me, that was part of the attraction I suppose. He had a Past.'

'What sort of past?'

'The usual sort. In other words, lots of mess. He lived in the most indescribable pigsty, till I came along. The first time I got into bed with him, I found a whole piece of toast in it.'

'In the bed?'

She nodded. 'With marmalade on it. The lazy slob. Terribly unfit – all that smoking and drinking, he comes from the generation when everybody did, only he kept on at it. He once acted out Erich Von Stroheim being the butler in that Greta Garbo film, *As You Desire Me*, you ever seen it?'

'No.'

'I hadn't, then. Well, he was showing me how Erich Thingy did it, with hardly any movements – just a flick of the wrist, a flicker of the eyes. And afterwards he was panting away as if he'd run in the Olympics.'

'Did you love him?'

Penny paused. 'I suppose so.' She smiled. 'Women like him because he's interested in the same sort of things they are. Gossiping. Sitting around talking about people.' Buffy had said that his ideal life would be to live in a brothel as a sort of mascot, like Toulouse Lautrec but bigger, watching the girls dressing up and hearing them nattering about their clients. Or else to be a salesman in the Harvey Nichols linger-ie department. He loved making up scenarios for himself.

Her mother had adored him. She still did. Her mother thought Penny was mad, leaving him, but then she didn't have to live with him did she? Hauling him out of the boozer at four in the afternoon, making excuses on the phone to furious producers, having his horrible dog tripping her up and weeing on the carpet.

'He had this revolting little dog which looked like a hair-piece – an incontinent hairpiece. He was a terrible driver too. Weaving all over the road. When it was dusk he'd start flashing his lights at the other drivers, the belligerent bugger, and then he'd find he hadn't put his own lights on in the first place. Typical Buffy. Or he'd try to flash them and squirt his own windscreen instead.'

'You left him because he was a bad driver?'

'No, no. I left him because I fell in love with Colin.'

'What happened?'

Penny looked at her. She was leaning forward, her face pale against the black leather of the chair. 'Now I see why you want to be a journalist. Funny, you didn't look the curious type.'

'Oh dear, I'm sorry. Do you mind?'

Penny shook her head. 'We had this cottage in Suffolk. Still have, though it's up for sale now. Anyway, I got a conservatory built onto it, for a feature actually. Always a danger sign, building a conservatory.'

'Why?'

'It's a displacement activity. I've always thought divorce lawyers and conservatory architects should go into partner-ship together, save a lot of bother.' She paused. Had she thought of this herself or read it somewhere? Either way, was there a piece in it? Could she stretch it out to 800 words? 'Anyway, I had it built – classy job, carpenter called Piers, that's how classy. And Colin came to photograph it. It was lust at first sight.'

'Did you grow carrots?'

Penny hesitated. Was this some sort of sexual euphemism?

Celeste said: 'I mean – I just meant – did you have a vegetable garden?'

Penny nodded. 'I did all the digging, of course. Buffy said he couldn't because of his back.' She smiled. 'When the film *Batman* came out he called himself Backman. Just about to do some daring feat, music playing da-da-da-da, then he'd groan and stop. *"Backman!"'* She was laughing, now. 'Anyway, I did all the work and he took all the credit, of course. I think he believed he actually did it. He has a bottomless capacity for self-deception.'

'Has he?'

'Bottomless. He can make himself believe anything. He's an actor, you see. I forgot to tell you that. They're even worse than journalists. They have to tell lies, and believe them. That's how they make their living. Then – poof! – it's all gone. In their case, into thin air. Not even wrapping up fish and chips.'

'You mean he's a liar?' Celeste paused. 'Can I have a glass of water?'

'You do look pale.' Penny jumped up and went into the kitchen. She opened the fridge and inspected the bottles of mineral water. 'Carbonated, decarbonated, double decarbonated, double-double decarbonated with a twist of lemon?' she called.

'Pardon?'

'Or just tap water?'

She gave Celeste the glass of water. The girl's hand was trembling. Maybe she was going through some traumatic affair, too. Must send myself a memo to ask her, Penny thought. She was in that sort of mood – skittish.

The cab arrived and they carried the parcels downstairs. Celeste was driven off. Penny returned to the flat.

Talking about Buffy had done it. On the one hand she was deeply relieved to have left him – not since she was a child had she offered up such fervent prayers of thanks. On the other hand she missed him too. Perverse, wasn't it?

She sat on the bed – they had got rid of the futon now. Gazing at the now-empty expanse of carpet she remembered one afternoon last summer, when she had still been married. She and Colin were making love in a field and she had suddenly burst out laughing. 'What's the matter?' Colin had asked, put off his stride. She was remembering something Buffy had said when they were discussing those yellow fields of oilseed rape. 'They smell like ovulating gerbils,' he had said. She couldn't tell Colin this, of course. She had simply replied: 'I'm so happy.' Which was true. It was just that two men happened to be making her happy at the same time: one in her head and one in her body.

Adultery: The Positive Aspect. She could write a piece about it. Soon, maybe. Just now it was too painful.

Thirteen

'Wasn't it you I heard on the TV last night?' asked Mr Woolley. 'I recognized the voice.'

Buffy was lying in a flat in Hans Crescent. He was having his prostate probed. Hunched on his side, staring at the moquette wallpaper, he felt Mr Woolley's warm finger goosing him. This was far from dignified, but not entirely unpleasant either.

'I said to my wife: that's him. Advertising something or other . . . relax . . . that's better. What were you extolling the virtues of this time?'

'Barbecued Niblets,' said Buffy.

'I never remember what it is, do you? Wonder anyone remembers what to buy.' His finger slid deeper.

'What's it like?' asked Buffy.

'Enlarged, yes. Feel that?'

Buffy nodded.

'Enlarged, but not inordinately so.'

Buffy had explained to him in detail his difficulties when passing water – a vaguely Biblical phrase he liked using with medical men. How the whole process, the scattered grapeshot nature of it, took so long nowadays that by the time he was finished it was practically time to start all over again. Mae West said *I like a man who takes his time*. But this was ridiculous.

'And then there's the dry rot.'

'What?' Buffy froze.

'Dry rot, isn't it? Rising damp, that sort of thing.'

79

'What? Where?'

'Always a problem, in old buildings. Dry rot, wet rot.'

For a moment Buffy thought he was being addressed in some hideous metaphor. Was the fellow trying to tell him something? Then he realized.

'Ah,' he said. 'The advertisements, you mean. Rot-Away Damp Proof Courses.'

'Must keep the wolf from the door. I said to my wife, I said with that voice our Mr Buffery could sell diet pills to the Somalians.'

Buffy's breathing had returned to normal. Not for the first time, he wondered why private consultants made such terrible jokes. The more expensive they were, the more tasteless their sense of humour. They looked so pleased with themselves, too, with their shiny faces and bow ties. Not surprisingly, really. How could one answer back if one's mouth was stuffed with cotton wool or one's spine was being ruthlessly pummelled? How could one interrupt the unfunny patter for which one was paying, as it were, an arm and a leg? He had had a wide experience with consultants – his heart, his teeth, his gums, his waterworks. Just when you thought everything was all right another bit of the old body packed up. He was familiar with all the properties for sale in *Country Life*, read tensely in waiting rooms from Knightsbridge to Wigmore Street. He even knew which Right Honourable was marrying which.

'No need for any further action at this point,' said Mr Woolley, 'but see me again in six months.'

'What further action had you in mind?'

'You really want me to describe it?'

'No, no!' said Buffy hastily.

Mr Woolley's finger was withdrawn; the glove crackled as it was peeled off.

'Haemorrhoids okay?' asked Buffy.

'Fine. Nothing much the matter with you, really, old chap. Only the things one would expect . . .'

' . . . at my age. I know, I know.'

Buffy paid a large cheque to the receptionist and emerged into the sunshine. Outside Jaguars waited, their engines throbbing. He felt both relieved and obscurely disappointed that there was nothing really wrong with him. Just the ordinary depredations of age.

He walked down the street. One didn't exactly grow old; it wasn't as simple as that. One just felt a growing irritation with a whole lot of things which nowadays seemed designed to baffle and frustrate, like the impossibly-sealed plastic around a Marks and Spencer sandwich. The way that books seemed to be published with smaller and smaller print. The way that when he switched on Radio 3 and got settled into something it promptly changed to organ music. It probably had in the past, but not with such crowing regularity. Did other people feel any of this, or was he entirely alone? Why, when he paid for something with a £20 note, did the sales assistant hold it up to the light and give it such a hostile and lengthy examination? Was there something wrong with him? There seemed no end to the small indignities of the modern world; each day another popped up, like the paving stones, to trip him over. Only yesterday he had gone to his local bottle-bank – he was a late but enthusiastic convert to this – and while he was flinging in his empties, glaring at the man next to him who was putting his green bottles into the clear receptacle, he had suddenly felt a trickle of cold wine travelling down his sleeve. He had ended up soaked; who would have thought bottles had so much left in them? Especially *his* bottles.

Even without meeting Celeste he would have felt this, but she threw the whole business into sharper focus. The thing was, she made him feel both incredibly young and yet incredibly old. Both at the same time. There was that leaping, breathless possibility of renewal which was so rejuvenating. The world reborn through her fresh young eyes, the miraculous prospect of the old engine coughing into life, as if he were a dusty Hispano-Suiza mouldering away in some garage; she had pulled off the wraps, polished him up and lo and behold! He roared into life. There was all this – the way she listened, wide-eyed, to the anecdotes that everybody else had got bored of by now. All this. Yet her very youth taunted him. He had taken her to Covent Garden, the week before, to hear *Cosi*, and the way she had bounded up the stairs, as lithe and thoughtless as a colt . . . How elderly he felt as she waited for him to dodderingly join her. And when she asked what the Home Service was he suddenly felt utterly alone.

He was aware of the sugar-daddy aspect of all this; of people either thinking he was a lucky old pervert or else simply out on the town with a doting niece. The plain fact was: nothing had really happened yet. He had known her for two weeks now. They kissed; she stroked his beard; he ran his hands over her firm young body – oh, her skin! So smooth, so elastic! But then she slithered like a fish from his embrace and said she must be getting home. Though inflamed by her – he was only flesh and blood, after all – he was also secretly relieved. How could he compare with the young men she must have known? (He couldn't bring himself to ask about them). Of course he had a wealth of experience behind him, marriages and liaisons galore, but he suspected that this didn't count anymore. The old body wasn't what it was; besides, maybe they did things differently now. Through Penny, and through his many hours spent in doctors' waiting rooms, he was thoroughly *au courant* with what went on in women's magazines, and he was only too aware that nowadays the sexual demands of young women were, well, demanding. The vigour of them, the shrill and taunting battle-cries! The strident right to multiple orgasms achieved by ever-more-gymnastic methods. Hadn't they heard of a hernia?

Celeste wasn't like this, of course. She didn't read *Cosmopolitan*. This was one of her attractions. But he still felt there was something to be said for a Dante-and-Beatrice-type relationship of unfulfilled yearnings. Possibilities, after all, were as infinite as the solar system; they had no boundaries and there was nothing to bring you down to earth. With no destination there need be no endings, and he had had a bellyful of those. By golly he had. Botched, ugly, drunken, keeping you up all night on the endless carousel of recriminations and home truths; neither participants possessing the energy to halt the mechanism and get off. There was a lot to be said for a soft-focus kind of celibacy, and a nice mug of Horlicks. He knew a turning-point had been reached the year before, actually, when he had taken Penny to a musical called *Blues in the Night*. When a delicious black girl had come on stage dressed in peachy silk underwear he had whispered to his wife: 'Couldn't we have stuff like that for the living-room curtains?'

He walked along Knightsbridge. Upper-class, rosy girls loped past. Shoppers were accompanied by tiny dogs. In this area you could even glimpse that endangered species, a woman in a fur coat. Sometimes he felt that this street was his spiritual home. He too could have been a man of leisure, living in Montague Square and buying *objets d'art* at lunchtime, if he hadn't been crippled by alimony. Prosperous-looking continental couples paused to look in the windows of Jaeger; the men wore leather trench-coats and the women looked pampered and ruthless, with burnished hair and Gucci boots. They were bound to have lovers. Why were the French so efficient in matters of the heart? They dealt with it as efficiently as they dealt with their digestive systems. Compared to theirs, his life seemed such a muddle – a Flodden Field compared to their Garden of Versailles.

On the other hand, what a rich full life he had had, the lucky bugger. One could look at it that way, the Chimes at Midnight way. That a marriage ends, does that make it a failure? After all, life itself ends, at some point or another. Does this make life a failure too?

It was in this reflective mood, always brought on by a visit to a doctor, that he downed a malt whisky in a mock-mahogany pub somewhere off Beauchamp Place. Two solicitors sat nearby. ' . . . not a lot of legroom, but that's the Nips for you,' said one of them. Buffy could spot a solicitor a mile off; he had known so many. These two were only about twelve years old, of course, but that was par for the course now. During their divorce proceedings, Jacquetta's solicitor was so young that Buffy had suggested he went to the lavatory before they started. Neither of them had laughed, but then Jacquetta had never been blessed with a sense of humour.

Solicitors, flat-rental agencies and removal men – how well he had got to know them over the years, what a good and trusty client he had been! Pickford's Head Office even sent him a Christmas card.

He downed another Glenfiddich. He would buy Celeste a present – something wildly extravagant, at Harrods. A nice repeat fee had come through that morning and he was feeling flush. It was funny; every now and then he earned quite a lot of money, usually for something he couldn't remember doing, but it didn't last long. All his wives had complained about his sojourns in the betting shop. 'It's so stupid!' they said. 'It's not betting that's stupid,' he had replied, 'it's losing.'

He emerged from the pub. It was already dusk. How quickly darkness fell, in the winter! He passed a Boots and thought fondly of Celeste, toiling away in her nylon overall. When he got to know her better he would take her away from all this, if she would let him. The whole strategy was rather vague so far because he didn't really know what she wanted. She spoke very little about herself. In fact he hadn't told her much about his own life, either, though she had asked him rather a lot about Penny. This seemed more encouraging than any amount of endearments.

What an adventure, to start again! A new woman, a new life. He felt optimistic and energised now. So energised, in fact, that he had another little drink to celebrate, in a hostelry across the street. He could hear about her past. Once again he would memorise the names of relatives, and hear about a childhood he painfully wished he had witnessed from a fly-on-the-wall position. He would learn that her father had never shown her enough affection – every woman he had ever known said that. He would become acquainted, through her upbringing, with a corner of England he had never known existed, but which would become a warm, glowing spot on the map – even when his relationships collapsed these places retained a tarnished sort of significance. First bikes; first bras. He loved hearing about all that. He would learn, agonizingly, of early crushes on the boy-next-door, and even more agonizingly of first affairs with men he might have sat next to, unknowingly, on the bus.

How mysterious they were, these forays into the past! Through women he had entered into a gambolling-over-the-hills childhood in the Brecon Beacons, into a fraught and chilly household in Leamington Spa. It was the most tender sort of history lesson. The cumulative effect was like *Old Macdonald Had a Farm*; one story added to another, a *quack-quack* here and a *bow-wow* there, more and more as time went on, wife after wife, until the song was so long it was quite a strain to memorise it. Especially after a few peerlessly unblended malts.

Buffy made his way across the street. He would become young again, he would get his mojo working, whatever that meant. He would even go dancing, if that was what she wanted, and make a complete prat of himself. And in return he would initiate her into the bliss of opera, in his experience totally unappreciated by the young – not that all the women he had loved had been as dewy as Celeste but none of them had understood the joys of Verdi, they had that in common. Thanks to him, there were at least seven women currently at large who could hum whole chunks of *Rigoletto*. That was an achievement of sorts, wasn't it?

He approached Harrods and stopped dead. Behind one of the windows a young man was busy working on the Christmas display; he adjusted a ball gown over the cleavage of a mannequin and stood back to look at the effect. It took Buffy a moment to recognize him.

Then he realized. It was Quentin, his son.

How tall he was! Tall and lithe. Neither Buffy nor Popsi had been slim, even then; how miraculous that this willowy creature had sprung from their loins. Quentin was dressed in black, like a modern dancer. His mouth glinted with pins.

Buffy hadn't seen him for some months now. Well, years. For a moment, the weirdness of his own son's name struck him anew. Popsi had insisted on it. At the birth – from which Buffy was of course absent but all chaps were in those days, they went to the pub – at the moment of birth Popsi had apparently said 'That's Quentin.' Not in general a stubborn woman, she hadn't budged on this one. 'He just is.'

Buffy waved, but his son didn't see him through the glass. He was about to shout *Quentin* but suddenly felt self-conscious. A couple, arm-in-arm, stopped to stare. Maybe they thought he was some pathetic old poofter, trying to attract the attention of this comely window-dresser.

Quentin knelt to fix a piece of fabric with some sort of staple gun. He looked graceful, and totally absorbed. The window was a tableau of family Christmases past – a handsome pair of mannequin parents, plus three offspring in velvet knickerbockers, flanked by reproduction furniture. Fake candlelight shone on their shiny, sightless faces. The smallest hint of a smile seemed to play around their lips as they gazed past Buffy. How superior they looked! Standing in the dark, he tried to collect his thoughts: last time he had seen Quentin he had been at St Martin's Art School, hadn't he? Was it really that long ago?

Buffy waved again but his son didn't look up. He tapped on the glass, but no response. Quentin was pinning up some ribbon, his head cocked sideways, his back to the window. He was totally sealed off in his aquarium. *Remember me?* Buffy wanted to shout. *Look, it's your father!*

Some more people stopped and stared. He hadn't really shouted it, had he? The traffic rumbled past. He tapped on the glass again but his son was speaking, wordlessly, to another young man who had just appeared, carrying a length of red ribbon. They nodded to each other, laughed, and just as Buffy was about to tap again, louder this time, Quentin slipped away behind a partition and was gone.

Buffy was in Harrods now, pushing through the shoppers. A woman stepped out, pointed something at him and sprayed him with perfume. How could he get to the window, inside the shop? All he could see were scarves and handbags and solid walls filled with shelves full of scent bottles. 'Can I help you?' somebody asked. He knocked over a stand of leather gloves, they fell like leaves around him. Maybe he wasn't even on the right *side* of the shop; he had lost his sense of direction. It was never that reliable, even at the best of times. He found himself squeezing behind a counter.

'Excuse me, sir.' A man in uniform took his arm.

Buffy laughed. 'Just looking for the exit.'

Now he seemed to be out in the street, hailing a taxi. He sat in the back, utterly exhausted, as it drove him home. Anyway, he could see Quentin anytime. He could pop round one evening for a glass of wine. Quentin lived in Leytonstone, didn't he? Or was that Maxine, Popsi's daughter by what's-his-name, the man she married after him, Terry? Buffy's head span; just for the moment he couldn't quite work it out. How many children had he actually got? There was Nyange, of course, his daughter Nyange. He hadn't seen her for quite a while, either. She lived somewhere awful too, almost as bad as Leytonstone. Where was it? Carmella, her mother, had told him when he had bumped into her in Shaftesbury Avenue, he was sure he had written down the address on a piece of paper . . .

He stopped the cab on the corner of his street. Suddenly, desperately, he wanted to see Celeste. Just to see her, even if he didn't talk to her. Just to see her face.

He hurried across the road to the chemist's shop. It was closed, of course; he had already realized that. He looked at his watch: 6.20. He stared into the shadowy interior of the shop. Nothing stirred. Women's faces stared at him, from the rows of packets. He tapped on the glass. No point in doing that, of course, but he had to do something. He seemed to have been tapping on windows a lot today.

'Left something in there?' Paddy, one of the regulars at The Three Fiddlers, had stopped to look in the window too.

'Yes!'

'By Jesus, the stink on you! You smell like a whorehouse!' said Paddy, flinching back. 'Coming for a drink?'

Fourteen

While Buffy was sitting in the pub that evening Celeste was in Frith Street, ringing Penny's doorbell. She didn't know her phone number, that was her excuse for coming round like this. Thank goodness Penny was at home. She opened the door; her face was plastered with yellow stuff.

'It's all right. It's mud from the Nile. Don't make me laugh or cry, else it'll all flake off.' She took Celeste upstairs. 'How nice to see your pure young face. It's been a perfectly ghastly day.' She opened the fridge and got out a bottle of wine. She was wearing a towelling robe with *Hotel Cipriani* embossed on the pocket. 'Everything's broken down. The expresso machine, the fax machine.'

'Perhaps you could grow mustard and cress in them.'

She laughed; her hand flew to her cheeks. 'Don't!'

'I opened all the parcels last night,' said Celeste.

'Already? How marvellous.'

'Some of them are ever so ingenious. There's a shower cap made out of a baby's plastic pants, stapled together. But it's going to take a bit of time. A lot of them are rather complicated. There's something made out of a colander and old hoover bags that I haven't got the hang of at all.'

'You're an angel. I can see you're going to be quite indispensible.'

It was easier somehow, talking to this masked woman. She looked so impervious. Celeste decided to plunge straight in.

'Talking of growing things, did you and your ex-husband, what was his name?'

'Buffy.'

'Did you and Buffy have any children?'

'God, no! He was a terrible father!'

Celeste paused. 'What do you mean? Was he married before?'

'Was he married? Taking over Buffy was like taking over a house full of sitting tenants.' She poured out two glasses of wine. 'All of them wanting rate rebates.'

'Who was he married to?'

'A ghastly, neurotic woman called Jacquetta. They had two delinquent sons who used to come round every weekend and wreck the place. I had to be nice to them, of course. Wicked stepmother and all that. All good copy, I suppose. Got a lot of pieces out of it.'

'What were they like?'

'Lounging in front of the TV all day watching *Neighbours*, amazing they haven't grown up with Australian accents. Crisp wrappers everywhere, horrible sticky things under the cushions. Table manners like baboons, of course. When they were little it was toys scattered all over the place with endless dead batteries, Buffy used to buy them terribly complicated things, guilt of course, but he never put them together, he was hopeless at that, and all the instructions were in Taiwanese or something. Then it was Walkmen, I kept treading on the headphones, and them being bored all the time and leaving the bathroom like a marsh, how do people get towels so *wet*? Adolescents! Lying on the floor, great bare feet, flicking the TV channels with their horrible horny toes.'

She paused, panting. *Hotel Cipriani* rose and fell on her breast. Celeste stared at her. Asking Penny questions was like pulling the lever on a fruit machine – masses of money poured out. She couldn't be lonely, could she? A sophisticated woman like Penny. She couldn't feel the way Celeste did when she sat alone in her flat, listening to the sounds upstairs from Waxie.

Penny took a gulp of wine. 'And nicking my hair mousse. And cleaning their fingernails with my forks.' She screwed

90

her eyes shut. 'And the *phone*. They were always on the phone, nobody else could get through, mumbling in mono-syllables in their awful cockney accents. They live in Primrose Hill, you see. Everybody's children have cockney accents there.'

'Is it a poor area?'

She laughed. Flakes of the mask fell, like plaster. 'Christ, no! Full of rich, liberal parents. That's why they have these awful children. Luckily the boys didn't come round so much towards the end, they said it was so boring. They wanted to go out with their friends. Trails of silent friends, all in black overcoats like undertakers, sliding into the flat. Totally silent! Long, black coats. They'd all go off to Camden Lock, masses of them, like a great black oil slick. Honestly Celia, it's such a relief now.'

'Celeste.'

'Sorry. Celeste.'

'What was she like, his ex-wife?'

Penny groaned. 'Oh, God. Jacquetta.' There was a pause. 'Jacquetta.'

'She ended up marrying her shrink, you know. Saved on bills, I suppose. Like an alcoholic marrying their wine merchant. He's quite famous – Leon Buckman, heard of him?'

Celeste shook her head.

'He's always on the box. When I first met Buffy his TV was broken. He'd kicked it in when Leon was on some pro-gramme about sexual dependency.' She dipped her finger in her wine, lifted out a flake, and wiped it on her robe. 'It's funny, I can talk about her now. She doesn't mean anything anymore. It's like looking at a photo of Cliff Richard.'

'She looked like Cliff Richard?'

'No, no. It's just, years and years ago, when I was young, he used to bring me out in goosepimples, I lusted after him so much, and now he's just a creepy old Christian covered in Panstick. You can't believe these feelings could die, can you, they're so fierce at the time.'

'Jealousy, you mean?'

Penny nodded. 'You ever been jealous?' Celeste opened her mouth to reply, but Penny went on. She had gathered momentum now. She talked in a rush, as if she hadn't talked to anyone in a long time. 'I used to drive past her house.'

'In Primrose Hill?'

'That's right. Buffy's old house, where they used to live together. Where she still lives. If her car was parked outside I looked into it, at the stuff on the back ledge. Apple cores. Leaflets for holistic centres in Crouch End. Whatever they were, even her kids' stuff, they were sort of charged. They made me feel faint. You probably think I'm silly – '

'No, I don't actually.'

'I've never told anyone this. Funny, isn't it? I used to look up at the house and imagine their life in it. The bedroom was on the second floor. I'd look at the window and try to work out how many times they must've made love in there. Hundreds? Thousands? Seven years, 365 days, say, on average twice a week . . .'

'That's 728 times.'

'But say they'd done it more often the first couple of years. Say, five times a week for the first three months . . .'

'That's sixty times.'

'Gosh!' Penny grimaced. 'And, say, three times a week for the next eighteen months . . .'

'216,' said Celeste, 'which plus the sixty makes 276 in total, for the first two years.'

'Hey, you're fast!' Penny looked at her with admiration. 'A mathematical genius. What a surprising girl you are.' She laughed. 'If you knew Buffy you'd think how ridiculous, but I was in love with him then, you see. I thought: maybe he'd been a lot more vigorous then, maybe she was marvellous in bed. I wondered whether he compared us. What her body was like.' She stopped. 'This is stupid. You're not interested in this.'

'I am. Go on. Hadn't you seen her?'

'Oh, yes. A few times. When I brought the children back.

Gosh, this is fun. I'm glad Colin's not here.' She drained her glass. 'Don't usually drink, either.'

'What did she look like?'

'Rather beautiful, I must admit. I didn't want to admit it, of course. Though in a funny way it made Buffy more attractive, that he'd been married to a beautiful woman. She was sort of bony and soulful. Thick, curly mane of hair when mine had always been boring and straight. I couldn't see much of her body because she wore so many layers, awful arty clothes, cobwebby shawls, Miss Haversham meets the Incas. But I imagined it. I wondered if her thighs were slimmer than mine. If she was, you know, *tighter* inside because of all her t'ai chi.'

'What's that?'

'Chinese martial arts. Terribly seventies.' She refilled the glasses.

Celeste's head was swimmy. She tried to catch everything Penny was saying, but she talked so fast. Larger pieces of her face pack had now flaked off, revealing areas of skin beneath.

'It was much worse in the cottage, of course,' said Penny.

'The place in Suffolk? With the carrots?'

Penny nodded. 'There were all these relics of her there, and I had to live with them. Things she'd planted in the garden, that always reminded me of her. Trees and things, that I couldn't pull up. I tried, once, but the roots were too deep.' She sighed. 'Curtains she and Buffy had chosen together. Stuff they'd got at auctions when they were probably happy, or as happy as you could be with such a self-absorbed cow as her. I had the whole place redecorated, of course – I did this feature on updating your second home, so I got it done for nothing. I even had the cesspit emptied. I said to Buffy *I don't want any old wife's droppings in there.*'

They sat in silence for a moment. Down in the street cars hooted, stuck in the traffic. Below them, people must be shovelling in pasta. Everyone was busy having an evening out. Celeste willed this Colin man not to come home yet.

93

'I threw out everything I found in cupboards and drawers, of course,' said Penny. 'Hairpins, boxes of Tampax, her dusty old packets of mung beans. Cassettes with her slopey handwriting on them. Joan Baez, honestly!'

'Who's she?'

'Soppy folksinger. Typical Jacquetta. You're too young to know about Joan Baez.' She paused, remembering. 'Shells from family holidays, and old espadrilles with sand still in them. Photos, of course. They're the worst.'

Celeste nodded. 'I know.'

'When Buffy was out one day, I found a photo of her sunbathing on the lawn. I burnt it. Then the next day I dug a vegetable patch there, to get rid of her.'

'Where you grew the carrots?'

'And later I got the conservatory built. The final exorcism. Fumigation. Whatever. But by then she'd sort of dissolved anyway, she'd lost her power, because I'd fallen out of love with Buffy.' Suddenly she jumped up. 'Gosh, I wish you'd taken notes. I must write all this down, before I forget.'

'Why?'

But Penny wasn't listening. 'Sally's gone to *New Woman*, hasn't she,' she muttered, searching for a pen, 'or was it *Woman's Journal*? She liked my thing on the Redundant Penis. Cut it to ribbons, of course, but still . . .' She grabbed a notepad. 'There's always Louise, she owes me one after that debacle over the menopause piece . . .' She stopped. 'Shit, they've sacked her.' The peeling mask gazed thoughtfully through Celeste. '*Options* might want it. I gave them lots of names for that *How I Lost my Virginity* thing . . .' She tapped the Pentel against her teeth.

Celeste got up. 'Shall I just get on with it then?'

'What?'

'The recycling thing.'

'Sure, sweetie. Some more arrived this morning. I biked them round.'

Celeste made her way to the door. The floor rocked gently

from side to side as if she were standing on a swing. 'Bye, then.'

'Wait!' Penny disappeared, and came back with a jacket. 'Have it. It's Saint Laurent.'

'I couldn't!'

'It's all right, it didn't cost me anything. We did some fashion shots. It'd look much better on somebody young.' She did, in fact, look ancient this evening, her face cracking like a monument.

'You sure?'

Penny put it on her. 'Boxy shoulders. I knew you'd look good in it. Power dressing!'

Celeste managed to climb onto the bus. The sliding doors hissed shut. Clinging to a pole, she swung herself into a seat. She thought: What's happening to me? I'm drunk. I'm wearing an ex-wife's clothes. I'm learning things I had no inkling of.

The man in the seat next to her leant towards her and said: 'Let's have a look at those titties.'

'Go fuck yourself!' she replied loudly.

He got off at the next stop and she sat there, blushing. How could she have said that? She had never sworn in her life. Where did those words come from? She started giggling and put her hand over her mouth.

She made her way up Kilburn High Road, past the boisterous Irish pubs and the glowing, rosy curtains of the Society Sauna and Massage. It was nine o'clock. A Rastafarian leant against a lamp-post, eating a drooping triangle of pizza. London alarmed her less, now. She was learning to deal with it. She stopped outside her flat and fished for her keys. I'm learning to lie, she thought, marvelling at herself. Well, I'm learning to keep quiet about the truth. I'm learning to drink Sancerre and wear power jackets.

In the hallway she stumbled over a large parcel. A note was sellotaped to it: *Whose is this? Waxie.* She carried it upstairs and switched on the light. But she didn't open the package, or even look at the heaps of objects arranged around the floor like the items for some demented jumble sale. She went straight to the phone directory, and opened it at 'B'.

In one sense, things were becoming more confusing. But she was learning to cope. *Buckman, Leon.* She found the address, in Primrose Hill Road, and sat still for a moment. Her heart thumped. She looked down at her jacket; it was a rich midnight blue and beautifully cut, even she could see that. She had never worn anything like it. Back home the neighbours wouldn't recognize her; they would think she had come to do a survey or something.

She fingered the stiff lapel. This was what actors did; they dressed up and became somebody else. Buffy knew how to do it; that was his job.

Suddenly she was ravenous. She made some toast, heated up some baked beans and poured them over it. As she sat she looked at her new self, hanging over the back of the chair. She felt strong and resourceful. Shy? No, not now. Not any longer.

Fifteen

In his basement consulting room, Leon was listening to a patient. Outside, children whooped on Primrose Hill. Indoors, there was a long, shuddering breath.

'I'm ready to talk about my father now,' his patient was saying.

Leon nodded. 'What do you want to tell me?'

'I've kept it buried, you see, all these years. What he did to me. I *know* he did it to me because I can't remember it.' She took a drag of her cigarette. 'I've buried it, I realize that now. I've denied it to myself, because it's so painful . . .'

She sat, wreathed in smoke. *Here we go again*, Leon thought. He wondered, for a moment, if the time would come when his two grown-up daughters in America would suddenly accuse him of sexual abuse, and take his protests as further proof of guilt. Everyone was muscling in on it now. Even Jacquetta had had a go, telling him she was sure now that her father, a mild, stammering academic, had fondled her in her bath when she wasn't looking. It reminded him of the sixties, when practically every woman he met had claimed some sort of sexual contact with Jimmy Hendrix.

' . . . he used to sit me on his knee, you see, and read me *Winnie the Pooh*. He used to read to me every night. I should have realized that was a danger sign. He wanted me close to him, he wanted power over me . . .'

The front door banged. There was a dragging noise along the ceiling. He and Jacquetta had the builders in. Well, Jacquetta had the builders in. They were building her a con-

97

servatory in the garden. A distant voice bellowed: 'Stavros! Where the fuck's those two-by-fours?'

His patient lit another cigarette. 'I see it now, of course, since I've been coming here. All my victim-dictated behaviour stems from that time when I sat there, his arms around me, giving me a hug and a kiss when he closed the book . . .' Her voice trembled.

Leon shivered. There was a draught in the room. Had somebody left the back door open?

She started to cry. 'That hug. I know now it wasn't just a hug. Oh no. It was a sort of rape, an assertion of his power over me, his male power, abusing my trust, my little girl's trust . . .'

Leon looked up. A man had come into the room. He wore overalls and was covered in dust.

'Sorry, mate. Just looking for a plug for me extension lead.'

Leon and Jacquetta didn't quarrel; they talked things through. When he went upstairs for lunch she was pouring boiling water onto her ginseng tea-bag. He went up to her and kissed her lightly on her forehead.

'Sweetheart, we really must do something about the noise.'

'*I* should, you mean.'

A mixture of hammering and Capital Radio floated in from the garden. He opened the oven. Maria had heated him up some cannelloni. God bless the Portuguese. His wife was too spiritual to cook. Too spiritual to pay her parking tickets either, he thought, as he glimpsed another couple of them amongst the opened mail on the table. He put them into his pocket and sat down.

'The builders, they've been using the patients' lavatory,' he said. 'The seat was up and there was a cigarette butt floating in it.'

'I knew you didn't want me to have the conservatory built. I knew you thought it was too expensive.'

'I didn't say that, actually.' At the time, he had just asked her if she was sure she wanted it. There had been a piece in the paper, only yesterday, about conservatories being a warning signal of marital unrest. On the women's page. Something about architects combining with divorce lawyers. He had only read it because it was next to an article about the dysfunctional orgasm, one of his specialities.

'You don't understand, Leon. You can seal yourself off in your, your . . .' She pointed towards the basement. ' . . . your ivory tower. I'm a *woman*. I have children. Things are needed from me all the time, little pieces of me. It's give, give, give. This place . . .' She gestured around the expanse of the kitchen . . . 'I feel hemmed in, Leon. Closed in.' She pointed out of the window, to the green slope of Primrose Hill. ' . . . that concrete jungle out there, all those people. I need to be just myself sometimes. I need somewhere to be alone, with growing things.'

'But you can't be alone in a conservatory. That's the point of them. Everybody can see you.'

She sighed. He noticed, for the first time, the grey threads in her hair. Not for the first time, exactly, but it always gave him a shock to see them. She was still a handsome woman – strained, fine-boned – but there was no doubt that they were growing old together. His own mane of hair had turned grey quite suddenly soon after he had married her. But he still had a certain Norman Mailer glamour to him, one of his female patients had remarked on this only recently. She was still in transference.

Jacquetta turned away, her beads swinging. She was wearing a mulberry, knitted two-piece he had bought for her in Monsoon. After they had married he had tried, gently, to tone down her wardrobe. This was for her sake as much as for his, she surely didn't want to be seen as a wrinkled Flower Power child at some conference in Stockholm. But then it turned out that she had no intention of coming on his conference trips anyway. Not for her, the role of appendage. Or, to put it another way, the role of supportive wife.

'I know we're not supposed to exist up here,' she said. 'I know we're not supposed to have a life. I couldn't bear *you*

99

having a life, when I was your patient. I remember hearing the radio through the wall. Your incredibly dreary wife listening to *The Archers*.'

'It wasn't her. She never listened to *The Archers*. It was the home help.' His ex-wife, in fact, was now a senior investment analyst on Wall Street but Jacquetta didn't like to be reminded of this. Even now, after nine years, she never called his ex-wife by her name. Jacquetta had an awe-inspiring capacity for self-deception, something they were just starting to do some good work on when their relationship slid from the professional to the personal, he had joined her on his couch (the floor, actually) and the analysis had to be prematurely terminated.

Jacquetta was nibbling a piece of celery in her abstracted way, as if she wasn't really doing anything as boring as eating. Sometimes he found this endearing; it depended on his mood. He loved her, he was sure, but on the other hand he was a man of science. What was love? A muscular spasm? A reassurance of the self? A need for lit windows when you returned home in the dark? He couldn't talk about this because she would take offence. She was extremely touchy. *Fiery*, he had thought at first, *artistic temperament*, but now he thought, touchy. *Difficult* was only something other people said. Despite all sorts of things, he still found her lovable. Contrary, but lovable. If, after all this time, he knew what love was.

He had been through so many marriages and so had she. That at least was something they shared. It brought them close, like children of army parents who had been brought up in trouble spots all over the world. Of course he felt the odd tweak of jealousy, but by hosting a Channel 4 series on the subject he had finally drained it of meaning, even for himself. Sometimes he still felt uncomfortable, too, living in her old marital home and working in the bottom of it, like a miner digging away in the depths of its subconscious, digging away at his seam of gold. But it was in a prime location, crammed with money and neurotic wives, and she had managed to hold onto the property with her own vague sort of ruthlessness, as if it were humdrum and somehow demeaning for anyone else, in this case poor old Buffy, to battle over the vulgar subject of money. She had managed it the way she nibbled the celery, vaguely disclaiming responsibility for what she was doing. Being on the profiteering end of this – his own wife having kicked him out, subsequently sold the house and gone back to the States – he had failed to ally himself with Buffy in any us-men-together sort of way. He wasn't that sort of pubby chap anyway. He had always been better with women. Besides, he had been sleeping with the man's wife.

He scraped his plate clean and stacked it in the dishwasher. Jacquetta was standing at the window, peering at the building site in their back garden. She wasn't wearing her glasses; she was always losing them somewhere around the house. Hunting for her spectacles was the only indoor activity that all the family shared. The workmen had suddenly disappeared, the way workmen do. Maybe for lunch, maybe for weeks. She was twirling a piece of hair around her finger. She was either spoiling for a fight or just waiting for him to leave.

'I know India's being difficult,' she said, 'but you could be more supportive.'

'I'm very fond of India. I'm very fond of all your children.'

'You hate her using our bathroom.'

'Only because she's in there such ages.'

'She's insecure about her looks. That's why.'

'I just wish she'd be insecure in the boys' bathroom.'

'She can't. It's too disgusting.'

That was true. Even Maria, their treasure, wouldn't go into the boys' bathroom. She wouldn't go into their bedrooms any more, either. Last week, ignoring a *Quiet Please! Examination in Progress* sign Bruno had stolen from school and pinned to his door, she had gone into his room and found him in bed with the girl from the dry cleaners.

'She is trying to find a flat,' said Jacquetta.

India won't move out, thought Leon. Not if she has any sense. Nobody's children move out anymore. In fact he *was* fond of India. She was the product of Jacquetta's first marriage to a man called Alan. They had been hippies together in the sixties; Leon had seen some painful but hilarious snapshots of them in bellbottoms. Their daughter was called India because she had been conceived in an ashram near Bangalore. He sometimes wondered if India's subsequent problems stemmed, in some measure, from this continuous reminder of the sexual activity that had produced her, twenty-three years previously. At the very least, it seemed embarrassing. Her father, Alan, had since gone into software.

'It's not India,' he said, 'it's the boys. One of them's been using my computer. I tried to call up a file yesterday – a patient's file, she was just about to arrive – and instead I got *The Pros and Cons of Bismark's Foreign Policy*.'

Jacquetta twitched her shoulders, as if a midge were bothering her. She wasn't really listening.

He went on: 'For people who don't ever talk to us they make an extraordinary amount of noise. And we've got to do something about their rabbits.'

'We can't get rid of the rabbits. They're *theirs*.'

'But they never go near them,' he said. 'They never even go in the garden. They never even open their *curtains*. They've forgotten they *exist*.'

'They wouldn't if they went. They'd be terribly upset, you know that. Remember what happened with their stick insects.'

'That was Buffy's fault,' he said. 'Anyway, they could've been dead for years by then. They were mummified. Everyone had forgotten about them.'

'The boys were traumatized, Leon! I talked it through with my group. I couldn't let it happen again.'

'But the things keep breeding, sweetheart, and getting out of their hutches. It's pandemonium out there, since the workmen arrived. Last week one of my patients was just starting to open up for the first time – five months it'd taken.

102

She was just starting to talk – to freely talk – when this baby rabbit hopped into the room and started to wash its ears.'

Jacquetta gazed out of the window. 'All right. But we can't get rid of the original pair. Not for children of a broken home. That would be too symbolic.'

Sixteen

That night the temperature dropped. The wood next to Lorna's cottage, already so thin and wintry, closed in on itself. Water froze in the ruts. Nothing stirred; the place was locked. The first frost, when it arrives, locks the senses; it is impossible to imagine anything changing. But Lorna, lying in bed, knew otherwise. She had read the sheet of paper, plucked from the photocopier. She didn't need to sleep to start this particular nightmare, for it was starting right now, without her. *My wood, my secret wood*, she repeated to herself, *how can they?* She turned over, and stared at the ceiling. *How can they bulldoze it up and turn it into a Leisure Experience?*

Brenda was dreaming of leisurewear, the flip-flip of the catalogue pages. She never remembered her dreams, the next day. Well, there was so much to do, wasn't there? It was all go, go, go.

Beside her, Miles slept. He had spiralled airily down into a place she could never reach. Nobody could meet him there except his uninvited guests, each night so eyebrow-raising yet so inevitable. He lay, trapped by Brenda and released by his dreams; outside the drone of cars, the arc lights. Beyond the ring road, Swindon slumbered.

He slept, dead to the world. He dreamt from the store of his past; none of the people in this story were alive for him yet though, who knows, he may have brushed against the shoulder of somebody who had brushed against one of them; he himself might have brushed against one of them. A car carrying somebody who had made love to one of them might even now be circling the roundabout whose sodium lights filtered through the curtains and bathed Brenda's humped shape in a flat and shadowless glow.

Way above the starter homes, above the orange glow of Swindon, the moon shone. It shone on the wood next to Lorna's cottage, its own reflection blurred in the frozen puddles. It shone on the white bones of Jacquetta's conservatory, curved like whale ribs over the black, matted garden. There is nowhere as secret as a London garden. Closed in by the cliffs of the surrounding houses, whose lights switched off one by one, it guarded its memories – of Buffy's children and the children before them, children who themselves had grown old and died. Beyond the houses, over in the Zoo, the wolves howled.

Jacquetta's dreams were incredibly vivid and powerful. She was proud of them, like a mother is proud of her surprisingly athletic children; the next morning she liked to recount them in detail to whoever she was living with at the time. Her first husband, Alan, used to roll his eyes and say 'Wow', but he said wow to everything. A man called Otto tried to interrupt and tell her his. Buffy, after they had been married for a while, used to get impatient. 'Bloody hell,' he would say, 'I've forgotten who everybody is. Hang on a bit. It's like some blooming Norse saga.' But then Buffy had never really understood her.

Leon did. Leon understood her creative unconscious, her needs and her insecurities, her fragile sense of self. He understood how, through her disastrous relationships with men, she was trying to make contact with the child in herself, the small girl trying to gain the love of the cold and distant father who had in all likelihood abused her in the past. Leon had explained it. How she needed constant reassurance from the men who she chose unerringly for the damage they would do to her. How she had to break those old childhood patterns. In

105

the group she went to, they called it Rewriting the Family Script.

The problem with Leon, if there was a problem, was that he understood too much. This was something else they discussed in the group. She had once had an affair with her gynaecologist – she had gone to him about her painful periods – and quite apart from the fact that he had turned out to be yet another sadistic bastard she had had the feeling that he was more familiar with her erogenous zones than she was herself. This had left her feeling helpless and disempowered, as if she were a bystander while he and her sexual organs just got on with it. Sometimes she felt that Leon was doing this, with her head.

He was wonderful, of course. He was a suave and accomplished lover; he was a regular visitor to their local gym and unlike some men she had known he hadn't degenerated into an overweight slob. That he earned a large amount of money wasn't important to her, she wasn't into possessions, but his wordly success made him content and she was happy to see that because she was a giving and generous Sagittarian.

The trouble was, he understood everybody. That was his profession. He called himself an enabler, a locksmith. He didn't give people the keys, of course. He enabled them to forge the keys themselves; working out their own combination was part of the process. From the upstairs window she could see the tops of his patients' heads as they made their way down the steps to his consulting rooms. After fifty minutes they emerged white-haired; older and wiser. This was no doubt caused by the falling plaster dust – there were usually builders around, for one reason or another – but for a visual person like herself those departing white heads made a vivid symbolic statement.

He almost understood *too much*. This was a ridiculous thing to say, she knew that, but sometimes she felt like a struggling novelist living with somebody who knew how to write the story better than she did. He knew the main character so well;

he was aquainted with all her early traumas and subsequent patterns of behaviour. She couldn't get angry with him for this – how could she? Besides, Leon never got angry. He would gently explain exactly what she thought and then ask, 'Are you comfortable with that?' Sometimes she remembered the rows she had had with other men and felt wistful, like a retired matador missing the stench of sawdust and blood.

No wonder she had such powerful sexual fantasies about her builders – priapic Greeks, ruddy young Geordies who would require nothing of her except her compliant, middle-aged body, who smoked roll-ups and talked about football teams she had never heard of. Who wouldn't understand her at all. Watching them toiling in her house, their chests slippery with sweat, made her insides melt. The rawness, the vigour, the muscles moving under their skin as they heaved up a floorboard! She was always thinking up ways of improving the house. She had had three bathrooms installed already and was going to get a fourth put in, for India.

This was one of the things she discussed with her group. There were six of them, all women, and they met in a room above a video shop in Muswell Hill. She could talk to them about Leon, her need for builders, everything. She didn't need to feel disloyal, because Leon understood why she went there. When she told him they did psychodrama – all of them acting him, in turn – he wasn't threatened, only interested. Besides, there were less and less opportunities to tell him things anyway because he was always so busy.

Sometimes she did something which she knew was just a cry for attention, a need for some sort of primal response. She was just recovering from a short but intense affair with her conservatory architect. He had the keys to a show flat in Battersea and they used to go there after hours. The place was exhilaratingly un*hers* – ruched curtains and *Interiors* laid out on the coffee table. Freed from the needs of her children, the puppet-string pulls of her life, the total comprehension of her husband, she had felt thrillingly liberated. There was plaster fruit in the kitchen and she had felt like Hunca Munca in the Beatrix Potter story, lawlessly exploring a toytown home.

There had been other episodes, quite a few actually, mostly with the disenchanted husbands of women she knew, and once with her pottery teacher. When she tearfully confessed, Leon understood. He always did. He took her in his arms. He told her the thing with her architect was quite natural, that we all needed our own private show flats in our heads, that in fact he had written a paper on it and read it out to an audience of two thousand psychotherapists in Baden-Baden.

Buffy, of course, would have bellowed and spluttered and got raging drunk. Other men she had known would have hit her. Leon just stroked her cheek and went downstairs, where he was dictating his latest book to his secretary. He had written several best-sellers. *The Blame Game and How We Play It* had been translated into twelve languages and his latest, *Guilt: A User's Guide*, had just been published. He was intensely proud of what he called his babies. Almost touchy, actually. Last Monday he had been on *Start the Week* and she had forgotten to tape the programme for him – she had been doing her postural meditation at the time – and he had almost got angry.

She had the vague feeling that he was going on TV this evening, in fact. Outside it was freezing cold. She could see the grey breath of the builders as they huffed and puffed in the garden, dragging panes of glass wrapped in brown paper. She was upstairs in her studio – her own room, her sanctum. This was her working time. She was working.

She sat at her desk. The trouble was, she had too many ideas. She had just been on a creative writing course and she thought she might write some prose-poems based on the seasons at their Tuscan house – a sort of contemporary *Book of Hours* – and illustrate them with drawings. The thing was, she had only been to their Tuscan house in the summer. Another idea that had been brewing for some time was an ecological children's story based on *The Tibetan Book of the*

Dead, but she had to be in the right mood for this. Various projects connected with her aromatherapy course, maybe with dolphins featuring somewhere, had also been simmering. Maybe she should ask her group if she were ready for this.

She was interrupted by the ring of the doorbell. Nobody else seemed to be around so she left her studio and went downstairs. She passed Bruno's bedroom door. There was a sign on it saying *STOP!!! DO NOT ATTEMPT TO MOVE THIS CAR!!!* It was one of those car-clamp stickers. They were always stealing things from the street – plastic cones, hideous objects like that – bringing them home and not knowing what to do with them. Adolescent boys . . . She couldn't begin to understand them. They were such an alien species that she sometimes forgot about them for days.

She negotiated the builders' planks, stacked in the hall, and opened the front door. A pale young woman stood on the step.

'Hello' she said. 'I've come about the rabbits.'

Jacquetta was miles away. It took her a moment to gather her wits.

'The sign outside,' said the young woman. '*Baby Rabbits Free to a Good Home*. I was just, you know, passing by and I saw it. I love rabbits.'

'So do I. It's awful to get rid of them but my husband insisted.'

A waif on her doorstep! The girl looked freezing. Her face was blanched white; only her little nostrils were pink. Jacquetta led her into the kitchen where she stood in front of the Aga, warming her hands. She was actually trembling with cold. Her coat fell open and Jacquetta noticed a tiny gold fish around her neck.

'It's the Year of the Fish,' she said, pointing to it. 'At least I think it is. Or maybe it's the Year of the Monkey. They go past quicker and quicker, the years, as one gets older. It's quite frightening.'

109

The young woman was still staring at her. Jacquetta wondered if she had a blob of paint on her nose. She took off her specs and the room blurred; she put them back on again. How dark and lustrous the girl's eyes were! Haunted. She had a delicate bone-structure too, like a ballet dancer. She would be marvellous to draw. The girl gazed around the kitchen as if she had never seen anything like it before – the dresser full of Jacquetta's pottery, the Georgia O'Keefe calendar. Despite the conventional clothes there was a vividness about her, an intensity, that Jacquetta felt she could identify with.

'Can I have a glass of water?'

Maybe she was going to faint. Jacquetta filled a glass and gave it to her. The girl's hand trembled; as she lifted it to her lips the glass dropped from her grasp and fell onto the floor.

'Oh, gosh, I'm sorry!'

Jacquetta picked it up. It hadn't broken; the builders' dust sheets had saved it. 'It's the last glass from a set I bought in Venice,' she said. 'On one of my honeymoons, actually.'

'One of them?'

For a moment Jacquetta couldn't remember which man it was. She adored Venice and had been so many times. 'Ah, yes. My second husband.' Russell. He had spent his whole time eating. In *Venice*. One didn't go to Venice to *eat*. She should have realized, then, that the two of them were totally incompatible.

'What was he like?'

What an odd thing to ask! 'A Taurus. Hopeless for me.'

Jacquetta put on her cloak and they went down the steps into the garden. It was freezing cold and the light was beginning to fade. The builders were packing up for the day.

'What a bore,' said Jacquetta, looking at the rabbit hutch. 'They've got out again.'

'They're under there somewhere,' said the oldest builder. She had an idea he was called Paddy. He was pointing at the frozen earth. 'They've made a burrow.'

'What shall we do?'

'Come on lads!' he said, 'Let's dig 'em out.'

The ground was frozen too hard, however. One of them suggested boiling a kettle, which they did. They poured it onto the earth. Steam rose. They started digging again.

The one called Paddy pointed to the ground. 'Know what we've got in there? Some hot cross bunnies!'

Jacquetta sighed, huddled in her cloak. When one had children, everything was so complicated. Even disposing of their pets turned out to be a major operation. And then the boys would probably make a fuss, when they came home from school. She sometimes wished she could just pack her paints and go to Goa or somewhere, somewhere simple, and just *be*. She gazed at the flushed sky. The sound of the spades seemed far away.

'Steady on, Stavros! Don't want to hurt the buggers.'

She loved this time of evening. The light from the kitchen, shining on the struts of her conservatory, reminded her of the temple at Karnak. She had gone to a *son et lumière* there once, with a man called Austin. Just for a while, he had seemed the man she had been looking for all her life; she was prone to these romantic impulses. She had sat there, in the Egyptian twilight, with his arm around her. Suddenly Buffy's voice had boomed out. '*It is said that, long ago, when Thebes was at its zenith, when gods were men, when Isis, she of the mischievous eyes, was beloved of Osiris . . .*' What a shock it was, to hear his voice! How rudely it had shattered her mood! Even worse, she had been married to him at the time. '*Let us journey into the past, let us unroll the scrolls of time and consider again these avenues, built by Rameses II and restored by the Ptolemies . . .* ' She'd had no idea he had recorded the soundtrack. How tactless of him! For a moment she had thought he had planned it just to spoil her tryst amongst the ruins.

'Got one of them! Here, Mrs Buckman.'

A struggling rabbit was shoved into her arms. One of the men was lunging after another one which was hopping away in the dusk. Her husband, disturbed by the shouts and

111

whoops, had appeared in the doorway of his consulting rooms.

'What on earth's happening?'

She had temporarily forgotten why they were doing this. Then she caught sight of the young woman. She sat like a spectre on the steps of the skeletal conservatory; her head swivelled from Leon to Jacquetta. She seemed to have no interest in the rabbits at all.

'Two down,' cried Paddy, 'one to go.'

'Don't catch the two big ones,' said Jacquetta, 'the parents. They're staying here.'

She looked at the girl again. I know, she thought. She's like a child, an unborn child, sheltered within the ribcage of an all-embracing mother. I shall paint that. I have been a child, a mother too. I shall paint her boldly, in acrylics. The struggling rabbit scratched her wrists but she only discovered this later. At the time she was so fired with creativity that she didn't notice.

The three baby rabbits were finally caught. Jacquetta and the young woman carried them into the kitchen and put them on the table. They lolloped around, their whiskers sparkling. They raised themselves on their hind legs and sniffed the copper candlestick; they sat on the *Independent*, washing their faces with their paws.

'Look at the light shining through their ears!' cried Jacquetta. 'The tracery of veins. Aren't they beautiful! This is the end of my boys' childhood, the last of their pets to go. Really, I can hardly bear you to take them.'

'You've still got the mother and father. The big ones.'

'Don't you see how symbolic it is? The young leaving; just a sad old mother left behind.'

'We all have to leave home. I did.'

'How could you know about loss?' said Jacquetta. 'You're far too young.'

'I'm not.'

The girl was sitting in the Windsor chair, looking at her

intently. How abrupt her voice was! With a funny flat accent. Jacquetta looked at the strong, raised eyebrows; the pointed face. In the room nothing stirred except the pendulum of Buffy's old grandfather clock, swinging from side to side, and the rabbits on the table. One of them had found a piece of apple rind, from lunch, and was nibbling it.

The builders clomped through the kitchen on their way home. 'Cheerio!' they called. In the hall they addressed each other loudly. 'What're you having for dinner, Stavros?' 'Rabbit kebabs! And you, mate?' 'My old lady's cooking my favourite.' 'And what might that be?' 'Bunnyburgers and chips!' The front door slammed.

'I'm glad you came today,' said Jacquetta. 'You'll never realize how momentous this is.'

'What do you mean?' asked the girl.

'It's a turning point for me. It's important to mark these moments, validate them.' The young woman listened intently. It was nice. Sometimes, in the group, Jacquetta had the feeling that the other members looked as if they were listening, but they were really just waiting their turn. 'My whole life's been geared to my kids, you see. Dictated by their needs.'

'How many have you got?'

'What?'

'Children.'

Jacquetta thought for a moment. It was so complicated. 'Three, basically.'

'*Basically*? What do you mean, *basically*?'

'Well, there's all those stepchildren and things.'

'How many?'

'Oh, lots.' Jacquetta gazed at the apple rind disappearing into the rabbit's hinged mouth. 'But today I've been released. I'm starting the process of separation, you see, of returning to myself. After all these years of being seen in terms of other people.' She paused, and then she announced. 'Now, I'm sure, I'm going to be able to *paint*.'

113

Seventeen

The front door slammed and two adolescent boys came in. They were dressed in black, and carried school bags.

'It's fucking freezing out there,' said one of them. 'What happened to global warming?'

For a moment Celeste didn't dare look at them. They stomped through the kitchen and opened the fridge.

'Half a tin of bleeding Whiskas. There's no fucking food in this place. There's never any fucking food.'

Buffy's sons. She looked at them now. They were poking their heads like crows into the fridge. They turned. Their faces were chalk-white, and spotty.

'You're a crap mother.'

'I've been working,' said Jacquetta.

'Oh yeah? You never work.'

One of them had his hair shaved at the back and a series of chains in his ear, looped together, like a little link fence. The other one had matted black hair tangled like a cat's coughball. Neither of them looked anything like Buffy, but then she hadn't known him when he was young. Their long skinny wrists protruded from their sleeves.

Jacquetta pointed to the table. 'This person, sorry I don't know your name, she's going to take your baby rabbits.'

'What rabbits?'

'Your pets.'

They looked at the baby rabbits, which now sat huddled together panting. There was a puddle on the newspaper.

'Don't be upset,' said Jacquetta.

'I'm not,' said one of the boys.

'Didn't know they'd had any babies,' said the other. He turned to his mother. 'Give us some dosh.'

'Why?'

'Going to get my nose pierced.'

The older one laughed – a startling, harsh sound like a corncrake. 'Nobody gets their noses pierced anymore. Only people who live in East Finchley.'

'The Tuaregs do,' said their mother.

'They live in East Finchley?'

'Africa,' she said. 'They're a tribe. Or maybe it's the Nubans. Incredibly statuesque and beautiful.'

'Tasmin Phillpott's got a ring through her nose,' said one of the boys. 'She looks like a pig.'

The other boy had opened a tin of grapefruit segments and was eating them with a serving spoon. 'My teacher says, why didn't you come to Parents' Evening?'

'Parents' Evening?' asked Jacquetta.

'You never come.' He rummaged in his bag and pulled out a damp, partially disintegrated piece of paper. 'Here's the reminder.'

'Did your Dad go?'

'Buffy? Christ, no. We didn't tell him. Last time he took out his hip flask. Anyway, he never knows what subjects we do.' He poured some cornflakes into the grapefruit tin and stirred it up. 'Nor do you.'

'I do!' said Jacquetta.

'You're both hopeless. Anyway I'm glad you didn't come. You'd do something really sad, like last time.'

'What do you mean?'

He snorted into his Cornflakes, and wiped his nose on his sleeve. 'You wore that sequin, like, headband thing. Everybody *stared* at you. And then you told our headmaster you'd had an erotic dream about him.'

'Did I?'

He shovelled in the last of the Cornflakes. 'My teacher only wanted you to come in case you brought Leon. She saw him on TV; she's got the hots for him.' He flung the tin in the direction of the swing-bin. 'She's that pathetic.'

A dirty white cat sprung into Celeste's lap. It was surprisingly heavy. She stroked it; as it purred, rhythmically, its claws dug into her thighs. She didn't dare push it off; she didn't dare *move*. Only an hour ago she had been standing, shivering, outside this fortress of a house, this creamy cliff five storeys high. Just standing there, staring at it, like Penny used to do. *I used to look up at the house and imagine their lives in it.* Then she had seen the sign, *Baby Rabbits Free to a Good Home* and rung the bell. On impulse, just like that. So much had happened, with such swooping speed and a distracted sort of intimacy, that she felt queasy. How easy it had been! She had been like a burglar, discovering a door was unlocked. There was so much she needed to ask, but on the other hand she didn't want them to notice her sitting there. She felt like a surveillance camera in a crowded shop.

As they bickered, she looked around. It was a huge kitchen. There were a lot of abstract paintings hanging up – violent and splashy, as if someone had been stirring a pot too vigorously and some of it had been flung onto the walls. Every surface was crammed with things – how different from her own neat home in Melton Mowbray! She wondered how much had changed in this room since Buffy had lived here. But then she didn't know what Buffy's taste ran to, anyway. She hadn't visited his flat yet; she hadn't let him take her there. She was so confused, so emotional, that she suddenly felt exhausted, like an overloaded electricity grid blacking out. But now somebody seemed to be talking to her.

'What are you going to carry them in?' Jacquetta was looking at her, eyebrows raised above her blue-rimmed glasses. She was wearing a sort of peasant's scarf wrapped around her head, and a lot of beads. It was only now that Celeste dared to have a good look at her. She wore a baggy sort of garment covered in zigzags and a long red cardigan. With all that jewellery she looked like a high priestess.

'Carry them?' asked Celeste stupidly. She had forgotten why she was supposed to be here.

'She can take them in that,' said one of the boys. He pointed to a cardboard box. 'Leon's crap book came in it. His author's copies.'

'It's not crap,' said Jacquetta vaguely.

They put the rabbits into the cardboard box. It had a label on it: *Guilt: A User's Guide, by Leon Buckman. 8 Copies.* One of the boys fetched some sellotape.

He was just taping down the lid when the doorbell rang. Jacquetta answered it. She returned with a big black man.

'Car for Mr Buckman,' he said. 'BBC.'

At the same moment a chunky young woman came down the stairs, yawning. 'What's happening?' she asked.

'Leon's going on TV,' said Jacquetta. 'Go and buzz him, somebody. He's downstairs. And this person's taking our rabbits.'

'You going to the White City?' the yawning woman asked the driver. 'Can you give me a lift? Drop me off on the way?' she turned to Celeste. 'Hi. I'm India.'

Celeste said she was just taking the rabbits away. India asked if she had a car; Celeste shook her head.

'Which way are you going?' asked India.

'Kilburn.'

'Want a lift? He'll drop you off.' India lifted up the box. 'Come on,' she said. 'Leon'll just be putting the finishing touches to his *coiffure*. He'll be here in a minute.'

'Where're you going?' asked her mother.

'Oh, just to see a friend.' India, the box under one arm, grabbed a coat in the hallway. Celeste turned to say goodbye, but Jacquetta was talking to her sons. They, too, were putting on their coats.

'We're going carol singing,' said one of them.

'But it's not December yet,' she said. 'Anyway, you can't sing.'

He laughed his corncrake laugh. 'Yeah, but they'll be so scared of us they'll give us the money.'

117

Celeste and India sat in the limo, waiting for Leon. They had put the box of rabbits in the front seat. Celeste hadn't a clue what she was going to do with them. She felt utterly helpless, swept up by events which were now beyond her control. One ex-wife, and now another! She had come in from the cold and sat in their rooms. Neither of them had thought it rude or odd. Children and step-children had appeared. So had rabbits – what on earth was she going to do with them? Buffy's past was like some complicated board game; she had opened it and taken out some of the pieces, but nobody had read her the rules. It was curiously exhilarating.

'Why are you called India?' she asked.

India took a card out of her wallet and passed it to her. 'I couldn't bear to tell anyone anymore, so I had this printed.'

Celeste read the card. It was printed in italic script. 'I see,' she said, reading it again. Conceived in an ashram in Bangalore. 'Gosh, how exotic.'

'That's what mum thinks. *I* think it's fucking embarrassing.'

'Who's your father, then?'

'He's called Alan. He works in Strasbourg. He only talks to his computer.' She snorted. 'He doesn't communicate with me, I'm not IBM compatible.' She wiped her nose. 'Fathers! Who'd have them!'

Alan. Celeste hadn't heard of him. Where did Buffy come into this? She couldn't work it out yet; Leon would be arriving any minute.

They sat there, looking at the bulgy folds in the back of the driver's neck. He wore a peaked cap. She felt comfortable with India. She looked about her own age, for one thing. She looked straightforward too, in a pissed-off sort of way. She had a square, suetty face; she hadn't inherited her mother's looks. She wore a woollen bobble-hat and a black, man's coat. It smelt of mothballs. Her fingernails were bitten right down. Celeste gnawed her fingernails, but only round the edges. Still, she felt a bond.

India leaned forward and addressed the driver. 'So what's he wittering on about this time?'

'Mr Buckman? I just take him there, miss.'

'Probably blathering on about his book.' She pointed to the box in the front seat. 'That's it.'

The driver read the label. '*Guilt: A User's Guide.*'

'Listen to it.'

'Listen to it?' he asked.

'Go on.'

The driver bent over the box and listened. 'There's something moving about.'

India sniggered. 'Smells a bit funny too, doesn't it?'

The driver sniffed. 'Now you mention it.'

At that moment the front door opened and Leon appeared. He was the man Celeste had seen in the garden. He hurried down the steps and strode briskly towards the car.

'It's all right,' he called cheerfully, 'I'll sit in the front.'

The driver lifted up the box and put it onto the floor. 'What *is* it in there?' He tipped the box; there was a sliding sound.

They drove off. Leon leaned over the seat and shook Celeste's hand. 'Hi,' he said, 'and who are you?'

Celeste told him her name. Leon's hand remained in hers for a moment; it felt dry and sincere. Even in the dark she could see that he had a terrific tan; at this time of year too. No wonder Buffy had kicked in his face, on the TV.

'You're not from London, are you?' he asked. 'You look far too wholesome.'

Celeste told him she came from Leicestershire. She said she worked in a shop – she didn't say where – and that it was her day off.

'You have any family here?' he asked.

She shook her head, willing him to stop. After all these weeks, he was the first person who had actually asked her any questions. Buffy mostly told her how beautiful she was, the light of his life, how could he believe his luck, an old has-been like him. Or else *she* asked *him* questions – about his past, how he had met Gene Kelly once, the thousands and thousands of interesting things he had done and the people he had worked with, most of whom she had never heard of, or only read about in magazines. They sat in teashops for hours, until the waitresses cleared the tables; they went to the theatre; they sat in pubs and talked until closing time. She had learned more, in the past few weeks, than she had learned in her whole life. Buffy had such a rich past packed into him, he was as concentrated as potted meat. Better, because he never ran out.

But Leon asked her questions. As the dark trees of Regent's Park flashed past he gazed at her with tender curiosity; she felt like one of the rabbits, mesmerized by the headlights of his eyes. No wonder his patients came back for more. She seemed to be telling him that she was an orphan. She must be careful. He would seek out any lies with his professional radar.

'So how do you like London?' he asked.

'Well, it's full of surprises.'

He smiled. 'Nice ones?'

She paused. 'More, like, unexpected.'

'If they weren't, they wouldn't be surprises, would they?'

The car stopped in the Edgware Road. Celeste and India got out, with their cardboard box.

'Let's meet again,' said Leon, leaning out of the window. 'I can see my family's taken to you.' The car drove off into the traffic.

India made a retching noise and pretended to vomit into the gutter. 'Isn't he creepy!' she said. 'Almost as awful as Mum. They deserve each other.'

'Why's he creepy?'

'See the way he letched all over you? He does that to everybody. He's always asking me about my sex life. I don't *have* a sex life but I make things up, really disgusting things to see if I can shock him.'

'Do you?'

She shook her head. 'He gets off on it. He's sex-obsessed.

120

He's always touching me, ugh. He screws his female patients and pretends it's therapy.'

Celeste stared at her. 'Does your Mum know?'

India shook her head. 'She never knows what's going on. She's too busy going to her groups and talking about it.'

'How do *you* know?'

'I found his condoms. He keeps them in his *Dictionary of Dangerous Drugs*. I'd gone down there to look up something. I borrow the keys to his cabinet, see, I can get all sorts of stuff there, and I was just checking to see if I'd done something really silly this time.'

'What do you mean?'

'Oh, mixing them. You know.'

'You steal his drugs?'

'LSD and Librium or something,' said India. 'I can't remember. So I looked in his book and there were these packets of condoms, hidden between the pages. Must've been in the L's. About six packets too, the randy sod.'

They were standing on the pavement, the traffic rumbling past. Celeste held the box; it was a lifebelt to stop her from drowning.

'You going this way?' India asked.

Celeste nodded. They started walking.

'They're such a fuck-up, aren't they?' said India. 'Parents.'

'Are they?'

'They make such a fuck-up of their lives. So bloody irresponsible.'

Celeste was about to argue, but she stopped. Hers had been too, in their own way. Their entirely different way. Strangely enough, her upbringing and India's had something in common.

'So bloody childish,' went on India. She walked, her hands thrust into her pockets, staring at the pavement. 'Mum used to nick Bunch to take to her Primal Therapy.'

'What was Bunch?'

'My teddy bear. She'd used him to help her regress. She'd regress to her childhood. But *I* was the child! It was *my* bloody teddy! He wasn't the same when he came back. One of his eyes was loose.' She veered left, sharply, and marched across the road. A van screeched to a halt. Celeste hurried after her and rejoined her, breathlessly, on the opposite pavement. 'Leon's a mega-wanker,' said India. 'Mega. Do you know, his answerphone has messages in English, German and Urdu? They think they're so trendy but both of them are really pathetic, lonely people.'

'Don't you like your Mum at all?'

'She doesn't know how to be normal. Parents should be normal. That's the point of them.'

'Mine were,' said Celeste. They weren't, of course. She realized that. But at the time she had thought they were normal. Boring, actually, though she wouldn't have used that word about them then.

'She's totally self-absorbed,' said India. 'She has to be the centre of bloody attention. She's always going on about her work. *My work*, she says in her suffering artist's voice. Any woman who talks about her work like that is bound not to do any. And if she does, it's bound to be awful. Have you seen her *paintings*? She just leeches off men, screwing them for alimony, screwing them for everything, and then going on about what a feminist she is. And sunbathing in the garden without any clothes on, every nipple on view. And asking bus conductors their birth signs, stupid things like that. And rushing off to Tunisia for three months. *Three months*! Leaving us with our nanny. Honestly, you're so lucky!'

'How do you know?'

'Because yours couldn't have been as bad as mine.' She stopped. 'God, I have been going on. Must be terribly boring.'

Celeste shook her head.

'This is where my friend lives,' said India. 'Where are you going?'

'I've got this flat in Kilburn.'

'Oh! I know somebody who lives round there.'

'Who?'

'He's called Waxie. He sells me coke.'

'Coke? You go all that way?' Celeste looked at her, puzzled. Was the whole family mad? 'Couldn't you just get it from a machine?'

India burst out laughing. 'A machine?'

'Or a shop or something?'

India paused. 'No, dearie. I mean Coke. Cocaine.'

Celeste didn't know how to reply. In their box, the rabbits were restless. They all slid one way, she could hear their claws scrabbling. Her fingernails used to make that sound, *scrabble-scrabble*, when she typed invoices on the Amstrad back at Kwik-Fit.

India put her arm around her, awkwardly. 'You make me feel awfully old.' She wiped her nose on the back of her glove; it was freezing cold. 'In my so-called family, all the kids are old. It's the grown-ups who're infantile.'

'Is that why you take drugs? You shouldn't, you know. Who's this friend you're seeing? Another drug-dealer?'

India laughed. 'No no. It's my step-dad. Well, one of them.'

There was a pause. They were standing outside a block of flats. Celeste looked up; the building loomed, heavy and monumental, against the suffused sky. The porch was lit. LOMFIELD MANSIONS, it said. The B was missing.

Buffy! She nearly said the name out loud. She had been so distracted, she hadn't noticed where they were standing.

'I said friend because I want to keep Buffy separate,' said India. 'They'd just get all psychological otherwise.' She stood there, huddled in her coat. 'I like him, you see. We *are* friends, actually. My Mum led him an awful dance, I'm really sorry for him. At least he's *human*. At least if I have a problem he doesn't read me the bloody *I Ching*. He takes me to the pub. Anyway, he makes me laugh.' She paused. 'Listen, why don't you come up and meet him?'

'No!' Celeste backed away, clutching her box. 'I mean, he sounds lovely, but . . .'

She had to get away. Maybe he was looking out of the window! Maybe he could see them standing there together. How could she possibly explain?

She turned to India. But India had already left. Suddenly energetic, she was leaping up the steps of the block of flats, her coat flapping.

Eighteen

'You old fool!' cried India, 'You old fart! What's her name?'

'I'm not telling,' said Buffy. 'Not if you take that tone.'

'How old is she?'

'Your age.'

India snorted with laughter and helped herself to one of his cigarettes. 'It's disgusting. Are you sleeping with her?'

'No. Unfortunately.'

'I should think not. How grotesque!'

'I adore her,' said Buffy. 'I've never felt like this before.'

'You always say that. You probably said that with Mum.'

'Don't I deserve a little happiness?' he bleated. 'After all these years? I've even given up drinking. More or less.'

They sat there, wreathed in smoke. She stroked his knee. 'I'm happy for you, Buff, I really am. Maybe this is the real thing. Does she know about all your repellant ailments?'

He nodded. 'Better than anyone. She knows about my piles and my constipation and my athlete's foot –'

'Gawd. She a doctor?'

Buffy shook his head. 'I'm not telling.'

India gestured around the room. 'Perhaps she can sort this place out. Look at it! When you're on your own you revert, don't you? Remember when you and Mum split up, and I came round after school to spring clean?'

'In your gymslip, with your little duster,' said Buffy. 'My angel of mercy. I remember. I burst into tears.'

'You were probably pissed.' She looked around. 'This flat really pongs. You'll never get your leg over, not till you do something about it. You can hardly get the door open, let alone drag some woman through it.'

They were silent for a while. From the bedroom came the sound of cracking bones. George must have discovered last night's Kentucky Fried Chicken.

'What about you?' asked Buffy. 'My Dark Continent?'

'If there was anybody, you'd be the first to know. But there isn't.'

'Is everything all right?'

India gazed down at her hands. He noticed the nicotine stains on her fingers.

'I wish you didn't smoke,' he said. 'It makes me feel guilty.'

'Don't.'

'Don't what?'

'Feel guilty.'

'Heavens, nobody's ever said that to me. Why shouldn't I?'

India was sitting on the floor. She pushed some crumbs into a little pile. 'Remember when you and Mum used to have those awful, awful rows?'

Buffy nodded.

'And Bruno stood up in his cot and cried and rattled the bars,' she said. 'I used to lie in bed with my eyes tight shut, but it never did any good, you still went on yelling, I could still hear you.'

'Don't!'

'Just like Mum was with Dad, but worse somehow. Maybe because I was older and I could understand what you were saying.' She flattened the pyramid of crumbs with her finger. 'Then you came in. You closed the door and sat beside my bed. And you put on Hammy's voice – you didn't put it on, you *were* Hammy. Or Voley or whoever it was, all those stupid animals. You took me somewhere else, along with you. We went off on our adventures.' She looked up. 'You were the only one who could do it. You let me escape.'

He sighed. 'So did I.'

'You're lucky. You're an actor, you can do it all the time.'

'Too bloody much of the time. That's what they all said. Your Mum, and all the others.'

She squashed the pile of crumbs and stood up. 'I can't, you see. Not any more.' Abruptly, she pulled on her woolly hat and picked up her coat.

'Don't go!' he cried. 'Come out and have a spaghetti!'

But she was at the door now. 'Got to see someone.'

'Who?'

'Just a friend.' She pushed aside some plastic bags and opened the door.

Buffy got to his feet and followed her out. 'Who?'

She wasn't taking the lift; she was hurrying down the stairs. Her voice echoed, as it floated back to him. 'Someone called Waxie.'

And she was gone.

Buffy sank back into his chair. He suddenly felt terribly depressed. How he longed to see Celeste's bright young face! But he didn't know where she was. It was her day off but she had refused to go out with him; he had wanted to take her to the Tate and introduce her to Bonnard but she'd said she had something planned. Same with her day off the week before. He had rung her flat, twice, but there had been no answer.

Maybe she was seeing someone else, a young vigorous man who wasn't a hopeless failure, who hadn't had the *chance* to be a hopeless failure. Whose future diasters weren't even written yet. Whose inadequacies were still in embryonic form.

Celeste was changing. She was wearing quite assertive clothes nowadays, fashionable clothes in strong colours. Last week, when he had taken her out to dinner, she had worn an almost intimidating jacket and a really rather seductive black dress. Was she just adapting to her habitat, or was there some unwelcome significance to this?

He wished India hadn't rushed off like that. It was five to eight. The sun was well over the yard-arm; in fact, it had been pitch dark for hours. No harm in a small scotch. He heaved himself to his feet and padded into the kitchen. It was freezing cold. He peered into the boiler. The pilot light was out.

Blithering hell and damnation. Penny could fix the boiler but Penny wasn't here. When halted at various obstacles in life's path he suddenly missed the various women with whom he had cohabited, different ones according to the nature of the aggravation. When he couldn't work the camera he thought of Penny; *she* would have remembered to remove the lens cap when photographing the pavement. She could get the car started, too; it was now rusting away in the residents' parking bay, its battery long since dead. Any electrical mishaps reminded him of Phoebe, a costume designer with whom he had lived for a short and not entirely harmonious time but who had been surprisingly deft with a fusebox. When his houseplants withered – they had all withered – he thought of Jacquetta, who used to talk to them or something; whatever dotty methods she used, it did the trick. Lorna had had green fingers too . . . *Lorna*. Goodness, he hadn't thought about her for years. She would be a middle-aged woman by now. Lorna . . . didn't he say, once, that she was the love of his life?

He drained his glass and poured himself another scotch, purely as insulation. He should have learnt how to do these things, fuseboxes and so on, when he had the chance. Trouble was, you didn't think about it at the time and when the final explosion happened, the appalling bust-up, it didn't cross your mind to say: *By the way, before you go, could you just show me how to set the timer on the video recorder*?

What had they learned from him, and he from them? Popsi had showed him how to cook terrific mince, hers was the best of all his exes' mince. Lorna had known the names of lots of birds, linnets and so on, she was always pointing them out, but most of the time he hadn't been attending. A woman called Miriam had taught him the words of all the songs in *Guys and Dolls*. But it didn't seem a lot, when you

128

looked back on it. In fact, it seemed pitifully little. Maybe what he had learnt from them had been so profound that he couldn't just at this moment put it into words.

He looked around the kitchen. On the shelf sat Penny's half-finished pot of Marmite. Lorna had loved Marmite too. So had nearly every woman he had known in a sufficiently domestic setting to discover this. No male acquaintance of his had liked Marmite, it seemed to be purely a female thing. He looked at the clutter of pots and jars. Would Celeste like Marmite? He would probably never know. He had been a failure, with his wives and his children and his step-children, how could he possibly crank himself up again for a lovely young creature like Celeste? How could he lumber her with someone like himself? If, that is, she wanted to be lumbered at all, which he was starting to doubt.

Why was she constantly disappearing, and with whom? Maybe his role had just been to get her going. It was like when you rented one of those holiday apartments in the Algarve. In your room there would be one of those starter packs – a couple of teabags, a bun, maybe an orange. That was him. She had eaten him up and now she had learnt the language she was launching off into an independent life of her own.

He made his way into the living room, knocking into India's tea mug and slopping its contents on the floor. She had hardly drunk any of it. What was wrong with her; was it his fault, like everything else? She had sort of implied that it wasn't, entirely; her words had deeply moved him.

He switched on the TV. Leon's face bloomed onto the screen.

' . . . *we must realize, Gavin, that for many people guilt is a fuel. They run on it, they can't function without it –* '

The smug git. Buffy switched it off. He no longer wanted to kick in the TV, however; Leon's face – fleshier now, and even more irritatingly handsome – no longer had the power to enrage him. It had been defused. Oh, the expense of spirit . . . They had all been defused. Even Penny, who he had recently glimpsed hailing a cab in Tottenham Court Road, even Penny had almost reverted back into a smart, glossy woman in an unfamiliar black coat. Eight years of sleeping in the same bed, of squabbling over the map in the car – eight years of everything had vaporised just like that, wasn't it alarming? They had vaporised as if they had never happened. Or, more exactly, they had been drained of meaning, they were full of sound and fury, signifying nothing. He must never tell Celeste this, never. One must never tell such horror stories to the young; they would never get to sleep at night. Keep to the woodland creatures.

He wasn't inebriated. Just cosmic. He put a Brahms quartet on the record player; he put on his overcoat and sat in front of the dead TV. A man he'd met in New York had once been walking past a record shop with Mia Farrow. The window had displayed a collection of Frank Sinatra records; she had paused, and nearly gone in to buy one. It was only then that she had realized *she had been married to Frank Sinatra, once.*

He thought of all the women he had known. Of course he could remember them; the hot agonies might have vaporised but the memories remained. He could draw nourishment from them for years, like a camel with water stored in its hump. He remembered the way Popsi poured Nescafé into the lid, instead of taking it out with a spoon – a habit either endearing or irritating, depending on his mood. Did other people do this? He hadn't met any. Penny's schoolgirlish wriggle each morning as she pulled on her surprisingly puritanical cotton knickers. Carmella's deft and impressive card-shuffling; their happiest hours had been spent playing gin rummy, with Nyange asleep in her cot. Who was Carmella playing card games with now? Where was his daughter, Nyange? Was Penny wearing lacier and more interesting knickers for that awful photographer, and pulling them on in a more lascivious manner?

Sometimes he wondered if they knew what they had in common, these women whose only similarity was, to some degree, he supposed, temporarily loving him. He knew what

130

life was like with each of them, that was his secret. He was like a computer database, with all this information stored in him. The way Jacquetta brushed her teeth, sucking moisture from the brush and spitting, never rinsing from a mug. Everybody he had lived with brushed their teeth in a different manner. Those intimate moments, in so many bathrooms! Lorna – yes, Lorna, now he remembered it – she used to dust herself with talc, a cloud of it, her hips thrust forward. She and Popsi, though they didn't know it, had shared a cheerful lack of inhibition in the bathroom, peeing while he shaved (he was beardless then), both wiping themselves daintily from the front rather than the rear, the only two women he had known who did it that way round. Popsi even used to insert her diaphragm when he was in the room, squeezing cream onto it with the skilled insouciance of a patissiere anointing a tartelet.

The temperature was dropping. He lit another cigarette, clumsily, with his gloved hands. Then there was the love-making, ah, the lovemaking. He shouldn't think like this but he couldn't help it. Even freezing cold, he blushed. The warm bodies, the chilly toes, the blind rapture and damp embarrassments . . . Jacquetta's thin, strenuous body, the way she climaxed whimperingly, turning her face away as if it were too precious to share. Penny's wholesomely gymnastic approach, at least during the early years, her smooth but hefty thighs gripping him like a vice, the surprisingly rude words she whispered into his ear, words she never used during daylight hours, like the louche company one only met in nightclubs . . . Popsi's boozy breath and gratifyingly multiple orgasms . . . Oh, the breasts he had known, the heaviness of them in his hand, the soft stomachs and hard shoulder-blades . . . the skin . . . the fingers . . . A girl called Annabel in that hotel room in Rye . . . Desperate and adulterous copulations in the backseat of cars, the windows steaming up . . . the indignities, the bare buttocks . . . The marital companionability and giggles, the familiar adjust-ments of flesh against flesh, limb against limb, year after

131

year, *ouches* on holiday when they were sunburnt, dear secret places where someone else was trespassing now, though they weren't of course, he himself had trespassed since . . .

Shut up. He could go on like this for ever. There was nobody, of course, that he could ever tell. And each woman he had loved, she held all those secrets locked within her, too – of other men who at the time he couldn't bear to contemplate, you blocked them out. What were they doing now, Phoebe and Annabel and Popsi and all the others? They stayed, fixed, at the age he had known them; such is the egocentricity of memory. In his head they were still young women though some of them would be grandmothers now. What were they doing – making tea for somebody else; opening a tin of cat food? Ten to one they weren't sitting in front of a blank TV thinking of *him*.

In some ways it was a relief, of course. It was a relief that he no longer had to visit Penny's testy old father in Ascot, that he no longer had to pretend to himself that Jacquetta's paintings were any good. These were other people's responsibilities now, and sometimes he felt a grateful warmth towards his successors. It was like passing on a troublesome car which sooner or later would start making that funny knocking noise. This wasn't a sexist comment because he felt exactly the same about himself. My God, the complaints about *his* performance! Women had used him and passed him on, ruthlessly in many cases. They had ransacked him en route like departing soldiers, stripping him of his home and his children.

Sometimes, however, he had felt barely touched. Some women, Jacquetta for instance, hadn't really registered him at all. She had never looked at his childhood snapshots or shown the slightest interest in his past. She was either distracted or prickly. Coming home from a dinner party, for instance, he would make some mild remark like: 'Isn't it odd how people who're wonderful cooks often make awful coffee, and vice versa?' Instead of companionably agreeing or disagreeing she would bark: 'What do you mean? *I* can't cook?'

Other women, less neurotic but as healthily egocentric, had blithely let him foot the bill and slipped from him into the traffic, into other arms. Sometimes he felt like a bottle of wine that travels from one party to another, passed from host to host, a bottle so undrinkable that nobody wants to open it. Hirondelle, say, or that stuff called *Red Table Wine: Product of More than One Country*.

He topped up his glass. Penny had once said: 'You're just an old soak. You're not even brave enough to be an alcoholic!' A remark he had felt was both glib and deeply meaningless; typical of a journalist.

Lorna wasn't like that. What had happened to Lorna the country-lover, the bird-spotter? He had loved her once. He could get quite maudlin, thinking about those missed opportunities. The right woman at the wrong time, and – my God – vice versa. No point in it, really. He was alone now. There was nobody just to be around, somewhere in the flat, when he opened his income tax demands. At certain moments even an unsupportive woman was better than nothing. He'd better go and see the blasted porter about the blasted pilot light.

Buffy tried to raise himself from his armchair. George, who had been sitting beside him, thumped his tail and climbed to his feet. Buffy sat down again; the whole operation seemed too complicated, just now. George sank back to the floor.

Celeste . . . oh, Celeste . . .

Nineteen

Celeste sat in the candlelight, drinking a glass of wine. She had got the idea of the candles from Jacquetta's house; she had bought them at the late-night shop and stuck them in saucers around the room. How magical! She could no longer see the damp patches on the wall, or the marks where the previous tenants had hung their pictures. Though she had put away her little crucifix, though the tentative faith she had once possessed had been rocked to its shallow foundations, the candles made her room feel sacred and somehow stiller than usual, even though the shadows danced elastically and the rabbits hopped around the carpet. Wine-drinking was a habit she had picked up from Penny. A glass or two in the evening, that was all. Sancerre, because that was what Penny had been drinking and Celeste didn't know any other kind. She tipped back her glass and drained it. If Buffy's exes could do all this, why couldn't she?

Since she had visited Penny, the week before, two more large boxes had been delivered. She had unpacked everything and laid out the objects on every available surface. She didn't know where these objects were going to be photographed, or when – nobody had mentioned this or indeed how much money she herself was going to be paid – but she needed to display them so that she could write down their descriptions and divide them into groups.

Growing Things was one. Flowerpots had been constructed from just about anything that was vaguely cylindrical, lampshades included. Seedling trays had been made out of the paper cups from boxes of chocolates and the cut-off fingers of rubber gloves. By pricking holes in the bottom of a sports holdall someone had created a capacious Gro-Bag – *with handy travel handles* said the accompanying note, though it didn't explain why one should want to take tomatoes anywhere. *Safety Aids* was another group. This included a pair of child's waterwings constructed from the styrofoam shapes used to pack a hi-fi. Broken rubber bands, knotted together, provided the straps. *Handy Hints* was a general sort of title, used for things like coffee-cup cosies made out of discarded sweaters and a stamp-moistener made from an empty roll-on deodorant bottle.

Just looking at them made her feel obscurely weary. She was starting to realize that no classification was really possible, even by a mind as logical as hers. Some of the objects seemed to have three or four uses and some seemed to have no use at all. Even if they had a use, she could never imagine anyone actually using them. And she still hadn't worked out the thing with the colander. Ranged around the room in the candlelight, they resembled religious offerings donated by a deeply confused congregation. One of the rabbits was already nibbling at a bundle of cut-up tights, which had been accompanied by a long explanatory letter she seemed to have lost.

She had a suspicion that the whole business was getting out of hand. Besides, there was something else that disturbed her, some symbolic meaning to it all that she didn't want to examine. It seemed to be to do with Buffy, and her place in his life. What had Penny said about 100 uses for a discarded husband? Maybe he saw her as a new shoot growing from the rubbish tip of his past – a rubbish tip which daily grew in size as she discovered more about it. Old tights and all.

She mustn't think about this; not now. She missed him desperately; she longed to pick up the phone. But she mustn't; not yet. Instead she looked at his sons' rabbits. One of them was eating a digestive biscuit which she had laid out on a plate, along with some lettuce leaves and a bit of cucumber.

Under the table stood their cardboard box. Its bottom was damp from their long voyage and littered with droppings like spilled raisins. The sticker saying *Guilt: A User's Guide* was peeling off. Not surprisingly, the rabbits showed no inclination to go back into it. If only somebody had sent something really useful, something that could be turned into a hutch! She would have to buy one tomorrow, in her lunch hour, if she could find a pet shop. The rabbits were all black, and larger than she had thought at first; they weren't really babies at all. But it was nice to have some company; she had always liked animals and had been devoted, as a child, to her guinea-pig Jonathan. His death had been her first acquaintanceship with grief. When she had needed to stop giggling – during school prayers, say – she only needed to picture his stiff little body to come to a shuddering halt.

She poured herself another glass of wine. She needed to talk to Buffy, soon. His voice was inside her head. He was so familiar that she felt she had known him all her life, that his voice had been there since she had sat in the armchair sucking her thumb. All the questions swimming around her brain, he could answer them or at least have a go. She loved him for that; she had never known a chatty man. Why do people's Walkmen always seem to be playing the same tune? Last summer she had wondered this, briefly; nobody she had met, then, would have been equipped with any sort of reply. Why do all French people's handwriting look the same? (Her whole class, at one time, had had French pen-pals).

But there were questions much more urgent than these, questions so painful that her stomach clenched. The trouble was, she couldn't ask them. He would just think her insane – insane with jealousy. He wouldn't even be flattered. *Why are you so obsessed with my ex-wives?* She couldn't tell him the reason – not yet.

There was only one person she could ask: Jacquetta. Jacquetta would know.

She could phone. She knew the number. A rabbit, sitting

on its haunches, was nibbling one of her spider plants. Celeste sat beside the phone, not moving. Nine o'clock came and went. Footsteps thumped up and down the stairs. India had come and gone but she didn't know that. Time passed. The ceiling creaked; music played. Her building was a-whisper with transactions.

Celeste didn't phone; she didn't dare. She blew out the candles and went to bed. In the house of secrets she lay, her eyes closed, vibrating gently to the underground trains. In the other room the rabbits were busy. At some point she heard the muffled thud of a plant pot, one of her spider plants no doubt, as it fell to the carpet.

The next day, energised by the bright shop, by being at work, she felt emboldened. There was a buzz in the air. Mr Singh's oldest daughter was sitting the exam for a private school, and he kept rushing to the phone to see if she was home yet. On their display stands the women's faces filled Celeste with courage. Such beauty, such miracles. Be a Vamp! Be a Blonde! Get into private school! Shake a bottle and anything could happen. Each package was filled with possibilities. She could change her life, change her accent . . .

Mr Singh put down the phone. She asked if she could use it.

She paused, her hand on the receiver. Her courage drained away. What excuse could she use this time? At some point, surely, even Jacquetta might get suspicious.

It was then, as she stood there, that the door pinged and a long black figure entered the shop. Its matted hair stood up, like a surprised person in a cartoon.

It was Tobias. Or was it Bruno? One of Buffy's sons. Just for a moment, as he stood there in the harsh strip lighting, she saw the resemblance – the nose, the posture.

'Oh,' he mumbled, surprised. 'Hello.'

Tobias had been going to visit his Dad. He did this secretly, creeping out of the house like a married man committing

137

adultery. It was not that his Mum and Leon disapproved.
Far from it. Leon in fact encouraged him to maintain a
relationship with his father – the main reason, of course, for
him to never let on that he did. Leon! What a wanker.

His half-sister India visited Blomfield Mansions quite a lot,
he knew that. But it was only recently that he had begun to
see why. His Dad's life was such a mess, that was partly
why. It made even *him* feel sorted-out. There was something
about his Dad's glaring inadequacies that made him, Tobias,
feel miraculously mature. Besides, now Penny was gone he
felt sorry for the old tosser. There was something sort of
simple about his Dad's ramshackle life. At home everything
was so muddy – his Mum so tricky and abstracted, his step-
dad so fucking understanding. What do you do when a bloke
gives you condoms? Where do you go from there? Didn't
Leon realize that the point about being sixteen was to be
misunderstood?

Oh, it was more than that. It was lots of things. He didn't
want to analyse it, they had enough of that psychological
crap at home. Basically, he was skiving off school and he
needed some dosh. His Dad always lent him money – if he
had any – because he was a soft touch and anyway he always
felt guilty about being such a rotten father. There was a quid
pro quo here.

So when Tobias rang the doorbell and just got the barking
dog he felt disappointed, for several reasons, that his father
wasn't at home. (In fact Buffy, who had a splitting hangover,
was down at the BBC narrating a documentary about pygm-
ies but nobody else knew that.)

Tobias took the lift to the ground floor, went out, and
walked round the corner to the local chemists. He needed to
buy some Phisomed for his pimples. He opened the door
and came face to face with the person who had taken his
rabbits.

'Oh, hello,' he grunted. He wiped his nose with the back
of his hand and shuffled his feet. How fucking embarrassing.
The point of buying zit stuff at this shop was that nobody

knew him. Now, if he were buying some spray, say, to curb the powerful sexual scent he gave off, something like that . . .

He edged towards the other assistant, the big plain one. She was sitting on a stool reading a women's magazine. He looked over her shoulder at the article: *The Pros and Cons of Stomach Stapling*. But it was no good; the other one came up to him.

'Hello.' She smiled at him. 'Your rabbits are doing really well. Bigger every day. Is there anything I can get you?'

Tobias felt his face heating up. You try to be cool and then what happens? You frigging *blush*. What a divhead! He liked her. She was older than the girls he knew, of course; she must be, like, early twenties. But it was the girls his age who seemed the old ones, with their boots and their loud dismissive voices and the way they looked bored all the time even when they were laughing about something he didn't understand. The way they wore badges saying *I Practise Safe Sex* and totally ignored him. He had grown up with some of them, he had been to primary school with them, but by now they looked as if they'd never been young at all.

He couldn't ask for the pimple lotion, not now. So he mumbled something he had heard the last time he had been listening to anybody at home.

'My Mum was talking about you,' he muttered. 'She said she wanted you to sit for her.'

'Sit for her? Where?'

'Like . . .' He rolled his eyes. He always did this when he talked about his Mum's work. 'Like, she wants to paint you.'

She stared at him. *She* blushed now – a pink glow that spread up her face and matched her overall. 'She does? Really?'

Twenty

At the Happy Eater it was lunchtime all day, breakfast time too, anytime. Meals looped and repeated themselves like the Muzak, ravelling and unravelling. Lorna walked from the kitchen to the tables, the tables to the kitchen. Her head was swimming with the names of plants. Birds she knew about, but plants . . . plants she was just learning. Her legs ached. She was getting too old for this.

Way across England, somewhere near Swindon, Miles sat in a Little Chef. He was mopping up ketchup with a piece of bread. Outside, traffic droned. He swallowed the last mouthful and lit up a cigarette. He had started smoking again. He knew it was unfair, to blame this on his wife, but that's what he did. After all, there was nobody to stop him. His marriage was like a cot-death. Barely begun, it had turned over on its face and stopped breathing. Nobody noticed, least of all his wife. Around him people carried on shovelling in mouthfuls of peas.

Meanwhile, in London, Penny sat in the Groucho Club nibbling a goat's cheese pizza. She was interviewing a blockbuster writer. As he droned on she watched the looping ribbon of her cassette recorder. Round and round it went, filling itself with his words. He was telling her about his Cotswolds mansion. As he talked about his tennis court she suddenly thought: *Rich people never have to write their initials on their tennis balls*. This struck her as so true, so witty, that she thought: *Must tell Buffy tonight*. Then she realized that she couldn't. This sensation still hit her. Months, it had been, and it still hit her.

Outside, a wintry sun shone. A mile away, shoppers in Knightsbridge were heading for sandwich bars. One of them was a middle-aged woman Buffy had slept with a quarter of a century earlier, an incident forgotten by both of them. She was emerging from Harrods, where she had just bought a party dress for her grand-daughter. Her reflection flashed against the window; behind the glass stood the mannequins Quentin had arranged. Her reflection flashed, and was gone.

Nearby, Quentin himself sat in a cappuccino place. He often came here in his lunch hour. Black and chrome, sharp and stylish, it made everybody look well-designed. It drained them of their past and re-created them as fashion statements. Stirring his coffee, he remembered when he was a little boy and how he pretended he had a limp. His ma, Popsi, would get exasperated and walk on ahead. Passers-by would murmur *poor little mite* and glare at her – glare at his mum, the most warm-hearted soul in the world. He knew he was making some sort of point, even then; that he was getting at her in some way. He closed his eyes, to concentrate. He must bring this up with his therapist. Closing his eyes, he pictured a shadowy figure – a man, striding ahead with his mother, turning to bellow at him to buck up. Was this Buffy, or one of the fathers who had come after him?

Quentin folded the fluff into his coffee. Talbot, the man he lived with, he always scooped off the froth first. For some reason this was starting to be irritating. Like the way his own ma, Popsi, poured instant coffee into the lid and flung it into the mugs without measuring it out with a spoon.

Quentin looked up and met the eye of a tall, good-looking man with a box of photographic equipment. Nope. No blip on the radar screen. Besides, he was too young. Quentin was irresistibly drawn towards older men. He knew why, of course; he hadn't spent a fortune on therapy for nothing. *I'm looking for my father; all these years, I've been limping to get his attention.*

Across the room Colin gazed, briefly, at the bloke who sat with his eyes closed. Good bone-structure; light him well and he could be a model. He gazed with the same detached interest at the Gubbio coffee-machine and wondered if he could ever fit one into his kitchen. 'There's no room for anything!' Penny cried. 'There's no room for me! If only I was hinged, you could fold me up and keep me in a box.' She was a tall woman, she needed to stride about. That's what had made her so attractive in the first place. Sometimes he wondered if he was going to be able to cope with her.

Buffy sat in his local, The Three Fiddlers. He was eating a Scotch egg. Well, a grey, loose piece of breadcrumbed cardboard that fell off a small, bluish, rubbery ball that had probably been hardboiled when he was still married to Jacquetta. Why hadn't he learned his lesson about Scotch eggs; why did he still order them? A bit like marriage really; you're hungry, you think it'll be different this time, it can't be as bad as the last one.

On the TV some satellite, Sky or something, was showing tennis. In November. Satellite TV, like central heating, rendered the seasons meaningless. Watching the ball fly, Buffy remembered watching a Wimbledon final long ago. Connors, was it? Or even Arthur Ashe? Years ago. Jacquetta was away, supposedly visiting her aunt in Dorset. Funny, then, that as he sat there he saw her quite clearly amongst the spectators in the Centre Court. Just to the left of the umpire. She was sitting next to a man. Their heads turning one way, then the other. And then turning to each other.

And she didn't even like tennis. In fact, she hated it. That was the worst thing of all. Oh, where was Celeste, who knew nothing of these things? Celeste his innocent girl, his comfort and joy? Not in the shop. Mr Singh said it was her day off. Where was she? His old heart ached.

Celeste sat, hunched on the concrete. Her buttocks were numb. Here in the garden it was freezing; the wintry sun had slipped behind the house and the conservatory lay in shadow. Wind whistled through the skeletal struts; the place hadn't been glazed yet and the workmen seemed to have disappeared. According to Jacquetta they had been gone for days. 'Builders!' she sighed. 'They always let you down in the end. Believe me. I know.'

Jacquetta was painting. Her hair was pulled back in a rubber band; she wore a spattered pair of dungarees which she said had belonged to a plumber of her acquaintance. 'What a man!' she said. 'Built like a shire-horse!' Her face was pinched with concentration; her arm flicked the paint to and fro in bold brush strokes. As she worked she hummed – a low, tuneless sound which for a while Celeste couldn't locate. Then she realized that it stopped when Jacquetta rinsed her brush.

Behind her spectacles, Jacquetta inspected her. *If she knew what I was thinking!* But Celeste guessed that she herself was just an arrangement of shapes and colours. She was just an object to be painted.

With Penny, too, she was just as unknown – a willing pair of hands, a person to wear Penny's cast-off clothing and deal with other people's cast-offs. Both women wanted something from her but neither of them had the foggiest idea what *she* wanted from *them*. It was funny, the way neither of them questioned the way she had popped up into their lives. Instead they just found ways of making her useful. Which was lucky, of course. Their lack of curiosity made the whole thing easier. No, not easier. None of this was easy. But for the moment it made everything more possible to manage.

Celeste sat in the conservatory, as instructed, her arms around her knees. Behind Jacquetta reared up the family home. Buffy had lived in there. He had eaten thousands of breakfasts with this woman. She, Celeste, had never even *seen* him eat breakfast. She didn't want to think about it. Now he was so familiar to her the thought of his unknown lives, so many of them, was becoming horribly painful.

Her arms ached, from gripping her knees. 'I want you foetal,' Jacquetta had said. 'What I'm seeing is a child, waiting to be born in the ribcage of her mother.'

Through the ribs the wind blew. Far away, wolves howled. Now Celeste knew they were wolves it made the sound even more desolate. It echoed around the world. She was lost; more and more lost as time went by. She gazed at the cliff-face of the house; at the curtained French windows of Leon's consulting room down in the basement. It was all closed, to her. Nearby, in their hutch, the two remaining rabbits were mating. They had been at it for hours, judder judder, the hutch rocking. The female's eyes were glazed in an enduring-it sort of way, but at least they had each other.

I must talk to her. Celeste opened her mouth to speak, but just then Jacquetta said: 'You make me feel quite broody. I'd love to have had another daughter. Sons are so . . . well, so male.' The brush flicked to and fro. 'But then Leon says daughters are so *female*. He's got some, you see.'

He's got some. It sounded like cufflinks. He's got some somewhere, can't quite remember where. In the chest of drawers? To these people children seemed to be produced with the carelessness of rabbits and scattered God knew where. Was it being middle-class and educated that made people so profligate? They didn't have to hoard because there was always more where that came from. And here she was, using words like *profligate*. She was changing. Buffy and his world were changing her.

'Leon's put in a lot of time with them. His daughters,' said Jacquetta. 'He knows how important that is. He's seen so much damage, that's why. Dysfunctional relationships. That's his speciality. I was very damaged when I met him, you wouldn't believe. Well, if you'd met my then husband you would.' Jacquetta paused. 'Er, can you keep still?'

Celeste was staring over Jacquetta's shoulder. She stared at the basement curtains. They weren't quite closed. In the gap, inside the consulting room, something was moving.

'He works on the child within,' said Jacquetta. 'We all have a child within us, a child we need to reach. That's what I'm trying to reach too, in my own work.' She squinted at Celeste. 'You're leaning to the side. Can you sit straight?' She went on painting. 'He's wonderful with his patients. It takes a lot of work, of course. Years, maybe, with some of them. They can be so resistant, you see. So terribly defended.'

Celeste stared, mesmerized, at the gap between the curtains. A pale shape rose and fell, rhythmically, as if it were being pumped by a pair of bellows.

'He's very persistent, very sensitive. He thinks of himself as a locksmith, an enabler. He's there to help them help themselves. It can be very exhausting. He gives so much of himself, you see. He works incredibly hard. When he comes upstairs, sometimes, he looks quite drained. The poor love.'

Frozen, Celeste watched. The pale shape was pumping up and down, faster now. She heard a faint cry, or was it just the wolves?

'Straighten up, can you lovey? You're leaning again.' Jacquetta's brush hesitated. She started to turn round. 'What is it?'

'Nothing!' Celeste pointed to the hutch. 'It's just the rabbits.'

'Ah. You're not embarrassed are you?' Jacquetta laughed. 'That's what I like about animals. They're so honest.' She paused. 'Excuse me, but could you open your eyes?'

Celeste had to get out of there. Anyway it was getting dark. When she opened her eyes a light had been switched on behind the curtains. They had been closed now; a mere slit of brightness shone between them, just a crack. Hadn't he realized that anyone was out here in the garden?

She couldn't ask Jacquetta questions now. She must have muttered something about it getting cold because the paints were being packed away and now Celeste was hurrying up

145

the spiral staircase, clatter clatter, into the kitchen. She stood beside the Aga. How could she find out what she needed to know when at any moment Leon might come upstairs? He didn't know she had seen anything, of course, but *she* did and that was bad enough.

She was standing there when the front door banged and Bruno, the other son, came in. He was dragging a large, battered metal sign. It said BUSES ON DIVERSION.

'Yo,' he said. 'Want to help me get this up to my room? It's for my collection.'

She lifted up the back end of the sign – it was surprisingly heavy – and they started upstairs.

'What're you going to do with it?' she asked breathlessly.

'Dunno.'

'What's going to happen to the buses? Won't they go off in the wrong direction?'

They stood on the landing, panting. All over the city wolves howled, rabbits juddered and buses careered into blind alleys. How did anyone cope? Quite apart from the other, much more embarrassing thing. She should have been warned when India told her about the condoms.

They had reached Bruno's bedroom. He pushed open the door – he had to push hard, there was so much stuff crammed against it – and switched on the light.

For a moment she thought the place had been ransacked. Clothes and lager cans were strewn ankle-deep all over the floor. Half-open drawers spilled more clothes. *Have I got children? I must have left them somewhere, look in the chest of drawers.* She stumbled over an empty vodka bottle and knocked into a traffic cone. Though basically a rubbish dump, the traffic signs gave it the air of a London Transport depot. There was a curious smell hanging in the air, too – a smell like burnt dung.

'Gosh,' she said. She thought: Buffy used to tiptoe into this room and kiss this boy goodnight. What earthquakes had happened since then! 'What a horrible mess!'

'Good, isn't it. Once I was asleep here for two days. There, under that stuff on the duvet. They couldn't find me. They ended up calling the police.'

In Melton Mowbray teenagers weren't like this. They didn't have his matted hairstyle and stupefied look. And, she was sure, his disgusting living quarters. The more money people had, it seemed, the more untidy they became. Back home people complained about their teenagers, of course, because they got on their mountain bikes and did wheelies around the phone kiosks. But overnight they turned into sober young wage-earners in Tesco's overalls. They had to.

'It's almost as good as my Dad's place,' he said.

'Really?'

'You should see it.'

'Should I?'

He smiled affectionately. 'He's hopeless, the old fuck-face.'

'You shouldn't talk about him like that.' She dumped the sign on the bed. 'Haven't you any respect?'

'With *my* parents?'

Just then there was the clump of boots on the stairs and the other one came in. Tobias.

'Hi,' he said. Then he sniffed and turned to his brother. 'What've you been smoking? Where did you get it?'

'Mum. I scored her some and she gave me a bit. My tithe.' He turned to Celeste and added, kindly: 'I know about tithes because we've been doing the Middle Ages.'

What was he talking about – his mum giving him cigarettes? Celeste gazed at the walls. They were black. Skulls and posters of leather-clad women hung there, along with signs saying ALTERNATIVE ROUTE and POLICE NOTICE:ACCIDENT. She felt weak, but there was nowhere to sit down. Her life was sinking into chaos, signs sending her off in all directions, the wrong directions, one-way streets and cul-de-sacs, rabbits eating her belongings and people's husbands getting up to you-know-what in basement rooms. Her feelings about Buffy were getting more confused every minute.

Who could she talk to now? His boys, maybe. She had a feeling they were more intelligent than they pretended. But not here. Besides, they had put on some deafening music and her head was throbbing.

There was only one person left, only one hope. She shouted at them: 'Where's India?'

Tobias laughed his corncrake laugh. 'Go to Pakistan and on a bit.'

'What?'

He turned down the noise. 'Just kidding. Sorry. She's out.'

'Where?'

'At work.'

'Where's that?'

Celeste, emerging from Leicester Square tube station, was assaulted by drunken yodelling and the smell of hot-dogs. A spotty youth was playing a saxophone. She walked briskly past him. Buffy had once said: 'Why does one only stop and listen to buskers when one's on holiday?' She stepped over a prone body; she hurried, bent double, past a Japanese man who was aiming with a video camera. By now she was learning the Londoner's duck and scurry, the swerves to avoid a drunk, the little skip over a puddle of sick. Only three weeks ago she had wandered dazed around Soho, flinching at the noise and smells. Only three weeks; how she had hardened up since then!

It was a big cinema, not one of the cupboards Buffy had complained about. She had meant to ask the manager if she could speak to India but *Citizen Kane* was showing, and Buffy had told her it was really good, so she simply bought a ticket and went in.

The ads were playing – a blue-jeaned rump was swaying on the screen, accompanied by loud music. Celeste paused in the dark. Somebody took her ticket; it wasn't India. But in the darkness other torches were weaving and dipping, up and down the auditorium. Which one belonged to her?

Celeste was shown to a seat. Once her eyes had grown accustomed to the dark she saw that the cinema was only half full. The curiously meaty smell of popcorn was in the air. Up on the screen the film began; an iron gate, turrets against rushing black and white clouds. One or two people were still arriving; in the aisles the torches still swivelled, shining on an empty seat here, an empty seat there. They flashed like fireflies. Soon they would be gone; the usherettes would disappear to wherever usherettes went. Where did they go? They just melted away.

She had never thought about this. She had never thought about so many things. Up on the screen a voice spoke boomingly. The audience breathed; they sighed, *en masse*, like a great dark sponge, settling down. They had ceased to function; the actors lit their faces, dancing across their irises. Celeste didn't really watch the film. For the first time she wondered what it must be like to be an actor. She hadn't really thought about this before. This was what Buffy *did*. He put on fancy dress and became somebody different. He escaped into it, leaving his various families in the dark, fumbling around while he entertained everybody else.

This wasn't fair. The seat next to her was empty. If only Buffy were here, he would explain. He would sit there, his bear-hand on her knee; he would feed her pieces of Bourneville chocolate. He would lead her into the story, into an adventure. Perhaps he would protest that he wasn't escaping; that he was returning people to themselves. He was filling their heads with reflections of themselves, he was filling them with answers. If not answers, then dreams. Who knows? He wasn't here.

India was, somewhere. Celeste couldn't concentrate on the film; she got up and went to look for her. There was nobody in the lobby except a bored-looking man selling hamburgers. He lounged beside the bubbling tank of orange juice. She went up the wide, carpeted stairs to the upper floor.

India was standing in the doorway marked *Circle*. Celeste could recognize her from the back, even in her maroon uniform. She was watching the film. Celeste tapped her on the shoulder.

India turned. 'Hi,' she said. 'What're you doing here?'

Celeste shrugged. 'I heard it was good.'

'I've seen it about a zillion times. My stepdad – Buffy – ex-stepdad – he used to take me to the pictures all the time. Specially the old ones. He knew the names of the actors; he used to whisper to me and everyone told us to shut up.' She tensed. 'Watch this bit.'

Celeste watched for a moment. India took her arm and led her to a seat. They sat down. There was nobody else up here, in the circle. India glanced around and took out a pack of cigarettes. 'Hope Mr Nathan doesn't see us. He's tried to sack me twice.' She lit a cigarette and sat back. She pointed to the screen, whispering: 'People don't really get old like that. Poor old Orson Welles had no idea what was in store. Bunged on a few wrinkles and whitened his hair.' She exhaled smoke. 'Little did he know that he was going to blow up like a balloon and his career crumble into pieces.'

Down below, actors bloomed on the screen. They lit India's face and her wreathing cigarette smoke. Celeste asked: 'So you came to these films with your step-dad?'

India nodded. 'It was our secret skive. *L'Atalante*, *Les Enfants de Paradis*, the only French I learnt was through sub-titles.'

'When did he meet your mum?'

India grinned. 'At a health farm. Mum was meditating in the garden, and he was creeping out to go to the pub. He was trying to squeeze under some barbed wire but his trousers got caught. She had to rescue him.'

'No, I mean how long ago?'

India put her feet up on the seat in front. 'She was married to my real Dad then. To Alan.'

'What about Buffy? Was he married?'

'Oh, Buffy's always married.'

'Is he?'

'He's such a romantic. Rather sweet really.' She inhaled deeply. She didn't seem to think it odd, Celeste questioning her like this. Maybe she was full of drugs and everything seemed natural. 'He was married to Popsi.'

'Popsi?'

'Popsi Concorde. Daft name, isn't it? Mum thought so, but I suppose she would.' She stopped, and gazed at the screen. Orson Welles was smashing up bedroom furniture. 'She was obsessed with her for a bit. As much as Mum can be obsessed with anybody except herself. Retrospective jealousy, I suppose. She kept on going on about how vulgar and brassy she was.' She blew out a plume of smoke. 'All I knew was Mum kept taking me to this pub.'

'What pub?'

'The pub Popsi worked at. She'd moved in there with her new boyfriend or husband or whatever.' The voice of Orson Welles boomed like Buffy's, boomed echoing from the past. It caressed the audience. India tapped the ash off her cigarette and turned to Celeste. 'Why're you so interested?'

'I just am. My life's so boring.'

'Don't·you want to watch the film?'

'This story's much better,' whispered Celeste. 'Go on.'

'We'd take the tube to Sloane Square. Gosh, I haven't thought about it for years. I was just little. Dunno why they let me in but Popsi was the easy-going type. It was called The Old Brown Mare, I remember the sign. I liked horses.'

They watched the film for a while. At least, Celeste pretended to watch it. Afterwards she couldn't remember a thing that had happened in it. She only remembered India sitting beside her, with the torch lying in her lap and the bluish light from the screen playing over her face. 'What was she like, Popsi?'

'Peroxide blonde, Barbara Windsor type. Buffy said she was the sort of woman who always had one too many buttons undone. I remember seeing her reflection in all the little mirrors around the bar. Mum would just sit there, watching her. She probably didn't even know who Mum was. I ate lots of crisps.' She laughed. 'The funny thing was, mum doesn't even *drink*. She never goes to pubs. Not usually. But jealousy makes people do peculiar things, I suppose. They get unhinged.'

Celeste hadn't noticed that the film had finished. There was a stirring, downstairs. Just then a man appeared, in a dinner jacket. He seemed to be shouting something at India.

When Celeste turned round, India had gone. Just a gauzy layer of smoke remained, hanging in the air. And then the lights came up.

Twenty-one

Miles pushed the trolley down the aisle. Muzak burbled, to sooth his troubled soul. Every now and then he consulted Brenda's list. Snicker Bars. Fiesta Kitchen Towels. Vosene Silk Hair Conditioner. Diet Tizer. He was never in the right aisle, but then her list wasn't in any sort of order. He kept retracing his steps and bumping into people coming the other way. Mostly women; it was the middle of the afternoon.

He was in a huge Tesco's just outside Chippenham. They were building a whopping Sainsbury's further up the road, too, in the middle of a field. They all had belfries and gables and clock towers; they were big brick leeches sucking the town dry. He'd said to Brenda: 'Just think. In hundreds of years archaeologists will say – what was that great religious revival? All those huge, huge churches. Vast car parks! We must have got it wrong, that it was a Godless age.' But Brenda hadn't listened, she had spotted a ladder in her tights.

Tesco Malted Wheats. He flung the packet into the trolley. Neither he nor Brenda ate Malted Wheats but that wasn't the point. He felt exhausted; his legs ached like a housewife's.

He made his way to the tinned fish. This was the big one, the one she had gone on about. Trouble was, they were clean out of pilchards. The word must have got around.

He loaded the groceries into his car and drove to Gateway's, the other side of Swindon. He searched along the maze of aisles. Pilchards. He almost whooped. He cradled the tin in his hand. To Brenda, this wasn't a can of Abbey Vale Pilchards in Tomato Sauce. It was a British Airways

Round-the-World Trip of a Lifetime for Two, with £100,000 thrown in.

He must have spent hours shopping, driving along ring roads from one supermarket to the next. By the time he got home it was dark and Brenda was back from work. From the sound of it, she had her friend Gail with her. He heard their voices in the lounge.

'So we're sitting in the cinema,' said Gail, 'and he started sort of sliding his hand up my skirt. Just a bit at a time. He thought I wasn't noticing.'

'Was that your pleated skirt from Marks and Spencers?' asked Brenda.

He dumped the shopping on the kitchen floor. Brenda was beside him in a flash.

'Did you get the pilchards?' she asked breathlessly. He nodded. 'And the other things?' She kissed him on the cheek. As she did so he noticed that the sink was full of water. Bottles lay submerged in it, to soak off their labels.

She carried the tin of pilchards, like a trophy, into the lounge. Gail's voice rose. They started giggling.

He stood there in silence. In the water the labels uncurled; some of them had already risen to the surface. The plastic bags sighed as they settled themselves around his feet. More and more strongly, nowadays, he felt as if he had wandered into the wrong house. These little starter homes all looked the same, it was an understandable mistake. He had actually done it once; he had sauntered, whistling, into the house next door and surprised the Widdicombes eating a fondue. He could just walk into another front door and begin all over again.

Did other men feel like this? He hadn't been a husband for long, only two years. He should have got used to it by now, but in fact the opposite seemed to be happening. Maybe it was the inside-out nature of their lives, Brenda working and him not. That was the most reasonable explanation. But he had started to feel this some time before he had been made redundant.

He started to put stuff away in the larder. On the shelves sat rows and rows of tins, stripped of their labels. They glowed, dully. Large ones, smaller ones, flattish ones. Choosing something to eat made him and Brenda seem like a blind couple; there was a dotty sense of adventure to it. You opened a tin and what would it be? Sponge pudding? Butter beans? There were ten cans of Bachelor Mushy Peas amongst that lot which nobody was ever going to eat. Brenda had only bought them for their labels – ten, so she could send off a multiple entry.

The whole house was silting up with things they were never going to eat, or condition their hair with, or squirt the furniture with. By now the larder was so packed he could hardly close the door. It made him feel breathless and congested, as if he had indigestion. Her craze for competitions was getting out of hand; it was an addiction, really. She quite cheerfully admitted that. And how could he have the heart to stop her?

She had such a boring job. Eight hours a day she sat at a console, tubes plugged into her ears as if she were in intensive care, staring at a screen that gave her a headache. How could he cut off her escape routes? All her friends at work were compers. During their lunch hour they scratched away at their scratch-pads of magic numbers. They washed butter wrappers. They collected bottle-tops as proof of purchase and squashed them under their chair-legs to make them flat enough to send off. They dreamed of cars and dishwashers and holidays for two in Bali; they dreamed of trips to the stars. They dreamed of the Long White Envelope sliding through their letterbox; they spoke of this in hushed and reverent initials – *the LWE*.

In the evenings they sat in each others' lounges and made up slogans. *Hovis and Half-Fat Anchor taste so good together because . . . BP Lubricants are the sportsman's choice because . . . It Asda be Asda because . . .* If they were in his house he could hear the sudden bursts of laughter, the excited voices as one of them was suddenly possessed with what they called

155

Winspiration. Before he met Brenda he had presumed that slogan-writing was a solitary activity, like masturbation, but she and her girlfriends did it together, a chaste orgy of voices chiming with insincere tributes to the goods they never used.

. . . because their porkers are corkers . . . because it keeps your food eatable at a price that's unbeatable . . . They were experts. They knew the combinations of flattery and humour that would win; they sneered at the tired old clichés like *Experts perfect them and connoisseurs select them.* One had to admire them for it. He did, actually. They won a lot. Only last September one of them, Phyllis, had calculated how many packets of Opal Fruits were piled up inside a Ford Escort GTi; she had won the car and all the sweets *and* had her photo in the local paper.

Oh, yes, they won. Brenda, in particular. That was the trouble. She was always hauling him off to presentations in hotels hundreds of miles away in the north of England, Stockport, places like that, where toupéed TV personalities whose programmes he had never seen put their arms around Brenda and called her *my love.* Then there were all the deliveries. Last week he had had the fright of his life when he had answered the doorbell to a man in green overalls who said: 'Hi there, I've come from Mars.'

That time it was a microwave cooker. Lucky he was home all day to take the stuff in. The house was filling up. At the top of the stairs was the little bedroom where he pictured their child would be; he had even papered it with a frieze of teddy bears. But they didn't seem to be able to have a baby and now the room was stacked with things he could never imagine anyone wanting, more and more of them, piled up: a thermos-gas barbecue, a Phillips foot spa, a digitally-controlled hostess trolley. In the corner was heaped £250-worth of Marley Cushion Flooring, consolation prize in the Shake'N'Vac competition. It was impossible to open the window anymore; it was wedged shut with a boxed set of Dunlop Maxfli golf club and balls. He had never played golf. 'Get on with you,' said Brenda, 'you could learn. I'll win you lessons!' She kept winning things for him; she thought they were in on this together and that they'd become Comping Couple of the Year. She didn't seem to notice his lack of interest. He had hidden some of the stuff in the cupboard – trouser presses, things like that. There was £100-worth of Denim Men's Toiletries in there; he got a whiff of it sometimes, when he passed.

She didn't notice because, like an addict, she was onto her next fix. Where did this hunger come from? Was it his fault? Maybe he had disappointed her and she was trying to fill the void. Maybe it was his fault that she hadn't got pregnant. He didn't dare ask; she didn't like questions. If he asked: 'What's all this for?' she would gaze at him, her eyes blank. And then he would get that hollow, lonely feeling again.

That night, in bed, she snuggled up to him. 'Poor Gail,' she said, 'she's always going out with such awful men. They think she's desperate, just because she's living with her mum.' She kissed his ear and pushed her hand inside his pyjama bottoms, caressing his buttock. 'Aren't I the lucky one? They all say so.'

Her bold familiarity made him sad. He willed her to go to sleep but her fingers were working on him, she was deft and businesslike. She could still arouse him even though his mind was miles away. He remembered the first time they had made love. They had just met, at a party. They were both drunk and fumblingly passionate, in bed at his flat. The local radio station was playing rhythm and blues. Just as they were shudderingly reaching a climax the music had stopped and the 2 a.m. news came on: *In Belfast, a publican and his wife were killed when an IRA gunman shot them at point blank range.* Even this had not checked their ardour, not in those days.

When they had finished, she curled herself against his shoulder and told him about the treasure hunt. It was the competition on the can of pilchards. 'Tomorrow I'm sending

157

off the entry form,' she said, 'just think of it – Hong Kong, Sydney, Disneyworld! Just the two of us!'

She fell asleep abruptly, breathing into his neck, her leg hooked round his thigh. It was cold. He wanted to put on his pyjama bottoms but on the other hand he didn't want to wake her up. A dual-choice question: Was this because a) he was so nice, or b) he didn't want her to go on talking? If she won the prize, could he send her round the world all by herself?

That night, gazing at the sodium light glowing through the curtains, he realized quite clearly that his marriage was a mistake. It was such an alarming thought that he didn't quite put it into words, even to himself. Life was so chancy; it was chancier than any scratch-card, and much more terrifying. Looking back, he could pinpoint the exact moments when he had made the wrong choice and set in motion a series of events he had been powerless to stop. One such moment had been standing at the school noticeboard and realizing that if he kept on with physics he could get out of games. The quickening momentum of this choice had propelled him into college and from there into the research labs of Glaxo's, six numbing years from which he had only just been rescued by redundancy. What on earth was he going to do now, with all his boats burned?

Another such moment had been bumping into an acquaintance called Neville Bowman at an off-licence one Friday night. Neville was buying a bottle of Hirondelle to take to a party, so instead of renting a video Miles had joined him and thus set ticking the count-down to that moment when he first glimpsed Brenda in the kitchen, nibbling a gherkin. She wore a strapless top-thing that exposed her plump, creamy shoulders. How lively she was! She chatted to him non-stop. Being shy himself, or maybe just lazy, he had always been attracted to bold, talkative girls and Brenda was certainly bold. By midnight they were pressed against the wall on an upstairs landing, kissing passionately as people squeezed past on their way to the loo. Briefly he had opened his eyes and seen her waving, over his shoulder, to one of her girlfriends.

Maybe even then it wouldn't have gone further. But when they paused for a breather he had felt obliged to back-pedal a bit and ask her about herself, what she liked doing in her spare time and so forth.

'Comping,' she had said.

'Really? So do I!' His heart had swelled. Suddenly she was dear to him. Not just sexy, but a friend too. He had never met a girl who liked camping. They could stride across the Berkshire Downs, ruddy-cheeked; she could help him carry his equipment, which had always been too heavy for one. They could bird-watch together and then, of course, there was that good old double sleeping-bag waiting. He had kissed her with real ardour then – with love, even. And by the time he discovered that he had misheard her – *comping* was a word unfamiliar to him then – it was really too late.

He lay there, his eyes open, visualizing drastic measures. A tornado swept up all the little houses in the Hazeldene Estate and blew them away, spinning, like Dorothy's house in *The Wizard of Oz*. His own house landed in such a distant land he could never find it, and Brenda would live happily there with someone else. The whole thing painless.

Or – he would simply go to sleep and realize that these past two years had been a dream. He would wake up and it would all be over. He had never gone to the party that night; he had rented the video and fallen asleep in front of the TV . . .

Or . . . or he scratched Brenda's back with his fingernail . . . under her skin, a message was revealed. What did it say . . . why couldn't he make out the letters? . . . Or was it numbers, a secret combination he must unlock . . . he tried to read it but he couldn't, and now it was blurring . . .

Miles slept, imprisoned and released, unaware that downstairs the can of fishes was going to take the decision out of his hands, just as the biscuit tin had done for Celeste, and that his life was already moving in a direction where everything would be changed, utterly; that in the future he would indeed look back on these years with the detached and vaguely affectionate curiosity of someone who had, in fact, simply dreamed them.

Twenty-two

'So what did you do last night, my treasure, my pigeon?' asked Buffy. 'I missed you.'

'I went to *Citizen Kane*.'

'Who with?'

'Nobody,' said Celeste. 'I feel so ignorant, I want to catch up. I went by myself.'

Could he believe her? She smiled at him – such a clear, candid face!

'I wish I'd taken you,' he said. 'I love watching you watching things.'

Celeste didn't reply. They sat down in the stalls. He had brought her to the Barbican to see *The Winter's Tale*. She rearranged his back-support cushion, wedging him in. Sitting in a theatre with Celeste made him realize how old he was getting – how the seats were getting smaller and harder, how the actors' voices were becoming more mumblingly indistinct. Celeste's youth was like a light being switched on in a house – the twilit garden was immediately plunged into darkness, her brightness edged it towards night. He was the garden, of course.

They settled down. Normally nothing would induce him to come to the Barbican, it made him feel like a prisoner of Stalinism, but he thought that she might be moved by the play, with its magic and redemption, its possibilities of miracles. Besides, Leontes was being played by an old rival of his, a reformed hell-raiser called Dermott Metcalfe who was rapidly becoming a Grand Old Man of the Theatre – a title earned by anybody if they stuck at it long enough, had one lucky break and kept out of the boozer. Dermott and he had been rivals in love, too. Long, long ago, on tour with *The Voysey Inheritance*, they had both fallen for the DSM, a comely redhead called Serena, and though Buffy had briefly enjoyed her favours it was Dermott who had finally captured her – indeed, who had married her. Probably was married to her still. Somewhere in Sussex she would be ageing beautifully – she had a splendid bone structure – and serving tea to colour supplement journalists who had come down to interview her husband.

The lights went down; the play began. Buffy took Celeste's small, cool hand and pressed it to his chest.

'Too hot, too hot!' cried Leontes, *'To mingle friendship far is mingling bloods. I have tremor cordis in me: my heart dances; But not for joy; not joy . . .'*

He had always been irritated by Leontes – what a stubborn, blustering old fool! Fancy suspecting a wife like Hermione. Anyone could see she wasn't the sort to two-time him; *she* wasn't going to plaster herself with Sudden Tan and fornicate above a pasta shop.

'Inch-thick, knee-deep, o'er head and ears a forked one!' Leontes shook his locks. *' . . . many a man there is even at this present, Now, while I speak this, holds his wife by the arm, That little thinks she has been sluic'd in's absence, And his pond fished by his next neighbour . . .'*

Dermott was doing the business in a sonorous, look-at-me way that seemed to go down all right with the audience, but they looked as if they all came from Kansas. Buffy turned to gaze at Celeste – the stem-like neck, the choir-boy profile. She seemed entranced.

'Is whispering nothing?' Bellowed Leontes. *'Is leaning cheek to cheek? Is meeting noses? Kissing with inside lip? Stopping the career of laughter with a sigh?'*

He wanted to tell her *it should be me up there!* The trouble was, the dramas in his own life had effectively eclipsed those of his career. Too many bloody dramas on the domestic front.

Rows and recriminations and, all right then, the odd blinder, but only when a chap was at breaking point . . . The chaos brought on by the defection of his various wives – Jacquetta, for instance, rushing off to Wales with that creepy Gestalt therapist when he was just preparing his Macduff. Her other escapade to Egypt. The hungover, cross-country trek to reclaim his sons from her mother, whose outrage seemed inexplicably directed at him rather than her nymphomaniac daughter . . . The bust-up with Popsi which sabotaged that film job. Only Popsi could barge into The Ivy, where he was lunching with the director, and manage to fling a bowlful of vichyssoise into the *director's* lap. Her aim had always been poor . . . The bloodsucking lawyers, barely out of their teens, who summoned him to court when he should have been in rehearsal, who bled him dry and forced him to turn down the BBC and take that mini-series job in L.A. that didn't survive the pilot. And yet nobody blamed the women. Well, they were women, weren't they? He was a brute, an egotistical bastard, an oppressor. *They* weren't, oh no! Their possession of fallopian tubes absolved them from any blame and to cap it all they stole his children too –

Buffy blinked. Up on stage, Hermione was speaking.

'Take the boy to you: he so troubles me, 'Tis past enduring . . .

She lifted up her son and gave him to one of her attendants – a slender, dark-skinned girl in an ochre gown. Buffy stared. Where had he seen that girl before? Waiting tables at the patisserie? She looked so familiar.

The girl put her arm around the child. *'Come, my gracious lord,'* she said, *'Shall I be your playfellow?'*

Working behind the counter at some shop he frequented? Where was it?

The girl turned, tossing her head. Buffy sat there, frozen. Oh, my God. Now he knew. Once, years ago, he had arrived at the place where she lived – a flat, three flights up, in the Elephant and Castle or somewhere. He had arrived to take her out to tea. She had opened the door to him – a skinny thing, pigtails, twelve or thirteen. She had turned, tossing her head like that, and called, 'Mum, there's a man here.'

'*Bear the boy hence!*' shouted Leontes. '*Away with him!*'

Nyange swept off-stage, taking the child with her. Buffy sat there, rigid, until the interval lights came up. He put on his spectacles and fumblingly leafed through the programme. There she was: *First Lady . . . Nyange Jamison*. His own daughter.

People were stirring. Beside him, Celeste was asking a question.

' . . . wife,' she seemed to be saying. Something about a wife.

'Hermione,' he answered abstractedly. 'That's Leontes's wife. He thinks she's being unfaithful, the old paranoid.'

'No. Your wives.'

'What?' He tried to gather his scattered wits.

'Your wives,' she said. 'I didn't know you had so many.'

He looked at her. 'You never asked.'

She shrugged. 'It just seems rather a lot to me.'

'Me too! I didn't *want* it, you know. I didn't *choose* to be married to lots of wives.' He closed the programme. 'I didn't think – when I grow up I want to get divorced three times, what fun!' He put his arm around her awkwardly, wedged in his seat. 'One day you might understand, my darling girl.'

She got up. 'Let's get a drink.'

Her voice was thin and sharp, almost commanding. Maybe she had noticed his attention straying. She looked at him coolly, as if, when it came to women, he suffered from some form of incontinence. How could he tell her about Nyange now? He wanted to point out his daughter's name in the programme but this was hardly the time to spring upon Celeste yet another instance of his supposed lack of control. In fact it had been Carmella, Nyange's mother, who had wanted a baby in the first place but it would doubtless seem churlish to point this out.

They moved towards the bar. He wanted to say: that was my daughter up there! Last time I heard she was a model but now look at her. Acting's in her blood, that's why; she got it from me. Oh, if only she had told me. I could teach her a tip or two, if she had come to me. She is my daughter, dammit.

If Celeste wasn't being so chilly he could put his arms around her and say: That was my daughter up there, I haven't seen her for years. I used to take her to the Soda Fountain at Fortnum's. I used to watch her shovelling in Knickerbocker Glory and telling me about her new step-father, oh, the pain of it! I used to send her birthday presents until I got disheartened by the lack of response. I used to send her presents that were too young for her; I only realized that later. I sent her a box of magic tricks and the next time I saw her she was wearing lipstick. When you have lost your children you stay forever a step behind. All over the world, banished fathers are sending their children clothes that are one size too small. Maybe we want them to stay young forever. To stop the clock. Then we'll start again and get it right this time.

'What's the matter?' Celeste held him arm. 'Are you okay?' She sat him down; her voice had softened. 'You look awful.'

During the second half he decided to brazen it out. When the curtain came down he would take Celeste round to the Stage Door and introduce them. Who knows? Celeste might even consider him racy to have fathered this exotic, dusky creature. Out of wedlock, too, for he had never been married to Nyange's mother. Up on the stage Camillo was speaking.

'I have heard, sir, of such a man, who hath a daughter of rare note: the report of her is extended more than can be thought to begin from such a cottage.'

Of course they must meet. How piquant! Besides, he himself was longing to meet Nyange again – at last in a setting that both of them understood: the theatre. A world that could bond them together at last. Watching his daughter move across the stage, poised and solemn, he felt a curious warmth. It was such an unfamiliar sensation that for most of

Act IV he couldn't identify it. Then he realized: it was pride. He was actually proud of one of his children. Would it be asking too much for them ever to be proud of him? Yes.

'You gods! Look down, and from your sacred vials pour your graces upon my daughter's head!'

The cast took their bows to loud applause. Buffy grabbed his back-rest and ushered Celeste out.

'There's someone I want you to meet,' he whispered.

'Is this the way?' asked Celeste.

LEVEL 8, said the sign. TIERS 1/2.

They hurried along a sodium-lit corridor. At the end was a gate. EMERGENCY EXIT. He rattled the bars; it was locked.

He took her hand; they hurried down another corridor and emerged onto a windy walkway. It was freezing. Their feet clattered on the concrete.

'I'm sure this is wrong,' she panted.

They pounded up a flight of stairs. GATE 2. Again they were stopped by a locked door. Beside it was a metal plate of entryphone buttons. NORTH STAIR. FLATS 28-46. Buffy's heart pounded; he tried to catch his breath.

They hurried down a ramp. LEVEL 8. An arrow pointed one way. LEVEL 7. An arrow pointed another way. FOLLOW GATE TO YOUR DESTINATION. They hurried down another corridor and pushed open a door. A stream of cars thundered by, choking them with exhaust fumes. They seemed to be in some underground road. What a nightmare this place was! Where was the Stage Door? Signs and arrows pointed them in all directions, NO ACCESS TO VEHICLES. ADVANCE BOOKING LEVEL 5. SPRINKLER STOP VALVE INSIDE. How could he get to his daughter when everything conspired to confuse him? Once, when he was visiting his sons in Primrose Hill, he had been allowed to go upstairs to Bruno's room. On the door was a large metal sign saying NO ENTRY.

They hurried across the carpeted, orange expanse of wher-ever they were, some level or other. The Barbican building

166

was emptying. Maybe he was losing his way on purpose. Maybe he was doomed to take the wrong turning, to find himself up a blind alley. To bang on the glass while one son, Quentin, slid out of sight, disappearing into Harrods. To gaze helplessly at Nyange, unreachable on a stage.

Celeste had stopped somebody and was asking them directions. She turned and grabbed Buffy's hand, pulling him along.

'This way!'

His chest hurt, his corns throbbed. Gasping, he followed her through a door. They emerged at the mouth of the underground car park. People were climbing into taxis and driving off in clouds of diesel smoke. Maybe he had missed Nyange; maybe she had already gone.

'There it is!' said Celeste.

Stage Door. Royal Shakespeare Company. One by one the actors were emerging, looking smaller than they had looked on stage. Buffy paused.

'Who are we looking for?' asked Celeste.

At that moment Dermott Metcalfe strode out. He was well wrapped up in an astrakhan coat and fedora.

'Russell, old cock!' He strode up to Buffy. 'Long time no see. Where've you been hiding? Enjoyed the show?' He turned to Celeste. 'Well, hello. This your daughter?' Buffy opened his mouth but Dermott was shaking Celeste's hand. 'Following in the family footsteps, eh?'

Not this one! Buffy wanted to shout. Not this one, the other one! But at that moment a car slid out of the mouth of the underground car park and stopped beside them.

'Darling.'

Serena's face, thirty years older but still recognisable, and indeed beautiful, smiled from the open window of the driver's seat.

'Russell Buffery, remember?' said Dermott.

She frowned for a moment, then her face cleared. 'Russell! Our children used to listen to Hammy. I told them, I used to know that man. Well, hamster.'

Dermott turned to Celeste. 'They were sweethearts once, these two. Before I staked my claim.'

Celeste stared at the woman in the car and turned to Buffy. '*Another* one?'

Dermott was talking. 'Every evening she drives me in from Gerrards Cross, isn't she a jewel?' He kissed the tip of his wife's nose. 'A pearl beyond price. I'm a lucky bugger.'

Suddenly Celeste took Buffy's arm. 'Oh, he's a lucky bugger too, aren't you Dad? What with Mum and all of us.' She turned to Dermott. 'There's lots of us, you see, but we're one big happy family. Isn't that right, Dad?'

Buffy nodded, dumbly.

She squeezed his arm. 'Trouble is, Dad's just too much of a stay-at-home. He's spent his whole time with us, playing with us, being a good Dad, that he's hardly had time for his career. Isn't that true, Daddy? That's why nobody sees him around much. But it's been worth it. For all those happy memories and happy times together.' She pulled him away. 'Come on, Dad. Time for bed.'

'My God, Celeste!' Buffy gazed at her. They were sitting in a taxi, driving home. 'That was terrific. What an actress!' He cleared his throat. 'Er, why did you do it?'

She turned to look out of the window. 'He was such a creep, I suppose. I'm fed up with people going on about how happy they are. Then you see them messing around in basements.'

'Basements? Who's been messing around in basements?'

She didn't reply. She was sitting huddled in the corner. He moved closer.

'Did you really mean it? About it being time for bed?'

She shook her head. 'Just drop me off in Kilburn High Road.'

'Celeste.'

She turned to look at him. The street lights chased across her face. Her eyes, how dark they were!

'My darling girl, what's the matter? I never know, with

168

you. That very first day, in the shop – your lovely face, it changes like the weather. Let me take you home.'

She sat there, gnawing her fingernails.

'I don't even know where you live!' he said.

'There's lots you don't know.'

He removed her hand gently. It was trembling. 'Tell me.'

'Not now. Not yet.'

Twenty-three

Celeste emerged into the sunshine of Sloane Square. Each tube escalator, she was discovering, propelled her into a different London. One day she might piece them all together. No drunks here; even the air smelt more wholesome and expensive. Women in tweeds strode past, carrying bags from the General Trading Company; one of them had a labrador in tow. A glossy Penny-type, wearing a designer suit, yelled 'Taxi!' in a carrying voice. Celeste herself felt smarter now; she had bought a new coat, russet red, from one of those shops she had once found too intimidating to enter. The coat had cost a lot – a whole month's rent from the people living in her old home, but that's the sort of thing she did now.

She consulted her map and walked down Sloane Gardens, past blocks of mansion flats which resembled Buffy's except there were BMWs parked outside. Her shiny new boots tap-tapped on the pavement; they sounded confident, but her heart was bumping against her ribs. Why had she been so stupid the night before? Buffy must think she was mad, suddenly jabbering on like that in front of other people. And what would he think if he saw her now? This was the third journey she had made into his past, the third and the deepest. Each one, she had thought, would be the last. How could anybody have had so many wives? Other women, too. She felt like an archaeologist, uninvited and illegal, digging through the foundations of an old building, through Victorian layers and then medieval layers and finally unearthing, way below, the broken mosaic of a Roman villa.

She was in an area called Pimlico. *Passport to Pimlico* was one of the old films Buffy loved; he had appeared in it, he said, as a talented juvenile. He had told her a rude story about one of the actors but she was in no mood to remember it now. She turned left and walked down Pimlico Road. There it stood on the corner: The Old Brown Mare.

She crossed the street and approached the pub. The sun glinted on its windows. Drawing nearer, she paused. It didn't look like a pub anymore, not quite. It looked too airy and clean. There was fancy script above the window: *Wine and Tapas Bar*. She pressed her nose against the glass; inside, the place was empty. Just a lot of chairs and tables, with pink tablecloths on them.

She hesitated. Then she pushed open the door and went in. Behind the bar, the mirrors were still there; the mirrors which had reflected multiple images of Buffy's ex-wife. She smelt garlic. A woman appeared, carrying dishes of food. She was so tanned and stylish that Celeste felt drained. She put a plate of squid on the counter.

'Yes, what is it? We're not open yet.'

Celeste said: 'I'm looking for someone who used to run this place. When it was a pub.'

'Dominic!' she yelled.

A man appeared from the kitchen. He, too, was extremely good-looking. 'Where's the effing enchilladas?'

'Talk to this woman would you,' she said, wiping her hands on her apron.

Celeste explained again, adding: 'It was years ago. She was called Popsi Concorde.'

'*What?*'

Celeste blushed. 'She was, really.'

He gazed at her. She felt embarrassed on Buffy's behalf, that he had married somebody with such a silly name.

'We negotiated with the brewery,' he said. 'I've no idea who the landlord was. Never met him.'

They turned away. They were like two racehorses, tossing

their heads and walking off while she stood there rattling her bucket.

Her knees felt weak. She stood outside; ridiculously, her eyes filled with tears. Nobody would talk to you like that in Melton Mowbray. If only Buffy were here; he would have bellowed at them. He would have thumped the counter, making the pimentos jump. She needed him so much that her chest hurt. She thought: I have no one else in the world.

Just then she looked at the row of shops opposite. One of them was a hairdressers.

A peroxide blonde. A peroxide blonde went to the hairdressers, didn't she? She needed frequent touchings-up. A peroxide blonde went to the hairdressers *a lot.*

Celeste crossed the street. Of course Popsi could have used one of the many preparations she herself sold over the counter. But no harm in giving it a try. She stopped outside the shop. In the window, the colour photos of models had faded. The place looked as if it had been there for years; that was a promising sign. It said *Unisex* but she couldn't see any men inside; just an old dear being combed out. A plump woman, well into her fifties, was standing on a chair pinning up a string of gold letters: MERRY CHRISTMAS TO ALL OUR CUSTOMERS. When Celeste came in she stepped down and approached her, smiling.

She looked so friendly – such a change from the people across the road – that Celeste said. 'Hello. I'd like some highlights. Do you think they'd look nice?'

How soothing it was! Long ago her mother used to wash her hair, cradling her head in the bath, massaging in the shampoo and gently lowering her into the sudsy water. Then the rubber hose, the spray sluicing her head. The shell tiles, glimpsed through stinging eyes.

The hairdresser was called Rhoda. All through the highlights operation, which had taken ages, she had chatted to Celeste and the other stylist about how she was going to decorate her new flat in Lechworth. With each new customer, she started all over again. The lease had expired on this place and The Body Shop was moving in. 'It's the end of an era,' she said. 'My regulars are gobsmacked. What do they want with Peppermint Foot Lotion?' Celeste sat while she blow-dried her hair. 'I'm giving you the tousled look,' she said, 'it's all the thing.'

Once, Celeste had seen a TV programme of a butterfly emerging from a pupa. It had pushed out slowly, straining and splitting the sides of its strong brown envelope. She too was making an effortful transformation. Once, she had just washed her face with soap and water and put on a track suit. Now she was learning how to apply make-up; how to buy grown-up women's clothes. She gazed back at the streaky, tangled mop on top of her head. *Your own mother wouldn't recognize you.* Was she more herself, or less?

Puff-puff went the spray. She looked at Rhoda in the mirror. 'Remember when the pub opposite was a pub?' she asked. 'Do you remember the woman who worked there? Years ago, it might have been. Do you remember her?'

Rhoda nodded. 'Course. Eileen Fisher. Oh, we had some laughs!'

'Eileen Fisher?'

'She was a lovely person. Big-hearted. A warm, lovely person, wasn't she, Deirdre?'

'With that little ratty husband,' said Deirdre. The place was empty now; she was fixing a paperchain onto the wall with a drawing pin. 'They put him inside, didn't they? Always thought he was dodgy.'

'It can't be the woman I mean,' said Celeste. 'Mine's called Popsi Concorde.'

'Oh, that was her stage name. She'd been in the theatre, see. Before she took up with what'shisname.'

'Terry,' said Deirdre. 'But give him his due, Rhoda, he was always nice to her little boy.'

'Little boy?' asked Celeste. The hairspray smelt so strongly of almonds and disinfectant that she almost swooned.

'Funny little thing, wasn't he,' said Deirdre. Her arms were full of tinsel. She gazed down at it. 'Never more, tinsel, will you embellish our walls. I think I'm going to blub.'

'Quentin,' said Rhoda. 'That was his name. She'd be sitting here, in this very chair, and he'd put on her shoes. High heels, she always dressed nicely. He'd put on his mummy's shoes and stagger about. He did make us laugh.'

'Not forgetting the ostrich boa,' said Deirdre. 'He's probably a transvestite now.' She giggled. 'Or worse.'

They laughed, then suddenly stopped. 'Lord, I'm going to miss them all,' sighed Rhoda. 'Every one of them, even the ratbags.'

'Where did she go?' asked Celeste.

Rhoda inspected her in the mirror. 'There you are. A small triumph, though I say it myself.'

'What happened to Popsi? Where is she?'

'This was years ago.'

'I know exactly where they went,' said Deirdre. 'When her old man was put away she got a job at that antique shop down the Fulham Road. She came back once, for her roots.'

'What antique shop?' asked Celeste.

'She said we mustn't lose touch. But you do, don't you?'

Celeste was standing at the till now, paying with her Barclaycard. 'Can you remember?'

Deirdre shook her head. 'But I go past it on the bus. It's next to that pizza place.'

Celeste signed the receipt. Her writing slanted; she couldn't control the biro properly. Her very name looked unfamiliar, as if it belonged to somebody else. She would have to get used to the hair too. 'Can you remember which one? You see, there were all these pasta places in Soho and I never found the right one.'

'Pardon?'

Celeste paused. It must be the hairspray. She really felt quite strange.

'I know,' said Deirdre. 'Pizza Hut.'

It was half-past three. Celeste ate a whole pepperoni pizza, deep-dish, she was that ravenous. Her hunger seemed to exist independently; it functioned, like a hospital generator, when everything else had broken down. The place was empty; outside the street lights were being switched on. She had already looked in the window of the antique shop next door, of course. There was no blonde woman sitting there; that would have been too much to hope for. Just a grey-haired old man and a lot of furniture.

She ate the crust; she always left the crust till last. Buffy had been married three times; each discovery made her feel she knew him less. Had he been a different man with each of them, somebody she wouldn't find familiar? Not just with the wives, with the other women too. He must have been really successful once, to have bought such an enormous house in Primrose Hill. How had he behaved in it, with Jacquetta? She herself had changed so much over the past few weeks, just by moving to London. The city had an unsettling effect on her. It was like living in a huge department store, not full of clothes but full of people. Maybe that was why its inhabitants married so many times. They couldn't resist going into the changing rooms to try on another person, and seeing how they fitted.

She paid up and went outside. The sun had long since gone; a light drizzle was falling. She stood outside the antiques shop. The man was on the phone. Some plates were displayed in the window. They didn't look any different from the plates back home. She thought of the ornaments on the mantelpiece, back in Willow Drive. One was a donkey with baskets on its sides; how she had loved it when she was little! Maybe it wasn't valuable, but it was valuable to her and that was the main thing. She had put away all the breakables, of course; packed them into boxes in the spare-room cupboard.

She peered through the glass. There was a big gloomy wardrobe at the back of the shop. Probably worth lots of money, but that didn't make it any prettier. Who had died, that their furniture had ended up here? The thought of people's pasts made her feel exhausted; she had had so much of that lately. Lumberyards of the past; children picking through the items, dressed in black like undertakers. Who was this Quentin? Was he another one of Buffy's children?

I'm not dressed in black, thought Celeste. I'm wearing a posh coat and I've just been to the hairdressers. Summoning up confidence, she pushed open the door. A bell tinkled and the man looked up.

She hesitated. She had seldom been inside an antiques shop, it wasn't her sort of place. But then Soho hadn't been, either, or Primrose Hill. The place smelt of polish. The man finished his phonecall. He was talking in German; she heard *deutschmarks*.

'Well, young lady, what can I do for you?'

He spoke as kindly as an uncle; she decided to brazen it out. She couldn't possibly pretend she had come in to buy something. 'I'm looking for a woman who used to work here. She's called Eileen Fisher. She had blonde hair.'

'Have a pastille,' he said, offering her the tin. 'There was an Eileen, but her hair was most definitely red.'

She put a pastille into her mouth. 'Are you sure?'

'Ah, Rodney. You can verify this.'

A young man had come in from the back room. He was tall and waxy-looking, with moles on his face. 'Seen the shipping forms?' he asked.

'My son, Rodney,' said the older man. 'Eileen Wingate, you remember. My eyes weren't deceiving me when I say she had red hair?'

'Wingate?' asked Celeste. Wasn't she called Eileen Fisher? 'Eileen Wingate? That was her name?'

'Dyed, Pops.'

Celeste stared. 'She's died?'

Rodney smiled. 'Not her. Just the barnet. *Sans doute* a bottle job. Definitely. Why're you looking for her?'

'It's a bit complicated.' A clock chimed; they waited until it had finished. 'Why was she called Wingate?'

'Must've been married to somebody called Mr Wingate. In truth, forsooth, I don't know. She nattered on but one didn't always take in every single word. Never get any work done.'

'What happened to her? Where did she go?'

Another clock chimed; a lower dong . . . dong . . . dong . . . dong. The father and son shook their heads. 'Moved out of London,' said the son, finally. 'She stayed in the business, I think, but not our line of the business. Where was it, Pops?'

'South coast?' he asked. 'That ring a bell?'

'I don't know!' Celeste sat down, heavily, on a spindly chair. 'When did she go?'

'Six, seven years. Haven't had a dickybird. Just a card at Christmas.'

'A card?' asked Celeste. 'A Christmas card?'

'Her son does them. Quentin. Frightfully artistic. Wood-cuts and whatnot.'

'Have you got one yet?' asked Celeste. 'This year?'

The two men looked at her. Maybe she was behaving oddly, but she was past caring.

'Only got a few, so far,' said Rodney.

He took her into an office at the back of the shop. On the desk, a fax machine beeped; it hummed, and paper slid out like a tongue. Rodney was sifting through a small pile of Christmas cards.

'It might have her address on it,' said Celeste. 'On the envelope – you know, one of those little stickers. It might have her address inside.'

He put down the pile. 'Not here yet. Maybe we'll get it at home.'

'Can I give you my phone number?' she asked. 'Will you phone me?'

She stood outside her flat, fumbling with the doorkeys. In one hand she carried a bag of cabbage leaves and carrots for the rabbits. After the beeswaxed order of the antiques shop the place next door looked chaotic – racks of coats, old saucepans, the female mannequin leaning against the wall as if she were drunk. MIND CHARITY SHOP, it said.

She felt deeply disorientated. How many names did this Popsi woman have? How many times had *she* been married? Upstairs, Celeste passed the mirror. A woman, topped with tousled hair, stared back. Who on earth was that?

She took the bag of food into the living room. She hadn't bought a hutch; she hadn't had time. Either she was working all day or else off on one of her voyages into the interior. The rabbits hopped up to her; they were becoming quite tame. She put the cabbage leaves on a plate and laid it on the carpet. Squatting there, she was suddenly aware of movement in the corner of the room. Just a tiny movement; something stirring.

It couldn't be a rabbit. All three were here, dragging the cabbage leaves onto the carpet and nibbling them. She climbed to her feet and walked across the room.

On the floor, jammed between the radiator and a box of recycled stuff she hadn't unpacked yet, was the bundle of cut-up tights. Half-hidden in it, she saw a squirming tangle of bald, pinkish-grey creatures. She gasped; just for a moment she thought they were maggots, but of course they were far too big.

One of the rabbits had given birth.

Twenty-four

It wasn't Lorna's wood, of course. It belonged to a local farmer called Vic Wheeler. He owned a lot of land, the whole secret valley and beyond, and was possessed of such entrepreneurial zeal that he was known in the village as Wheeler-Dealer Victor. Already, over at Barstone, a 2000-bed international hotel was being constructed, plus industrial units and an Asda superstore. One of his woods had already been bulldozed to create a roundabout and another had been sold to a Japanese firm which specialised in male bonding. Each weekend executives arrived from London, wearing flak jackets, and rampaged through the trees shooting each other with red dye and learning how to relate. That Vic Wheeler's son had married the daughter of the Chief Planning Officer had done no harm at all, squire.

It was mid-December. By now Lorna knew the full extent of the plans. Vic Wheeler had set up a consortium to build a Leisure Experience. It was to stretch over 300 acres. A theme park was planned, though the theme itself had not been decided yet. There was to be a bowling alley, skating rink, three fast-food outlets and, where her wood now stood, an eight-screen multiplex cinema. The pace was quickening. In the Happy Eater besuited men spread maps across the table and cockily bandied numbers to and fro; outside, their Ford Granadas were spattered with mud from their forays through the fields.

Lorna was a solitary person, an independent spirit. Various protest groups had been formed but she had devised her own plan. She had got the idea from a short story. She had read it, years before, in an old copy of the *Times* which she been using to wrap up chicken bones. In the story a woman, to save a local wood, had planted it with rare plants and filled its pond with an endangered species of newt. The wood had been declared a Site of Special Scientific Interest and nobody had built anything at all.

The plans were going to be put before the council in the spring. By that time the wood had to be planted up. Lorna felt surprisingly energised. It was like petty squabbles and complaints – who's going to do the washing-up, say – vanishing the moment war is declared. Looking back, her whole life seemed to have consisted of botched relationships and missed opportunities – men, her acting career, the other thing she didn't want to think about. So much had slipped through her fingers for reasons that now seemed laughable, if they were not so sad. Now she could actually do something, something positive and complete.

It was a misty Sunday afternoon. She sat on her veranda, sorting through the catalogues that had arrived during the week. There was one from a wild plant nursery in Herefordshire; another from a specialist orchid-grower. With mild interest, she looked at her legs. She was wearing men's corduroy trousers; she had found them years before in the potting shed. They were tucked into mismatched woolly socks, one red and one striped, with another pair of socks on top. They didn't match either. She supposed she must look odd, but then oddness only exists in the presence of other people. The same applied to her age and her sex; she was both ageless and sexless, there was nobody to mirror her back to herself. She didn't know if she were amusing or not because there was nobody around to laugh. She simply existed. After all, human behaviour is only born in company; how does one know a burp is rude if there is nobody there to flinch? She had lived alone for a long time now. Stepping into the Happy Eater was like stepping into the world, like suddenly appearing on stage, but nobody really knew her there, customers passed through, staff came and went. It seemed like a dream and this was the real thing: the hazy sky, the tracery of trees, her cat rubbing its head against her trousered leg.

Some of the plants had already arrived and lay in a row, waiting to be planted, misting up their polythene bags as if they were breathing in there. They were her allies, her limp, green troops. She had bought some more plants at garden centres, and had even found a rare species of poppy at a Texaco station. Suddenly she thought of Buffy. He would say: *Funny, isn't it? Garden centres are full of furniture and garages are full of plants. And tandoori chicken sandwiches. And bags of potatoes. Amazing one can get any petrol in them at all.* She hadn't thought about him for ages. His voice spoke to her sometimes; other people's voices too. They were all there, even if she didn't hear them, like a radio that happened to be switched off.

She shook her head, to clear it. She put on her overcoat, tying it around her waist with string, and fetched her spade. She must get going; weeks of planting lay ahead of her. The sun was sinking; soon it would be dark. She worked in the dark, when nobody could see her.

There had been no frost for days; the ground was soft and ready for her. Beyond the garden lay the wood; thin and airy except for its fir trees and the clotted, dark ivy thickening the trunks. She only noticed the ivy in the winter; it was revealed, now, like a silent person at a party one only notices when the other guests have gone.

Twenty-five

They were one big, happy family. That's what they said, Popsi and the traders in the antiques arcade. Always a laugh somewhere; always a drama. They helped each other out; they minded each other's stalls when one of them went to spend a penny. Nobody went upstairs to get a bacon butty without asking if their neighbour fancied one too. They knew each others' life stories and what stories they had! Even Popsi's ups and downs – and she had had a few – even her ups and downs were par for the course here. Put it on the TV, they were always saying, and who would believe it? Take Margot, who had the china stall opposite; who would believe, looking at her now, that she had once been principal trapeze artiste with Gerry Cottle's Circus? Not only that, but she had won a battle against ovarian cancer and spent three years living in a caravan with a manic depressive? That was a long time ago, of course, before she had put on the weight. She had seven grandchildren now, but she didn't look a day over forty-five.

That's what they said about Popsi, too. People took them for sisters, in their matching sheepskin coats. She and Margot had both done their hair the same colour too – Plum Crazy. Popsi had always believed in ringing the changes, hairwise. They both believed in making the best of themselves, in keeping time's wingèd chariot at bay. Live life to the hilt, that was their motto. Popsi fondly watched her, across the aisle, talking to a customer. 'It's a very rare piece,' Margot was saying, 'it's very unusual, of course, for it not to have a handle.'

Popsi loved it here. Their little band – it was like being in rep. Better really, because nobody went away. Every Thursday to Saturday here they were sitting in their stalls, blowing on their hands, their little heaters glowing. Every week she looked forward to it. The rest of the time she would be away on buying trips – antiques fairs in conference hotels, places like that. Sometimes a call came and she had to drop everything. They were only walk-on parts, of course, but it was good to keep your hand in. Unlike her, producers were getting younger and it was sensible to keep in the swim. Only the week before she had been a *'harassed shopper'* in *Inspector Morse.*

But at the end of the week, when she drove along the promenade and unloaded her car, when she came into this chilly hall with *hellos* all round and its low beams saying DUCK OR GROUSE, each week she felt she was coming home. She felt herself here. That was why she had called herself Popsi again. Women's Lib, she had always been for it though she hadn't known at the time. Get out of life what you put into it, that was another of her mottoes, and have a laugh on the way. She had always felt like a Popsi, that was why she had given herself the name in the first place. She had only changed her name to please her husbands and now she didn't have one anymore she was staying Popsi Concorde until she dropped off her perch.

It was even jollier now, with Christmas coming. Trade had picked up; it was really quite brisk, with people coming to find that special present, that personal something that showed you cared much more than a gift pack from Boots. *You're buying a little bit of history*, that was what she told people, *a little bit of someone's life. Recycling's all the rage, isn't it?* When she thought of all the things she had thrown out, all those times she had moved, she wanted to weep.

Down the aisle Walter, who sold military paraphernalia, was playing *I'm Dreaming of a White Christmas* on his wind-up gramophone. He lived with his mother in a bungalow up on the Downs. He had taken Popsi to a traction engine rally once but he really wasn't her type. When he had tried some hanky-panky on the way home, in the back of his vintage bus, she had patted him on the head and told him to find a nice girl more his age.

Customers tried to pick her up too – men had always tried it on with her, God knows why. Only the week before, one joker had lifted the receiver off one of her phones and pretended he was ringing her: 'How about coming out for a swift half, you voluptuous pussycat?' She would have, once – give her a drink and she was anybody's – but now all she wanted to do was put her feet up in front of the TV. Her joints were playing up. They ached more this time of year, with the fog rolling in off the Channel. In fact, they ached more *each* year. Sooner or later it would be hip replacement time; everybody here swore by them.

Margot was doing very well. 'It's only a hairline crack,' she was telling a customer as she wrapped up a sugar bowl, 'put on a spot of Araldite when you get home.' She had run out of carrier bags and Popsi had given her a few from her stock of Sainsbury's ones. It was quieter in her stall. She sold period phones and radios. Her line wasn't so seasonal; she catered more for the bona fide collectors and they didn't believe in Christmas. In between customers she and Margot nattered all day, only pausing briefly to make a sale and then carrying on where they had left off. They didn't stop for browsers, of course; china-teases, Margot called them. From long experience they could both spot one of those and Margot could deal with them as she went along. ' . . . so then he really started getting violent – *yes it is pretty isn't it* – he got me down on the settee, the kiddies yelling their little heads off, I thought he was going to *kill* me – *no dear, I'll be making a loss on it as it is* . . . when they got me to Casualty they'd never seen such bruises . . .'

A lot of the people here were browsers, actually. On holiday, maybe, and just getting out of the rain. Because it was a seaside town they got a lot of retired folk, too, who didn't like the new shopping centre because it was full of lager louts. They fetched up here, sucking in their teeth when they saw the prices on the old biscuit tins and spinning out the morning over a cup of tea in the café. Just occasionally real dealers visited: Germans and Swiss, in fur-collared coats, with Mercedes estate cars parked outside. They knew exactly what they wanted. When they walked down the aisles everybody else looked amateurish and dowdy; a hush fell, as it does in a hospital ward when the consultants sweep in.

She was expecting one now, actually: a Mr Fleischmann, but he hadn't turned up yet. She had met him in an antiques fair in Birmingham and she had found him the items he wanted. Dealing with him made her feel suave and international, part of a network. Most of her customers were ordinary nostalgia-buffs who just liked bakelite – young blokes with gelled hair, probably designers, or else anonymous, solitary collectors who wore anoraks and looked like train spotters. She imagined them alone at night, sitting next to their collection of valve radios. It made her feel motherly.

She would kill for a coffee but Margot was busy and Duncan, the clock specialist in the next booth, was talking to a testy-looking customer. 'Well, it was working this morning,' said Duncan.

Just then Elsa appeared. She ran a period clothing stall and believed in an Afterlife. She was always trying to tell Popsi hers but Popsi said no thanks, this one kept her busy enough.

'I saw this piece of watered silk and I thought *Quentin*,' said Elsa.

'You are a dear.'

'Well, it's Christmas, isn't it?'

See? That was what they were like. Elsa left and Popsi put the piece of material into a carrier bag. Margot, who was wrapping up a teapot, was telling a customer about one of her grandchildren. Sometimes it irked Popsi, that Margot treated complete strangers to the intimate details of her family life, grabbing them with the same breathless confidentiality with which she grabbed Popsi. Did five years of friendship count for nothing? Or maybe Popsi was just irked by the knowledge that, things being what they were, it was unlikely she herself would ever be a grandmother at all. Quentin was you-know-what (she said the word quite openly to other people, she was quite broadminded, but it still pained her to say it to herself) and her daughter Maxine, a big girl, had gone to veterinary college and showed far more interest in horses.

How did Quentin get that way? It certainly wasn't inherited. She herself had always been healthily heterosexual and though Buffy said he had been something of a tart at boarding school – according to him he had been angelically beautiful and passed around the sixth form like a plaything – when he left he had soon reverted to a lifelong interest in the opposite sex. She blamed the whole thing on the carrier bag episode; that had been the turning point.

Even now she blushed to think of it. Remembering moments like this warmed her up better than any electric blower. She had been living with Terry, above the pub. However, she had also been having a little hows-your-father with a lovely man who lived in Chelsea. He like to see her dressed up. So two afternoons a week she crept off to his flat, with her carrier bag. Quentin was at school then. Trouble was, one day she had picked up the wrong carrier bag. Arriving in the gentleman's bedroom, she had unpacked it: out came some muddy shorts, a packed lunch and a stout pair of football boots.

Margot had hooted with laughter at this but it really wasn't funny. 'What about little Quentin?' said Popsi. 'There he is, in the changing room, opening his carrier bag and taking out my suspender belt and my satin corset.' 'Don't forget the split-crotch panties!' shrieked Margot, who liked to hear this story again and again, 'and the whip! Don't forget the whip!' Quentin had always been a sensitive boy; sometimes she felt this had sent him right off the tracks.

She had come to terms with it now, of course. In fact she

had become very fond of some of his menfriends and one or two of them still came down to visit her long after they had split up with him. She was devoted to Talbot, who currently lived with him. Maybe she was a sort of Judy Garland, a fag-hag. From long heart-to-hearts with them she discovered the problem usually stemmed from the father anyway, so she could always blame it on Buffy. He had been a hopeless example to a son.

Margot was still busy. A customer was holding a cruet. 'Think it over dear,' said Margot 'but it probably won't be here next week. They go very fast, particularly if they're missing the pepper pot. That makes them a collector's item.'

Irritated, Popsi called 'Margot!' and tapped her tooth. It had an immediate effect: Margot stopped talking and whipped out her mirror. The two of them had an agreement: Margot rationed Popsi's cigarettes and Popsi told Margot when she had lipstick on her tooth. Margot's front teeth stuck out, that was why, and she always put on too much lipstick in the first place.

When she turned back, Popsi noticed a young woman standing near her stall. She wore a reddish coat and a black scarf. Her hair was streaky. Maybe I should try streaks, thought Popsi. She had dyed her hair for so long she could no longer remember what colour it was. Then she realized: of course, it would be grey. This gave her such a jolt that she came to a standstill.

The young woman stepped closer, picked up the receiver of one of the phones, looked at it, and put it down again.

'Nice, isn't it?' said Popsi. 'That's a Pyramid, Second Series. I've got one in red, too.'

She didn't look like a browser. Nor did she look like a customer. She looked fidgety; Popsi's children used to look like that, fiddling around with things, when they wanted to ask her for some money.

'This one's nice,' said the young woman. 'I've seen them in old films.'

'That's a Candlestick, pet. An early one, probably 1920. Interested in period phones?'

She pointed. 'We used to have one like that at home.'

'Yes, my love, they're the most usual. Cheeseboards. Made right through the forties. You wouldn't remember those days of course, fresh young thing like you.'

'Do the radios work?'

'Do the radios work, she asks! Or course they work. Need to warm up, but then don't we all? Lovely tone; warm and brown.'

'I used to listen to the radio.' She touched the walnut veneer of a Ferguson; her finger made a mark in the dust. 'I used to think there were real people in there.'

'Well they are, aren't they? In a manner of speaking.' She laughed. 'Only too real, some of them.'

'What do you mean?'

'You really want to know?'

The girl nodded.

Popsi looked at her. 'How long have you got?'

'I was playing Doll Tearsheet. First day of rehearsals the director, what was his name? Lovely man. He came up to me and said, *Darling, this is Russ Buffery, our Hal.* And there was this fellow, black polo neck, very racy in those days, very debonair, and he took my hand and kissed it. Something clicked. My knees turned to jelly. I thought: *can't wait to see you in tights!* It was danger ahead, I knew that. Spontaneous combustion. Ever felt it?'

Celeste didn't reply. They were sitting in the little booth; smoke wreathed up from their plastic coffee cups. Popsi took out a packet of Silk Cut. The women in the stall opposite called, 'Popsi!'

'Just telling her about my first.'

'That's your fourth,' called the woman.

'*Husband*, I mean,' said Popsi. She lit the cigarette, holding it in her mittened hand, and turned to Celeste. 'Have to smoke when I talk about Buffy. I called him Buffy, there and then, and it stuck. Oh, he was charming, the rogue! We were both so young, of course, your sort of age, pet. We had our lives ahead of us, or so we thought.' She inhaled, and blew out smoke. 'You don't want to hear all this.'

'I do!'

The other woman shouted across. 'She doesn't, lovey. She's just being polite.'

'I'm not,' said Celeste. 'Honestly.'

'Don't tell her the rude bits!' called the other woman. 'Not till I can listen! I've heard it all before but I still like it.' She turned to her customer. 'Sweet, isn't it? Very unusual pattern.'

'Well, we fell for each other,' said Popsi. 'We fell in love. I've never been happy like that before or since. We toured all over Britain, he got lovely notices, he was a lovely Prince Hal, and, oh, he made me laugh! I adored him. So did everybody – the cast, the landladies, he could wrap them round his little finger. See, like the Bard said, he was not just witty in himself, he was the cause of wit in others. Oh, we heard the chimes at midnight all right.' She stopped for a moment, coughing her gravelly smoker's cough. 'Course later, when he put on weight, he could've played Falstaff himself. But then . . . I thought this is my man, for life . . .'

Celeste was sitting on a camp stool. The aisles were full of people; sometimes somebody bumped against her but none of them stopped at the telephones. Over the other side of the hall somebody was playing *I'm Dreaming of a White Christmas*. She seemed to have heard it before; or was it just this story that seemed so familiar?

'So we're married now, two rooms in Bloomsbury, it was a palace compared to where I'd grown up. And then our little boy was born and, well, it all started going to pieces. You know what it's like.'

'No I don't.' She gazed at Popsi's rouged face. As she travelled back in time she was discovering progressively older ex-wives. Popsi, however, though the oldest, was holding out gamely against the ravages of the years. She wore a thick layer of orangy make-up and her hair was dyed an interesting colour Celeste had never seen before – if forced to pin it down, she would say mulberry. Her face was still very attractive.

'Maybe it wasn't the kid,' she said, 'maybe it happens. You think it's the end of the world at the time. Anyway, Buffy and me, we started making other friends.'

'Hadn't you got any already?'

'I mean, special friends.'

Celeste paused. 'Oh.'

'We did misbehave, I admit it. Lord, the boozing and the screaming matches, and one of us slamming out, and me picking him up next morning from Bow Street station, drunk and disorderly. Then one of us moving out and going to live with someone else, then coming back and having another bash. It was the sixties, see. Everything was hanging out, hanging loose, whatever, everything was up for grabs. Didn't know what we were doing, half the time.'

'Why not?'

'You wouldn't understand, my love. You were just a twinkle in your mother's eye.'

The woman opposite stepped across. 'Got any more carriers, ducky?'

Popsi rummaged under her chair. 'What's your name again, pet?'

'Celeste.'

She said to the other woman: 'Just telling Celeste about what we got up to in the Swinging Sixties.'

'Don't listen. X certificate!' The woman clapped her hands over Celeste's ears. Celeste wobbled, on her camp stool. When the hands were removed *I'm Dreaming of a White Christmas* was playing again.

The other woman went back to her customers. Celeste looked at Popsi's face, her rouged cheeks and bright blue eyeshadow. The whole thing felt unreal. Outside it had grown dark; in the roof, the skylights were black. The little booths, cluttered with their props, looked like stage sets. She felt she was a child watching an incomprehensible pageant of ex-wives, a costume drama in three acts. They had been paraded before her: Penny, Jacquetta, and Popsi – the Career Woman, the Neurotic, the Good-Time Girl. So quietly did she sit, an audience of one, that nobody noticed her. What were those lines from school? *They strut and fret upon the stage.*

Popsi was massaging her legs. 'It's the circulation that goes,' she said. 'Still, cold hands warm heart.' She wore a sheepskin coat and fur-lined boots; still she shivered. 'Funny to think of it, how it just goes. Just like that. We met off and on, of course, for Quentin's sake. No hard feelings really, there was fault on both sides, I'd be the first to admit that. But all you have left is a few memories, and the kids.'

'Kids? Was there more than one?'

'Nyange was born by then, by the time we split up.'

'*Nyange?*'

'Buffy's little girl. Weird name, isn't it? He'd had a short sojourn with somebody called Carmella. Way out of his league, I told him so at the time.'

Celeste paused. She fiddled with the dial on a radio, turning it to and fro. Nothing happened, of course. 'What happened to her? Nye . . .?'

'Nyange. I see her sometimes. On packets of shampoo and things.'

'What do you mean?'

'She's a model. She was, anyway. Ever so gorgeous. But then they often are, aren't they?'

Behind Celeste, a man cleared his throat. 'Those work?' he asked, pointing to the shelves full of phones.

'Of course,' said Popsi, 'just plug them in.'

'Oh,' he said, and went away.

Celeste asked: 'What do you mean, they often are?'

'Half-coloured people. See, they get the best of both worlds.'

'Her mother was – '

'Black, dear. She was a dancer, legs up to her neck. Way out of his league, like I said.' She sighed. 'Wonder what happened to her. She was in the chorus of *Hair*. What happened to them all. Mine, his, everybody's. You can't help wondering, can you?'

'What happened to you?'

Popsi laughed; it sounded like pebbles being shaken in a jar. 'You got all week?'

Celeste looked at her watch. 'Got to get back to London, actually.' She looked up. 'You had any more children?'

'Depends what you mean, *had*.'

There was a silence. Down the aisle some thin, reedy voices were singing *Good King Wenceslas*. She heard the rattle of a tin.

'I don't see,' she said, 'I don't understand!'

'I've got Maxine, of course. I had her with Terry, that's my second husband. And there's Quentin. But my little boy.' Quite suddenly, her eyes filled with tears. 'My little boy, he'd be a grown man by now.'

The tears spilled down her cheeks; they literally spilled, as if someone were tipping a cup. Behind them the voices grew louder; the tin rattled. They were singing *Oh, Come all ye Faithful* now. Celeste didn't turn. For an alarming moment she thought Buffy's two sons might be standing there, dressed in black and glaring at her. All his children, rattling tins and demanding God-knows-what.

'He'd be forty this year,' said Popsi. Her mascara was sliding down her cheeks. 'When I see a middle-aged bloke in the street, I think *that could've been him*.'

'You mean you don't know where he is?' Celeste had to raise her voice above the noise.

Popsi shook her head. 'I had a you-know-what when I was sixteen.' She rubbed her eyes; the mascara smudged. 'He's still there, in my heart. And all my little unborn grandchildren. Sorry, love. When I think about him I just start to blub. I remember, once, in John Lewis's . . .'

A tin was thrust in front of Celeste's face. A small girl looked at her coldly. 'It's for battery chickens,' she said.

Celeste searched in her bag. Popsi seemed in a dream. She

looked at the little girl. 'Aren't you a poppet,' she said, vaguely.

Celeste gave some money to the little girl, who went away. Popsi woke, and fumbled for her purse. 'Wait!' she called. She heaved herself to her feet and went off down the aisle, after the carol-singer. The singing grew fainter.

Just then the phone rang. Celeste stared at the shelves of telephones. There were at least thirty of them – cream ones, black ones, the things called candlesticks, with a separate mouthpiece on a string, like the ones you saw in Westerns. The ringing continued. She stared, panic-struck. Which phone was ringing? She lifted up the nearest one – a brown thing, covered in dust – but it was dead.

Popsi hurried back to the stall and rescued her. She grabbed a modern phone, hidden amongst the others, and spoke into the receiver.

'Ah! *Guten morgen* or whatever.' She blew her nose. 'Pardon, *guten tag*.' She listened. 'London? You can't come down here?' She paused, thinking. Her tears had dried now, though her face was still a mess. 'Wait. *Uno momento*.' Putting her hand over the receiver, she turned to Celeste. 'You going back to London? Can you do me a favour?'

'What is it?'

'It's this dealer, see, and he's flying to Hamburg tomorrow. There's a couple of phones for him here. Could you take them to London and he can pick them up from your place?'

'But you don't know me.'

'Oh, I'm a trusting soul,' she said. 'Always have been. That's the trouble really.'

Twenty-six

Celeste sat in her room, waiting for the phone to ring. The German man, she had forgotten his name, was supposed to be phoning before ten; he was going to come round, give her a cheque and take delivery of his two Pyramid phones, one brown and one black.

At 10.15 the phone rang. It was Buffy.

'Light of my life,' he cried, 'my little plumcake. Oh, I've been missing you! Where've you been all day?'

'Just out.'

'What's happening? What have I done wrong? Can I come and see you?'

'Not really. I'm expecting a call.'

'Who from?'

'Just somebody. I'll be in the shop tomorrow.'

She put down the phone. Her hand was trembling. It was so painful, hearing his hurt voice, but she couldn't talk to him yet. Not yet.

Buffy put *Death and the Maiden* on the record player; the slow movement always made him cry. He gazed at his glass of wine. His latest method of cutting down drinking was to buy such disgusting stuff that even he couldn't finish the bottle.

Why was Celeste being so cold? Christmas was only ten days away and she still wouldn't say if they were going to spend it together or not. She had nobody to go back home to; nor did he. They were both orphans in this big, blustery world. They loved each other, didn't they? He constantly told her how much he adored her. She never actually said she loved him but she hugged him, she sat on his knee and picked little bits of fluff out of his beard; she laughed at his jokes and she showed an all-consuming interest in his previous marriages. For the time being, this was enough. That events had not yet taken a more carnal turn had something to recommend it – after all, look what had happened to Humbert Humbert. Just sitting next to her in a tea shop filled him with joy. If for once in his life he had an unconsummated love affair, surely that meant it need never end?

December was the cruellest month, with Christmas looming. It was a month of gathering pain. Soon the day of reckoning would arrive, the day when it became all too clear that nobody else wanted him anyway. The rest of the year he could fool himself, but not on December 25th. He was an outcast, shivering in the cold whilst all over Britain loving families sat beside the fire opening presents and playfully trouncing each other at board games.

That it had never really been quite like this, even when he had been secure in the bosom of his various families or allied arrangements, didn't tarnish the nostalgia with which he gazed back to the past. If he were honest, he could remember the most monumental rows. They were often sparked off by something small, but then the whole day was a tinder-box, wasn't it, ready to flare up at any minute. Only the previous Christmas, when he had actually been allowed to have his sons (and that only because Jacquetta and Leon had gone on a second honeymoon to Israel), only the previous year the meal had disintegrated when he had, whilst berating Tobias for his table manners, leaned across him to grab a roast potato. Not a venial sin, surely, but something must have been bottled up in Penny for her to yell at him about his appalling double standards, what a pathetic example he was, how belligerantly self-righteous and he could at least have used a spoon rather than his hand. This had led seamlessly into what was known as a lively discussion on his shortcomings as a parent, even his sons chiming in – which was an improvement, he supposed, on their usual mutinous silence.

His various Christmases had come in all permutations, most of them uncomfortable and some so disastrous that he would have preferred to have spent the day in a Salvation Army hostel. At times like that, how preferable was the charity of strangers to anything muddier! In fact, looking back, the more tenuous the link the more successful the day. This was no doubt because expectations weren't that high to begin with. After Jacquetta had left him, and he was at one of his lowest ebbs, he had actually spent a surprisingly happy Christmas with an old lesbian aunt of hers who he had always liked and who, oh, bliss, demanded nothing of him except an inexhaustible stamina for a card game called Spit.

Then there were the various bizarre times when he had, as it were, gone back a notch, shunting excruciatingly into his former life with a slight change of cast. This happened after a few years when the wounds had healed, or were supposed to have healed, and it was considered beneficial for the children to have some seasonal get-together. On one occasion Leon had flown to America to spend Christmas with his ex-wife, shunting back a notch himself, and Buffy had returned to his old home for a parody of Christmases past – a grand-guignol occasion which had effectively squelched any future shenanigans with the girlfriend he had brought along with him, he supposed as an act of bravado. Mercifully he could remember little of the day, except his drunken ransacking of the Christmas cards on the mantlepiece to see which of their mutual friends had sent a card to Jacquetta and whether they had included Leon in their message of goodwill.

Another occasion, almost more desolating, was long ago when Jacquetta had temporarily deserted him and he had looked up Carmella, the Caribbean dancer with whom he had had a brief affair. After all, she had borne him a daughter. Christmas with these two comely near-strangers, in a shawl-festooned room in Deptford, had been unbolstered even by alcohol for there was nothing in the place except apple juice. They were vegetarians, too, and though Carmella had cooked him a pheasant wing Nyange kept saying, 'poor little bird, just think it could be flying around the woods'; in the end he had had to barricade his plate from her offended eyes, propping up the book Carmella had given him as a Christmas present – a volume called *Women's Woes: A Look at Gender Tyranny*.

It was better, really, if these sorts of gatherings didn't take place on the day itself; it placed too much of a strain on everybody. Such was his network of ex-families that he had sometimes eaten several dinners on the evenings leading up to Christmas – two or three of them, like dress rehearsals for a performance from which he himself would be absent. Though reasonably festive, salmon would be served as a stand-in for turkey and fruit salad as a stand-in for the Christmas pudding; there was the unmistakable sense of everybody else eating lightly in preparation for the blow-out to come, the next day or the day after that. Unopened boxes of crackers would be waiting on the sideboard, tactlessly in full view. The children's hand-made table decorations would only partially be finished. As he opened his small – sometimes very small – gifts, he could see the larger, more lavish parcels stacked around the base of the Christmas tree, ready for the big day when he himself would be absent.

The problem with this, of course, was that Christmas Day itself would be left gapingly vacant, though India had once come round with a doggy bag, saying she would much rather have spent it with him. Besides, there were worse things than being alone. During his marriage to Penny he had been forced to spend the day with her parents in Ascot, an experience that had made the whole trauma of his divorce worthwhile.

Buffy lifted up the phone. It was eleven o'clock. He couldn't ring Celeste again. She had sounded so dismissive. Who was phoning her, that she expected their call so keenly? Her new hairstyle was a worrying sign. She looked fetching, but more tousled and beddable somehow. Almost randy, in fact. She had acquired a new mannerism to go with it – she shook her head, like a dog emerging from a pond, and then ruffled up her hair with her fingers. He didn't trust that.

George had farted. Buffy hurried to the window and struggled with the catch. The trouble with dogs was that, unlike humans, the process was totally silent. This meant one only became aware of it gradually and by then it was almost too late to take any action. He flung the window open and gazed across the Edgware Road at the block of flats opposite. In the windows, festive lights pinpricked the darkness. Where the rooms were lit he could see the shapes of the Christmas trees themselves, placed squarely in view to make him feel unloved. What was she doing? If he knew where she lived he could jump into a taxi and accost her, flinging himself at her feet. But what happened if he looked up, and there was a man standing beside her?

He hadn't rung. He wouldn't now, it was 11.30, far too late. He had obviously decided to forget about the whole thing and go back to Germany.

What did it all mean? What did anything mean? Celeste hadn't moved for some time. She was sitting on the carpet, freezing cold. Already, her afternoon seemed as lurid and unlikely as a dream. Had she really been in Hastings? She could have been to the moon. Events were so out of control that she felt paralyzed. Another batch of baby rabbits had been born. She had put cardboard boxes on either side of the room, like hi-fi speakers, and filled them with torn-up newspaper. Bits of paper had already spilled onto the carpet; within the boxes the bedding moved as the babies stirred. The first lot – six of them – were stronger now, lifting their blind blunt heads. Soon they would be shakily venturing forth.

Along the edges of the room were stacked the recycled items – a jumble of plastic containers, lampbases, hair curlers – like an insane obstacle course. The room was starting to smell. What was she doing with all these relics from Buffy's past? The rabbits, the colander, the two silent phones – what meaning was locked within them? Her life was slipping into confusion and squalor. Her heart beat fast and she could scarcely breathe; she felt as if she were underwater, trying to swim to the surface. The water pressed down on her, filling her lungs.

She struggled to her feet, put on her coat and left the flat. Music thumped from behind a closed door. Why, when the place was so obviously full of tenants, did she never see anybody? She hurried into the street. The cold air hit her. Suddenly she was wide-awake.

Twenty-seven

Buffy opened the door. He was wearing pyjamas and a very old dressing-gown.

'Celeste, my love!' He put his arms around her. It was midnight; he looked surprised but delighted. 'How wonderful to see you!'

She disentangled herself and inspected him. How seedy he looked! Grey and unshaven – even though he was bearded he managed to look unshaven.

'So this is where you live.' She looked around. 'Crikey.'

'I would've tidied it up if I'd known.' He hugged her again. 'My tonic, my life! My heart implant, you little ticker.'

'Don't be silly. Can I have a drink?'

'Don't try that wine, it's disgusting. Let's have a scotch.'

She negotiated her way into the room. It was a terrible mess; worse, even, than his sons'. There were things all over the floor. It looked as if he were camping here. Perhaps that was all he had ever done – just camped. She cleared away some newspapers and sat down in an armchair. Dirty grey dog hairs were matted into the fabric.

'There's a funny smell in here,' she said.

'I know. Don't know where it comes from. I need somebody to look after me.'

'Aren't you old enough to look after yourself?'

'Nobody's old enough to look after themselves.'

Women must have said that to him so many times. She thought of all the quarrels he must have had – everything she accused him of must be so familiar to him by now. How exhausting it must be! No wonder old people looked so old. It was all the repetition. She herself had had hardly anything duplicated yet – words of love or words of blame.

He gave her a glass of whisky. 'I want to sit close to you and lay my head on your knee, but my back hurts.' He sat down in the other chair; beneath him, the stuffing had disgorged onto the floor. He patted his knee. 'Come and sit on mine, you little sparrow.'

She didn't budge. She looked at him, across the littered hearthrug. 'Who did you love the most?' she asked.

'What?'

'Of all of them?'

He got up and came over. He pulled her to her feet. 'You silly.'

'Tell me about them.'

'They don't mean anything.'

'Well they should!' Her loud voice startled her. The dog pricked up its ears. 'You married them, didn't you?'

'Who have you been talking to? What have they been saying about me?' He put his hands over her ears, like the woman had done that afternoon. 'Don't listen to them,' his muffled voice said.

She removed his hands. Everyone seemed to be treating her like a baby. He gripped her; they collapsed into the armchair.

'Did you tell them all the same things?' she asked. 'Are you just a clever actor?'

'My dear girl, if I was a clever actor I'd be getting some work.'

They were wedged awkwardly in the chair; he was a big man. She spoke to an egg stain on his dressing gown. 'I don't know what to believe anymore.'

'Don't be jealous of anybody. Ever. *This* is important. *This*. *Us*.' He lifted her face and looked at her. 'Nothing else matters.'

'But don't you see? It should! I want them to matter. I want all of them to matter! Else, what's the point?'

She had never really needed a drink in her life, or known she had needed it, until tonight. Trouble was, she couldn't reach her glass. She was wedged in. Oh, the great breathing bulk of him, smelling of warmth and tobacco. When he talked she could feel the reverberations, like the tube running beneath her room.

He said: 'Everything matters, but nothing matters that much. You'll learn this, one day. It's not depressing, sweatheart, it's not depressing at all. But you might not understand yet. When I die, I want you to put it on my gravestone – *Everything matters, but nothing matters that much*. Will you promise?'

'That's not fair, talking about dying.'

'Looking at you makes me think about it. Since I met you I think about it all the time.'

She struggled out, from under him, and walked to the mantlepiece. She suddenly felt stagey, as if a director had told her to stand there.

'All right,' she said. 'Let's just talk about the *everything matters* bit. If that's the case, who were you with, say, in the summer of 1968?'

'Who? You mean, a woman?'

She stared at her reflection in the mottled mirror – her set jaw, the floppy mop of hair. She nodded.

'Well,' he said. 'I was sort of married to Popsi.'

'Sort of. What do you mean, *sort of*?'

'Sweetie-pie, you've never been married.'

'No.'

'Well, then.'

'So *sort of* means somebody else,' she said. 'Who was it?'

He sat there. His eyebrows went up and down, as he frowned. He was thinking.

'I know,' he said. 'I was married to Popsi, but I was vaguely with Lorna.'

She turned from the mirror and stared at him. 'What do you mean, *vaguely with Lorna*?' *Basically*, that was what Jacquetta had said: *Basically I've got three children*. What had Popsi said? *How many children? Depends what you mean.* 'Vaguely! Basically! What on earth do you all mean?'

He sat, slumped in his chair. 'You're young,' he said. 'Certainty is the luxury of the young. When you get older there's no such thing as a straight sentence. It's all qualifiers. Parentheses sprout out all over the place.' He pointed to his ears. 'Like hair, sprouting out of these.'

'I just want to know what vaguely means. Who was she?'

There was a pause as he lit a cigarette. 'She was a lovely girl. Very young, younger than you. Very ambitious.' For a moment, his face was obscured by smoke.

'Ambitious for what?'

'For the same thing I was. Fame, success, all that. She was going to be a great classical actress.'

'Was she? Is she?'

He shook his head. 'The world's full of people who're going to be great actors. Now they're, I don't know, running country hotels and writing cookery books and . . .'

'Selling antiques.'

'Selling antiques. And getting divorced and doing all the things everybody does.' He smiled at her. 'Trying to make beautiful young girls fall in love with them. Life's a very time-consuming business. You have to be super-humanly talented or ruthless to push through all that. If you're not superhumanly talented or ruthless, but only a bit, then everything else comes flooding in. All the parentheses. The *vaguelys* and *sort ofs*. If you see what I mean.'

There was a silence. She took a sip of whisky; it burned her throat. She looked across at him. He raised his eyebrows. His hair was greying, his beard even more so, but his eyebrows were still black. His thinking bits, moving up and down to the fluctuations within. Puppet eyebrows, worked from machinery that was dear to her. She loved him very much, but she didn't move towards him; she stayed at the mantelpiece. She hadn't finished with him yet.

'What was her whole name?'

He had to think for a moment. 'Lorna Kidderpore.'

'Lorna Kidderpore.'

'Her father was a distinguished something or other. Mathematician.'

'How long did you know her?'

'Just a month or two.'

'Did you love her?'

'Of course,' he said. 'I'm not a womanizer, darling, I'm a romantic. A romantic falls in love for life. Trouble is, they know no past and no future. They learn from nothing and anticipate nothing. That's what they share with the very stupid, who in many ways they resemble. A romantic actually believes in possibilities. That's why my life's been such a mess.'

'What happened?'

'She was offered a job. Touring Europe with some theatre company. She had to choose between the job and me and she chose the job.'

'What happened to her?'

'I don't know.'

'Did you ever see her again?'

'Once. I saw her once.' He flung his cigarette into the grate. It was full of old cigarette butts.

'When?'

'Five, six years ago. In Dover. Penny and I were taking my boys on holiday, to France. Not a great success. In fact, an unmitigated disaster. Penny got food poisoning and Bruno got into trouble with this gendarme, and then the car broke down –'

'Get back to Dover.'

He smiled. 'That's what I always imagined my children saying.'

'What children?'

'The ones I never met. The ones who listened to me on the radio. You should've seen all the letters I got, the cards coloured with crayons, hundreds of them! They loved me much more than my own kids did, but that's because they didn't know me.'

'We did! You made us feel we did. You told us stories. Our parents just told us to mind our table manners. Tell me the story. Tell me about Dover.'

The dog got to its feet, padded over to Buffy and sat down again, next to his bedroom slippers. 'Are you sitting comfortably?' said Buffy.

'Yes' said Celeste, though she was standing.

'Then we'll begin. It was a bright sunny morning and Buffy and his family were going on holiday. Gosh, what an adventure! They were off to meet the frogs. The two little animals in the back were fighting as usual. *"Stop it, you little scallywags!"* said Buffy, with a twinkle in his eye. Just then, as they were driving through Dover Town, lo and behold! Bless my cotton socks! There was his ex-mistress, coming out of a greengrocer's shop.'

'What happened?'

He took a sip of whisky. 'I shouted at Penny to stop and she did, but everybody hooted at us. And by the time she had found somewhere to park and I'd rushed out, well, Lorna had gone. Disappeared.'

Celeste yawned, though her heart was thumping. 'That was a lovely story,' she said. 'Now it's time for beddibyes.'

Buffy jumped to his feet. 'Yes, yes!' He put his arms around her. 'Oh, I've been longing for you to say that for the past six weeks. Ever since I saw you in your little overall.'

'Not here.'

'Look, I promise not to do anything. Scout's honour. I probably couldn't anyway. I peak at about ten and by five past it's all over.' He rubbed his beard against her cheek. 'We can just sleep together. I washed the sheets last week. Last month, anyway.'

'No, I must go.' She pulled away from him.

'But it's half past two!'

'I'll find a cab.'

'You can't go alone, it's not safe.'

She grabbed her coat and made for the door, tripping over

a carrier bag. It tipped over, clankingly, and empty bottles fell out.

'I want to talk to you about Christmas!' he cried.

She kissed him, and ran downstairs.

'What about Christmas?' His voice echoed in the stairwell, fainter and fainter.

Back in the flat, the three phones sat in a row. She picked up the receiver of her own phone, the one that worked. Music was still thumping through the walls; she heard a banging door and muffled laughter. People here stayed up all night.

So did the people at directory enquiries. 'Which town?' asked the girl.

'Dover,' said Celeste.

'What name?'

'Kidderpore, L.' Celeste spelt it out. There was a pause. She waited, tensely. This Lorna woman had probably changed her name about three times since then. Everybody else had.

But then the voice answered.

Twenty-eight

London was revving up for Christmas. There was a quickening in the air, a Friday night quickening but every day of the
week now. People double-parked their cars and dashed into
shops; restaurants were crammed with secretaries in paper
hats. Postmen, opening postboxes, stepped back at the ava-
lanche of envelopes and children in nativity plays squirmed
inside their sheets. All this and more, dread and joy and
loneliness. Stalls appeared in Kilburn High Road, selling
wrapping paper, and in the shops CD players were strewn
with tinsel. Buffy's wine merchant was doing brisk business.
Buffy himself had bought two bottles of Leoville Lascalles '71
but was Celeste going to drink it with him? He had bought
her a pair of silver earrings for her dear pierced ears but
when was he going to give them to her? Just as he and
Celeste had become more intimate – the events of that night
had shifted them into something more raw and personal,
something that more resembled a love affair – she seemed to
have gone to ground.

The next couple of days she hadn't been in the shop at all.
Mr Singh said she was doing his VAT. 'She's too good for
this place,' he said, 'she has a brain, that girl.'

'I know that!' said Buffy. 'Please get her to call me.'

He had phoned her, and got no reply. He had sat beside
his phone like a teenager, waiting for her to ring. The next
day there she was in the shop. His heart lurched.

'Please bear with me,' she said. 'I've got something to sort
out first.'

That evening he put on the answerphone and went to a Christmas party, at which he had hoped to show her off. When he lurched home the machine said o. What was happening; why was she being so mysterious? From long experience, of course, he knew the answer.

All Sunday he fretted. He bought all the papers, as a displacement activity, but he couldn't concentrate. Listlessly, he turned the pages. A treasure hunt competition had grabbed the public's imagination, with thousands of people haring all over the country searching for the prize. *My Room* was a concert pianist, with a wife and a brood of blond, smiling sons. They sat in an immaculate lounge, looking safe. The woman said '*My husband is my best friend,*' one of those statements that for some reason had always filled him with rage.

He took the dog for a walk, shuffling past the columned villas of Little Venice. Range Rovers, the ultimate fuck-the-rest-of-you vehicles, were parked outside; as he passed, people drew their curtains closed. He stood on the bridge, gazing down into the canal. If he threw himself in, would she care? Would any of them care? Would they even notice?

His eyes filled with tears. Does anyone love me enough, he wondered, to look in the paper when I'm abroad and see what the weather's like in the place I'm staying? That sort of thing? Have they ever?

Christmas was coming and Quentin was alone. Alone in his flat with a *Serves One* Tagliatelle. Back to serves one, back to square one. Talbot had moved out. Quentin gazed at the swagged and beribboned room, its damasks and velvets. It was his own place again; his home had been returned to him and no trace remained of Talbot – nothing, after two whole years. At the moment this was deeply disorientating; one day, when he was feeling better, maybe he could find it invigorating. He had in the past.

The split-up had been a mutual decision really, if such things could ever be mutual. The moment someone voiced their doubts Quentin always convinced himself he had been feeling this way too, all along. He did this for self-protection. The moment someone said 'It's not working, is it?' or 'We've got to talk,' things were changed for ever. This happened in other spheres too. Somebody once said his wallpaper was vulgar and he had never been able to look at it in the same way again. In the end he had stripped it off and redecorated the entire flat.

Quentin switched on the microwave. He hadn't told his Ma yet. He dreaded her disappointment; she had liked Talbot. 'This one'll last,' she had said. But nothing lasted, not in his family. No wonder he found it difficult to sustain relationships; with his parents' example, who could? His past resembled some ramshackle lodging house, people coming and going, strangers installing themselves at the breakfast table and then inexplicably disappearing. His therapist called it, 'emotionally rented accommodation'. He said that Quentin's failure to sustain relationships was his way of staying close to his father and mother. By repeating the pattern he stayed their child forever, bonded to them. And it was true. Each time he broke up with somebody he thought about his father and wondered how he had felt. It was like an accident making you aware of all the other people who must be in hospital.

Quentin laid the table for one – he always did this properly – and uncorked a bottle of Chardonnay of which he would only drink half. Popsi, his mum, said, *look on the bright side.* She said, *every person you meet, you learn a little something.* He tried to remember what he had learnt from the men with whom he had lived. Derek? Derek had taught him how to make marmalade. He had also taught him more than he really wanted to know about old blues singers, Blind Somebody This and Blind Somebody That, to tell the truth they all sounded exactly the same to him. Talbot? Talbot had taught him the rules of American football and how to play *Take my hand, I'm a Stranger in Paradise* on the piano with one finger. Quentin was sure there must have been more than this, but the thought of Talbot was still too raw.

What had his Dad learned, from all his wives? How had he coped? He would like to see him, but by now a meeting would be so strange and artificial that he didn't want to risk the terrible sense of loss such an encounter might cause. Maybe his father was disappointed in him because he was gay. But he didn't even know that. Big things like that, let alone the little things. A whole universe of little things which, even if they met now, it would take a lifetime to bring up in conversation.

Long, long ago his Dad used to visit. This was during the Pimlico period, when Quentin was little. When he lived above The Old Brown Mare. In retrospect, maybe his father only visited because it was a pub; maybe it was less to do with parental love than with the magnet pull of the booze. He and Ma had the most appalling rows. Then Terry, his stepdad, would storm across from the Saloon Bar and throw his father out. The bellowings in the street! The shape behind the frosted glass, banging on the window! The fist, battering against the inlaid lettering, PUBLIC BAR written the wrong way round, RAB CILBUP. The bellowings fainter and fainter as the years passed.

The visits petered out. As time went by, each meeting became a paler repetition of the one before, each one more indistinct until the image of his father almost faded away. Maybe his Dad felt the same, that Quentin gave less of himself each time, said less, until they were like two near-strangers exchanging small talk. Barely remembering, after the event, what the other person looked like. His Dad was like a rubber stamp which was never dipped in the ink pad. Stamp, stamp, each time fainter.

Quentin sat down with his tagliatelle. What was he going to do for Christmas? Each year he dreaded it. Each year the friends his age dispersed to their families in Northumberland or Surrey; temporarily they became dutiful sons, people he would hardly recognize if he saw them, chaps who hadn't brought home a girlfriend yet but there was plenty of time for that, wasn't there dear? The men with whom he had lived, who were mostly older, had sometimes taken him somewhere hot, Morocco or somewhere, but this had often ended in tears.

Sometimes there had been nobody at all in his life and he had simply gone home to his Mum. These Christmases, though cheery and alcoholic, had often ended in tears too. It never failed to amaze him that, considering she was such a simple woman, their relationship was so complicated. Had his Dad ever felt this? Being a son was a peculiar condition with its own network of snares and traps, but then, no doubt, being a husband was a peculiar condition too. He himself had been a sort of husband to Talbot, who had been rather female in his moods. He would like to discuss this with someone. His Ma wouldn't understand. He adored her really, despite the tears, but she would take it personally; she wouldn't understand.

His Dad would. This year, for the first time, he didn't just wonder: what will Buffy be doing? He always wondered that, briefly. This year he thought: wouldn't it be interesting if we met?

Christmas was a time of miracles. That was what Miles had been brought up to believe. Brenda believed in it too. Beneath the tree, in their little house near Swindon, the floor was spread with Ordnance Survey maps. She crouched there, muttering under her breath. How dumpy she was! Once he had considered her curvacious but his inner vocabulary had changed. *Curvacious* to *dumpy*, *vivacious* to *wittering*. It was the same thing, really, just lit from the other side. He wished he weren't voicing this, even to himself. It was a terrible thing to put into words.

'Framshill . . .' Her stubby finger moved across the map. 'Six-Mile Bottom . . .' She looked up at him, her face flushed. 'Gail thinks it's in the Peak District but I'm keeping my trap shut.'

A gold key. That's what lay buried somewhere or other. The key to a trip of a lifetime, to a fortune, to happiness. Brenda didn't look happy; she looked flustered. Already, all over Britain, people were tramping over ploughed fields. They were armed with torches; they went out after dark, when nobody could see them, to dig for the treasure.

'Where's Tiverton?' she muttered. 'Devon. Blast.' She tapped her biro against her teeth. 'What's an anagram for *sepia*?'

'Despair.'

'Don't be silly, there's no town called Despair. Anyway, that's got a *d* in it. And an *r*.'

Celeste was spending the night with somebody. How did he know? Because she looked flushed and radiant – her actual features looked subtly different – and under her overall she wore the same sweater two days running. Because when he phoned her, first thing in the morning, there had been no reply. When questioned she had shrugged her shoulders – assumed nonchalance, he knew it well – and said: 'I must've just popped out to get some milk.'

Red alert! Warning bells! *Popping out* always meant trouble. That airy, throw-away phrase, what betrayals it had concealed! Jacquetta just *popping-out* to the shops. Such housewifely diligence, how very uncharacteristic! Him running out to remind her to buy a bottle of soda and seeing her at the end of the street, in the public call box.

He was sixty-one, with a lifetime of *popping-outs* behind him; he was something of an expert on the subject. He knew when a woman was having an affair, just as he knew when a woman was pregnant. He had heard the ping of the phone extension, that tiny chime at midnight. He had seen that closed, secret look on her face; that look a child has when they have got a forbidden sweet in their mouth and stop chewing when a grown-up comes into the room. Oh, the over-elaborate explanations of where they had been! (He should have smelt a rat with Penny's trips, he had slipped up there.) The fact that they always seemed to be having a bath when he came home from work. The sudden and totally uncharacteristic acts of generosity – *no you go, you'll have a lovely time* – and lunches in town with female ex-schoolfriends whose name he didn't quite catch. The sudden alertness when the phone rang, like a fox stiffening at the sound of a hunting horn.

Oh he could go on for ever, he could give master classes in it. And here it was, starting all over again. In the season of goodwill, too.

Come and Behold Him, Born the King of Angels . . .

Five days to go. In Blomfield Mansions, Buffy was sleeping. Down the road, in one of the large houses with ruched curtains, one of the houses he passed in his walks, Annabel lay sleeping too. Annabel, from the hotel room in Rye. He hadn't met her since; indeed, he never would. But what did it matter now? Women he had touched; women he had wanted to touch. Women who had arrived too early or too late, just missed on the stairs, just missed at the bus-stop. Women he had just glimpsed in a swing door and dreamed about later, waking in the night damp with desire, with evaporating conversations. Who cared if it never happened, what was the difference? He was alone now, asleep, with his dog snoring beside him.

While he lay dreaming, India and Nyange were emerging from the Subterranean Club. It was a smoky basement near the Charing Cross Road, its floor slippery with beer and flyers. They emerged, their eardrums singing. Downstairs the music thumped; muffled, now, like heartbeats.

They met occasionally in the West End, when India finished work at the cinema. They were fond of each other; after all, they were sort of family.

'Your Dad's been very strange recently,' said India.

'Which dad?'

'Your real one.'

213

'Oh. Him.'

'He's obsessed with somebody half his age.'

'Not with me though. Oh, no.' Nyange tossed her head. 'He hasn't even come to see the show.'

'How could he, when you've never told him about it?' They stood at the stop, waiting for the night bus. 'It's up to you, too,' said India.

Men, passing, turned to stare at Nyange. She turned her head away. An empty Marks and Spencer's carrier bag bowled along the pavement, its handles raised like arms. A gust of wind blew it into the air, up, up above the parked cars.

'What're you doing for Christmas?' India asked.

'Mum's going to Kingston, but I can't go because I'm working.'

'Kingston's not far.'

'Kingston Jamaica, peabrain. Visiting the grandparents. Doing some consciousness-raising amongst the women. She's really boringly political now.'

'Go and see Buffy.'

'I can't,' said Nyange. 'I haven't seen him for years. Last time it was really depressing.'

'Why?'

'He smoked all through Christmas dinner.'

'Perhaps he was nervous,' said India.

'Mum had to cook him pheasant, yuk. He bit on a shotgun pellet and cracked his tooth, blimey he made a fuss. We said poor little bird, it didn't want to get shot. It would rather be flying round the woods and things, wouldn't it? And then he gave half of it to his dog.'

'Maybe you'd put him off. Maybe it was disgusting.'

'Then his dog was sick on the carpet.'

'Exactly.' India's bus hove into sight, its interior blazing with light. 'Actually, I like him better than my real parents.'

'That's because he's not your real parent,' said Nyange.

The bus slowed down. India rummaged for her purse. 'It's the season of forgiveness. Whatever your Mum's been saying

214

about him, all these years, that's not to do with you. He's in quite a state.'

'I *can't*.'

The bus doors folded open with a hiss. 'Come and have Christmas with us then,' said India. She hugged her and stepped on the bus. 'I wish you would. It'll be much more fun if you're there.'

The doors closed, with a sigh. India sat down. The bus was empty. DO NOT SPEAK TO THE DRIVER, said the sign.

As the bus carried her home, India dozed. She dreamed it was Buffy up there, sitting at the wheel. The bus wasn't empty now, it was crammed with children and ex-wives. DO NOT SPEAK, it said, but they were all speaking at once, their voices deafening. They were shouting that he hadn't a clue where he was going, he hadn't passed his test and how could he take them home when he didn't live there anymore?

O Come, All Ye Faithful . . .

Three days to go. When Buffy went into the shop, Celeste was on the phone. She muttered something into the receiver and put it down quickly.

'Who was that?' he asked, a pleasant smile stretching his lips.

'Nobody.'

He tried to rally. 'Let me take you out tonight. *The 39 Steps* is on at the Everyman.'

'Oh, dear.' She reddened. 'Sorry, I can't.' She stood behind the counter, gnawing her fingernail.

'Know what Picasso said? One starts to get young at the age of sixty, and then it's too late.'

'Don't be silly,' she said, smiling.

He paused, then he said casually: 'Would you believe, I don't even know your address! What happens if I want to send round a little Christmas something?'

'How lovely!' She told him her address. 'I'm up on the second floor.'

When the snow lay round about, deep and crisp and even . . .

Three days to go . . . but no snow lay. The weather was mild. The ground was soft, perfect for digging.

In the dark, solitary figures toiled. The moonlight caught the flash of their spades. One on Dartmoor; one in a field just outside the glow of Basingstoke. All over England people were digging for treasure.

In Bockhangar Wood, in deepest Kent, two figures were digging, side by side. They weren't digging for treasure; they were planting, hoping for their own miracle.

Last winter I went down to my native town, wrote Dr Johnson, *where I found the streets much narrower and shorter than I thought I had left them, inhabited by a new race of people, to whom I was very little known. My playfellows were grown old, and forced me to suspect that I was no longer young.*

Added to that, thought Buffy, a drowsy numbness brought on by duplicity and drink. At his age it was hard to stay awake until the small hours. He managed to, until two in the morning. Then he went downstairs and hailed a cab.

It was a tired-looking street. His darling angel lived here; his darling, treacherous angel. There was nobody about. He got out, telling the taxi-driver to wait, and crossed the road.

There was a junk shop, at street level. Up above music thumped. Pink light glowed through a torn blind. But on the second floor, Celeste's floor, the room was dark. The curtains hadn't even been closed. Nobody was there. And by this time of the night, nobody would be.

He stood there, shivering in his bedroom slippers. There was a note stuck with sellotape to the front door. *Liam, I'm at Chog's.* Behind, the *mutter-mutter* of the taxi-engine. *Mutter-mutter, cuckold-cuckold, that'll be £3.50 squire, from Heathrow ho-ho, mutter-mutter, bit of a wally aren't you? Always have been, eh?*

God rest ye merry gentlemen, Let nothing you dismay . . .

The Three Fiddlers was festooned with streamers, the ceiling practically groaned with them. The lunchtime roar was swelling in volume; beside the fire the two old girls, Kitty and Una, were singing. Behind the bar the impossibly young Australian was wearing a Santa Claus hat.

Buffy was having a drink with Celeste. Men leered at her – even more so, with the new haircut. Oh, my God, did *he* look at her like that?

'Who're you seeing?' he asked.

'Who?'

'What's his name?'

'Buffy, I told you!' She patted his knee. 'He doesn't exist.'

'Is it Liam?'

'Who's Liam?' she asked.

'Or Chog?'

'Who're you talking about?'

She got up and went out to the loo. Or was she making a phone call? While she was gone he rummaged inside the pockets of her coat. The things he had discovered, in his previous lives! Train tickets to Bristol Temple Meads; a screwed-up note, in unfamiliar writing, saying *Bell broken, bang on door, xxx*. No actual love letters, he had never slept with a woman that stupid.

He pulled out her darling woollen gloves and a packet of Polos. He felt around in the bottom and pulled out some empty, earthy polythene bags and a plant tag. *Cypripedium calceolus*, it said. *Lady's Slipper Orchid.*

He bundled all the stuff back. Who was she having an affair with – a gardener? She returned.

'I am coming for Christmas, aren't I?' he bleated.

'Of course. I said so.'

'I've bought the turkey.' He had insisted on this. He hadn't bought one for years; it made the whole thing seem more domestic – more possible, somehow.

'I'll come and fetch it on the morning,' she said. 'Then you can come to my flat. I'm cooking us all Christmas dinner.'

'What do you mean, *all*?'

She blushed. Whoops, a slip-up there. What was she envisaging, some ghastly show-down?

'Who're you talking about?' he asked.

She said: 'I've got a lot of rabbits.'

'Why?'

'I'll tell you some day.'

He put his arm around her. 'Let's have lunch tomorrow. It's Christmas Eve. Let me take you out somewhere swish.'

She stroked his knee, running her finger down the lines of the corduroy. 'I can't,' she said. 'I'm getting off work early.'

'When?'

'One o'clock' she said.

'Why?'

'I've got to go somewhere,' she said.

Twenty-nine

Christmas Eve and the streets were crammed. People were leaving, their cars piled with gifts. *Better fill up now, no petrol tomorrow.* People were going home, gathering in their children, battening down the hatches. People were rushing out making last minute forays – cranberry sauce, paper napkins. Oh, God, some Ferrero Rocher chocolates for Thingy. The rustling of wrapping paper behind closed doors, whispers, giggles. In heated rooms trees silently dropped their needles, and unwatched TVs announced that snow was forecast.

It is not just what you wear, it's the way you wear it. This was Buffy's profession, of course. Still he was taking no chances. Shaving off the beard was the obvious thing but he couldn't bear to do that. God knew how many chins lurked under there by now; that was one of the reasons he had grown it in the first place. But he wore a black trilby hat; he had purloined it, long ago, from the BBC costume department and nowadays he only wore it to visit his bank manager. He wore dark glasses. Christmas Eve had dawned cold but sunny too, so they didn't look too ridiculous. He had wrapped a black scarf around his face; as he hid in the bushes, waiting, his hot breath breathed back into his face, dampening it with the condensation of his anxiety. His coat – well, Penny had given it to him, say no more. Charcoal-grey, satin-lined, from Aquascutum. *Her* sort of thing, like all her presents. One look at the coat and you could see why

219

his marriage had failed. He hadn't worn it for years; Celeste, of course, had never seen it.

Through the sooty leaves he could see the corner shop. At one o'clock sharp Celeste emerged, putting on her coat. She called 'Happy Christmas!' as she closed the door and hurried into the Edgware Road, crossing when the green man was lit.

His old heart was thumping. He sidled out, through the shrubbery. A bus was approaching. He crossed the road, saunteringly, like a stockbroker. Or was he a bit of a spiv, with the shades? Whatever, she didn't notice because she had shuffled in, with the rest of the queue, and by the time he climbed in she had gone upstairs.

She liked sitting on the top of buses. How painful it was, to remember her childish confidences now! He mustn't think of that, it was too upsetting; he had to keep alert and keep in character. His skin tingled with the old actor's adrenalin – it had been so long since he had done any proper work. Down here he was in a good position to see her leave. The woman next to him had a pile of parcels on her knee. 'They all want those Nintendo things, don't they?' she said.

Celeste got out at Victoria Station. He got out, following her through the crowds. The place was packed. Everyone was fleeing the city; they carried suitcases and Christmas presents. Just for a moment he lost sight of her, then he glimpsed her standing in line for a ticket. She stood motionless, her face blank. What was she thinking? He felt uncomfortable, watching her. When people are amongst strangers they revert to themselves, they look smaller. Her breathless charm, her very Celesteness, had drained away; she was just a slim, abstracted girl consulting her watch. She could be visiting an aged aunt, instead of setting off to meet her lover.

She got her ticket and hurried across the concourse. On the way she stopped at W H Smith; he watched her buy a magazine. She had no luggage; she must be returning that night. Besides, she had to cook him dinner the next day. She had said she would come round in the morning to fetch the turkey.

All of a sudden, such domesticity seemed utterly unlikely. She was leaving him for ever. She was taking the boat train; she was travelling to Gatwick. She was going to fly away and he would never see her again.

She hurried towards the platforms. Blithering hell, he hadn't bought a ticket. He didn't know where to buy a ticket *for*. Too late now. Too late to go to the ticket office and ask the man her destination. He should have thought of this, but his own boldness in this enterprise and his growing sense of unreality had paralysed him. Quick! Action stations! He hurried after her. He would have to pay on the train. He was swept up in a hurrying surge of people; thank God he had told the porter to take the dog around the block, if he wasn't home by six.

'But it's Christmas Day!' Miles stared at her.

'Not till tomorrow.'

'It's Christmas Day tomorrow. All your family's coming!'

'We'll be back by then. Come on.' Brenda already had her coat on.

'But it's miles!' he said. 'It's hundreds of miles. It's East bloody Kent!'

She was trembling – actually trembling. He had never seen anything like it. The woman was mad. 'If we don't get there first, somebody else'll find it.' She switched off the Christmas tree lights. She dashed to the window and checked the catch. 'Don't you see, nobody'll go out tonight!'

'No, because they're not totally insane.'

She switched off the light in the little crib above the fire-place. She turned round to face him. 'I've found it, Miles. I've worked out the place where the treasure is. If you're not coming, I'll just go by myself.'

Celeste was in the next carriage. Through the interconnecting door, Buffy could see the top of her head. He had bought the *Standard*; he pretended to read it, but he had forgotten his spectacles. Outside the suburbs slid past. The sun was already sinking; poplars cast long shadows across a wintry sports field. Next to him, a woman nudged her child: 'Stop that, Lottie, or there'll be tears tomorrow.'

He was Gervais, a crooked merchant banker. He had been involved in some dubious insider dealing. The dark glasses were to conceal his identity; he was fleeing the country – Dover-Calais-Basle. The climax of the episode was a fight to the death in the snow-covered Alps. It was a European co-production, Klaus-Maria Brandauer, the works.

'Don't stare!' hissed the woman. 'It's rude.'

He smiled at the child, and rewound his scarf. *Close-up*, here, of his noble profile.

This is why I love acting, he thought. Anything's better than being me.

The car, with Miles and Brenda in it, sped along the M4. They had left their home, which was already in shadow. Miles was trying to remember Christmases past but he couldn't manage it. Unhappiness plugs our ears, it presses its fingers into our eye sockets. He was a lump of matter, no better than putty. He had no past and no future. Only the car was moving.

The train stopped at Dover Priory. Celeste got off. Outside, people greeted each other with open arms. Nobody was meeting her, however. He followed the rust-coloured coat as it made for the taxi-rank.

She drove off. Ducking into a taxi, he leant across to the driver and repeated the line from a thousand movies.

'Follow that cab.'

The sun was sinking. Beside Miles, in the passenger seat, Brenda leaned forward. 'Oh, hurry!' she said. She looked like the witch in *The Wizard of Oz*, leaning forward on her bicycle. The sharp nose; the sharp voice. They were hurtling through Kent. He was driving so fast that soon, surely, they would spin off into the sky.

Buffy had removed his dark glasses. He was in the middle of the countryside, the middle of nowhere. He stood shivering in the lane, watching the cab leave. The driver hadn't switched off his inside light; it glowed, a bright lozenge against the flaming sky. For a mad moment he wanted to shout *stop*! Civilization was driving away, leaving him totally alone. He was freezing cold.

Celeste had disappeared down a muddy track. She hadn't seen him; he had told his taxi to stop further up the lane. What on earth was she doing here in the wilds of nowhere? Who was she seeing? It was getting darker by the minute. Why did it always get so dark in the country, so soon and for so long? How did anyone stand it? Near him, something was rustling in the hedge – something bulky. Far away, across the fields, a dog barked; the loneliest sound in the world.

Buffy had always had an equivocal relationship with the countryside. It was best experienced – indeed should only be experienced – during a hot June afternoon with a glass of Chablis in one's hand. The cottage in Suffolk had been bought for Jacquetta's sake; she had said she felt trapped in London and at that time he would have done anything to please her. He had had visions of the boys romping through the woods and returning home with sticklebacks in jam-jars; of Jacquetta transformed into a smiling, wife-type person. Of himself transformed into a manly paterfamilias, chopping wood and presiding over games of charades during their TV-free evenings. It hadn't turned out like that, of course. It hadn't turned out into anything remotely resembling that.

He walked along the lane – even that made him breathless – and stopped at the track. It led downhill, between thick hedges. There was still enough daylight to see that it was muddy – tyre-ruts glinting with water. On the other hand it was too dark to see with any accuracy how to step around the muddiest bits. At the end of the lane – far away, impossibly far, in his condition – he could see the lights of some sort of habitation. Celeste's love-nest. He felt suddenly, achingly, lonely. If only she were here, to keep him company! Impossible, of course. She was his enemy now; the very person he was stalking. Another treacherous woman. His darling Celeste, she had turned out to be just like the others. Oh, the weariness of it, the plummeting predictability!

He listened to the silence. Far away, there was the hum of the main road. No other signs or sounds of human activity. On the other side of the hedge, startlingly close, something coughed. It sounded horribly human. What a cold, wet, horrible place the countryside was! And there was so much of it, miles and miles of it, going on forever. Oh, to be back in London, in his cosy flat!

Stumbling and slipping, he inched his way down the track. His feet sank into the mud. He heard the bronchial cough again, then a rustling noise and some bleating. There must be sheep in there. Christmas Eve: in other circumstances the whole thing could be quite Biblical.

Who on earth lived down there, and what exactly was he going to do? All he knew was that his socks were sodden; his shoes were hopelessly inadequate for this sort of thing. If he had known, he would have brought a pair of wellington boots.

It took Buffy a long time to inch his way down the track. It was quite dark by now, though a moon had risen. Through the trees he could see the lit windows of a dwelling, nearer now. The yellow rectangles reminded him of an advent calendar, of years of children squabbling about whose turn it was to open the next little window and then, quite suddenly, growing too old to bother. An arctic wind sliced across his cheeks; it sliced through his thin, city coat. Was that a twinge of angina? Faintly, very faintly, he heard the sound of music. He slithered and grabbed at the hedge, tearing his hand.

Maybe he should turn back. What had knowledge ever

brought him but pain? So many betrayals. Was there anyone one could grasp, in this world, and hold close to your heart?

He couldn't turn back, of course. He was lost in the windy night. There was nowhere to go, and nobody to take him there. And it was too late now. Sodden and scratched, he was standing on someone's spongey lawn.

The black bulk of a building loomed up. It looked like a cottage. The front door opened, with a blaze of light. *Donna é mobile* swelled out, Pavarotti, and spilled across the lawn. The light shafted across the garden, illuminating the trunks of trees. He heard laughter.

Celeste came out. She was with a man, who was muffled up in a hat and greatcoat. They were laughing together. Arm in arm, they hurried off down the garden; they seemed to be carrying bags.

He watched them, in the moonlight. They crossed the garden, the lit, theatrical set; they climbed over a fence. And then they were gone.

The blood drained from him. Tears filled his eyes. Another man – he had guessed, of course. But no amount of steeling himself could prepare him for the staggering voltage of the truth.

Miles, obeying Brenda's instructions, stopped the car outside a Happy Eater.

'Can't we have something to eat first?' he asked. Through the window he saw Christmas decorations, brightly-lit tables, and people putting food into their mouths. We may not be happy, he thought, but we could at least eat.

'You've had your sandwiches,' said Brenda. Shaking, she pulled open the Ordnance Survey map, yet again. 'Three fields, and we're there! Come on!' She got out of the car and pulled out the spade and the trowel. 'It's a full moon!' she whispered. 'A hunter's moon! Get the torch!'

He got out. The wind slapped his face. They seemed to be on some sort of ridge, miles from anywhere. A large elephant stood nearby, its back silvered by the moonlight. Beside him the parked cars were dimmed by condensation. Brenda pulled his arm; he stumbled across the tarmac.

Buffy stumbled blindly across the garden. He collided with a barbed-wire fence. Breathing hoarsely, he wriggled through it, tearing his coat. He seemed to be in a tangle of brambles now. Trees reared up above him. The moon was hurtling through clouds. Lower down, an orange glow seeped up, like a stain, from the horizon. That must be Dover – civilisation. A thousand miles away. Now he was deeper into the wood he could hear the traffic on the main road, louder somehow. Why? A trick of the air. Amongst the trees some creature – a bird? How the hell did he know? – something made a scraping sound, again and again. The sound of a knife being pulled through a sharpener. Himself, sharpening a knife for the Sunday roast. So many roasts, so many Sundays. Through the trees, in the moonlight, he could see the two figures. They were walking together, close to each other. His brain roared. He stumbled towards them.

Miles stumbled after his wife. She was galloping down the hill. On either side of her, rocks detached themselves from the ground and scampered away, bleating. He heard her voice. 'That's it! There it is!'

She pointed. A wood rose up, ghostly in the moonlight.

'Fifty feet inside the perimeter,' she called, 'due south!'

I'm not here, he thought. This is a dream. I'm asleep, in Swindon. In a moment I'm going to wake up. There'll be no Brenda; nothing.

She was running down the hill towards the wood. He heard the thump thump of her gumboots. The moon was so bright he could see her breath, puffing.

Buffy pushed through the brambles. A thorn caught his scarf and pulled him back, temporarily throttling him. The sky had cleared. Above, the moon shone in a vaulted dome of stars.

'Oh, shit!' hissed Brenda. She pulled Miles behind a fir tree. 'Look!' she whispered.

He peered out. Between the trees, fifty feet away, something moved. It was two figures, a man and a woman. He could see them quite clearly. They were toiling, amongst the trunks. Digging. He saw the glint of a spade.

'Oh, no!' gasped Brenda. 'Somebody's there already!' Her voice broke. 'I can't bear it!'

Suddenly she launched herself off, crashing through the undergrowth.

'Brenda!' he hissed. Slithering and stumbling, he followed her.

Buffy stared. What was happening? There seemed to be four people now. He heard the faint sound of voices. Through the trees, in the moonlight, the couples looked quite Shakespearean. Lovers in the Forest of Arden. And what bloody part was he supposed to play? He stood there, numb with cold. He had been thrust upon this stage; he had forgotten his lines.

A fight seemed to have broken out; two of the people were struggling. He heard a shout.

Brenda was wrestling with the overcoated figure, trying to pull the spade out of its hand. Miles heard it shouting: 'We're not digging things up! We're putting things in! We're putting plants in!'

'Stop her, can't you?'

A girl stood in front of him. She grabbed his arm.

'Stop that horrible woman!' she said. 'Who is she?'

'It's my wife.'

He stared at the girl. Moonlight shone on her wild eyes and tangled hair. She was utterly beautiful – the most beautiful woman he had ever seen. Gazing at her, he felt a curious sensation. It was as if his body was being both drained and refilled – a tender transfusion. He woke up from his long hibernation. It was as if he were suddenly face to face with the lost half of himself, with somebody so utterly familiar he didn't have to speak. His heart swelled, filling him, blocking his throat. Gently, he pushed the hair off her forehead.

'What's your name?'

'Celeste.'

He couldn't speak. He wanted to put his arms around her. He wanted to open his coat, pull her in and button her up close to him; he wanted to press her against his beating heart.

At that moment there was a crashing noise, like an elephant approaching. A bulky figure was charging towards them. It wore a black hat and a black coat; it was trying to push through the undergrowth but a fallen tree blocked its path.

The girl turned. 'Buffy!' she cried.

The man was squeezing under the bough of the tree, trying to crawl through. Suddenly he bellowed – a bellow that echoed through the wood, silencing them all. With a flapping sound, birds flew off.

He lay on the ground, groaning. 'My heart!' he groaned. 'My back!'

They approached him. He lay there like a beached whale, moaning with pain.

'It's a heart attack!' he moaned.

Celeste knelt down beside him. 'Buffy! What are you doing here?'

'What the hell are *you* doing here?' he yelled. He lifted his head, grunting, and pointed to the figure bundled up in the greatcoat. 'Who's that tramp?' His head fell back.

'That's not a tramp,' replied Celeste. A twig snapped as they all stepped nearer. The wind had died down; far away, there was the sound of singing.

She shone the torch onto the face of her companion. No, it wasn't a tramp. It was a middle-aged woman. She wore a woolly beret thing pulled over her ears. She stared down at the figure lying at her feet. He stared up.

'My God,' he said. 'Lorna.'

'That's not a tramp, you silly billy,' said Celeste. 'That's my mother.'

Thirty

It was Christmas Day. Freezing cold, heavy grey clouds, the first flakes of snow falling. The trees were locked like iron in the grip of winter; the only movement was the flutter of birds, swinging on the strings of bacon rind. Outside Keeper's Cottage, in deepest Kent, several cars were parked.

In the cluttered little living room Buffy was laid out on the floor, his head resting on a cushion. He was surrounded by his ex-wives, all three of them. Lorna was rummaging in the cupboard, looking for some sherry. Celeste was bringing in some glasses.

'We thought you were dying,' said Popsi.

'So you care!' cried Buffy. 'You all care!'

Nobody replied to this. Celeste put the glasses on the table, removing a pile of gloves and scarves. 'I didn't realize it was only his back,' she said. 'He seemed in such a state. That's why I phoned you all.'

'I *am* in a state,' said Buffy. 'It's agony. It's completely locked.'

'It did that in Kendal, remember?' said Popsi. 'On our honeymoon. You were as helpless as a baby.'

Penny looked down at him. 'It did that when we were supposed to be going to Daddy's seventieth birthday party. Purely psychosomatic.' She nudged him with her boot. 'What an old hypo,' she said. 'Buck up, you self-pitying old buffoon.'

'Don't be so heartless!' said Popsi. She ruffled his hair. 'You poor old sausage. Shall I light you a cigarette?'

Jacquetta gazed at him vaguely. 'You should centre your spinal fluid,' she said.

The room was so crowded it was difficult to move without bumping into somebody. Tobias and Bruno were jammed between the sofa and the bookshelves; like all adolescents, they seemed to take up more space than fully-grown people. They were sorting through Lorna's pile of cassettes.

'Rough!' said Bruno. 'It's all bleeding opera.'

'You can thank me for that,' called out Buffy. 'I taught all these women to love opera.'

'No, actually,' said Lorna. 'I taught *you*.'

'Oh, oh, he's re-writing history again,' said Penny. She looked down at Buffy. 'He's good at that.'

'I am here, you know,' said Buffy. 'You can address me. I'm here, I'm in pain.'

Eleven people were squashed into the room. Some of them had never met before; most of them had never met Lorna. Summoned from their various Christmases and thrust into this cottage, miles from anywhere, they still wore a dazed look. But they were starting to settle down. Quentin and Nyange sat in the window seat. He was holding a skein of her hair as she demonstrated how to plait cowrie shells into it.

Penny gazed at the brown-skinned girl and the homosexual, sitting side by side. 'Very Channel 4,' she remarked. 'All we need is somebody who is physically challenged.' She stopped, and looked down at Buffy. 'Whoops! Forgot. We've got one. In fact, looking back on it, he was frequently physically challenged.'

'Just what do you mean by that?' demanded Buffy.

Penny laughed. So, disconcertingly, did some of the other women.

'Sherry?' asked Celeste, handing round glasses.

'I'm dying for a pee,' said Buffy. 'I've said it about eight times. Will somebody please carry me to the lavatory?'

There was a silence.

'Come on!' said Buffy. 'Who's going to volunteer?'

'Not me,' said Penny. 'No fear.'

Popsi said: 'Last time I carried you, remember, when you were drunk? I did me back in. And – well, pet, there's a bit more of you now, isn't there?'

Penny looked around. 'Any offers? Jacquetta?' But Jacquetta didn't seem to hear.

'For God's sake!' cried Buffy. 'After all these years. Is it a lot to ask?'

'Yes,' said Penny.

India got up from the floor. 'We'll do it. Come on, Celeste.'

All over Britain, families were sitting down to Christmas lunch. In Buffy's flat, George had found the turkey. The fridge door hadn't closed properly for months; the dog had simply nudged the door open with his nose and dragged the turkey out. Half-chewed portions of it were strewn over three rooms.

In Celeste's flat the rabbits had found the vegetables. Bits of carrots and Brussels sprouts lay scattered over the carpet. The rabbits sat there, munching; they vibrated to the trains below and the thumps of the music above.

The fire blazed in the grate. Penny, sipping her sherry, was looking with interest at the other women. 'Isn't this fascinating! We're like a reunion of old girls who've been to a particularly ghastly boarding-school.'

'Thanks!' said Buffy, who was back in position on the floor.

Popsi laughed her gravelly laugh, and ended up coughing. She was wearing a gold lurex sweater, cut perilously low. She had sprayed glitter onto her hair; she called it her Christmas decorations.

Penny gazed at Popsi. 'I always wondered what you looked like,' she said, 'but you were so much before my time. You were just a lot of crossings-out in Buffy's address book.'

'Oh, the places I've lived,' said Popsi. 'Gypsy isn't in it. Had two husbands after him, Terence and Ian, but he was the nicest.' She lifted Buffy's head and inserted a cigarette between his lips. 'You were, you know. Course you were slimmer then.' She lit the cigarette for him. 'But so was I.'

She sat back in her chair, panting. Whenever she moved, glitter scattered.

Jacquetta waved her hand. 'All this smoke . . .' She vaguely batted it away.

Lorna and Celeste, the hostesses, refilled glasses. 'Sorry there's only this,' said Lorna. 'I'm sure there's some Twiglets somewhere. I wasn't expecting company, you see. I was supposed to be going up to London, with Celeste. After we'd done some planting. We were going to go up to London and give Buffy a surprise.'

'Oh, you've done that all right,' he said.

'This is much more fun,' said Penny, holding out her glass. 'I wouldn't have missed it for the world. Better than going to visit Colin's father in Nantwich. I've got a feeling he's just like Colin, only more so.'

It was a crowded little room, even with no people in it. Plants and old sheeps' skulls crammed the window ledges. Holly had been thrust behind picture frames. The curtains were closed against the cold grey day.

Quentin fingered the fabric. 'Damask would be super here. Gold and russet, can't you see it?' He turned to Lorna. 'I can get you some with my discount. I work at Harrods.'

'Harrods?' replied Lorna. 'Last time I saw you, you were in your pram. I just sneaked a look. You were a lovely baby.'

'Wasn't he just!' said Popsi. 'When was that, dear?'

'I was meeting Russell in a tea shop,' said Lorna, 'and he was looking after him.'

Popsi looked down at Buffy. 'You never looked after Quentin.'

'Of course I did!' said Buffy. 'I looked after him all the bloody time, while you were off with your fancy men. Now who's re-writing history?'

Nyange ran her finger along a beam. 'I've always dreamed of a place like this. A little cottage. A place with roots. Mum and me, we've been all over.'

233

'Emotionally rented accommodation.' said Quentin. 'Join the club.'

'Don't blame me,' said Buffy. 'Blame your mothers. There's two sides to this, you know. You've never heard mine.'

'Yes,' said Nyange, 'because you were never there.'

'Whose fault was that?' demanded Buffy.

Popsi raised her glass. 'He's here now. We all are. Better late than never.'

They drank. Jacquetta gazed around. 'This house has an incredibly strong sense of history.'

Popsi said: 'We're history, aren't we? All of us.'

'You're my history,' said Buffy.

'That's it in a nutshell,' said Penny, 'the Russell Buffery World View.'

'Oh, shut up!' he said.

'Did you colour wash these walls?' asked Jacquetta. 'I'm thinking of getting the builders back in. I've just found a marvellous decorator. He's called Kevin. I thought I'd get my kitchen done.'

Lorna looked around. 'That's not colour wash,' she said. 'That's patches of damp.'

Penny turned to Jacquetta. 'I had the cottage repainted, after you. I was so jealous.'

'Really?' asked Buffy. 'How gratifying!'

'Oh, it didn't last,' said Penny. She looked at the women. 'Funny old harem, aren't we.'

'A roomful of women, what bliss,' said Buffy. He tried to raise his head, groaned, and relapsed onto the cushion. 'Wouldn't it be wonderful if you all started fighting over me.'

Penny nodded. 'Like, last one to leave has to take you home.' She took another sip of her sherry. 'Three wives, one for each decade. A sixties one, a seventies one and I suppose I was the eighties one.'

'Don't you dare write a piece about it, you bloodsucker,' said Buffy. 'This is Christmas. A sacred day. A private, family occasion.'

'Ex-family, thanks very much' said Penny.

'Not for me,' said Buffy. 'I've found a daughter!'

Penny laughed. 'I know. The way you've been going on, anyone would think you'd given birth to her yourself.'

'It's a miracle. A miracle birth!' Weakly, he patted the carpet beside him. 'Come and sit here, Celeste. Can I call you daughter? Budge up, everybody.' Celeste sat down beside him, wedged in. 'Look at this beautiful young woman,' he said. 'A new slate, a clean broom. We're starting today, from scratch.'

'Yes. And you won't have to go to all the trouble of traumatising her childhood,' said Jacquetta. 'Running off with other women – '

'Me?' shouted Buffy. 'What about you? Rushing off to Tunisia with your art teacher, creeping off to Egypt with that asshole Austin, shagging your shrink when I was paying for the sessions, know how much they cost – ?'

'Children, children!' said Popsi. She turned to Lorna. 'Go on, lovey, show it to us again.'

Lorna had been sitting beside the fire, feeding it with logs. There had never been so many people squashed into this room. She had been turning from one to another, her head swivelling as if she were at some marital Wimbledon, the ball of blame flying to and fro. She felt oddly detached from it all; so used was she to being alone that she needed to be by herself to catch up with it all. Though she had changed into a skirt for these ex-rivals or whatever they were, though she had tidied herself up for the arrival of these various sort-of-siblings of her own astonishing daughter, she was still wearing a lot of clothes. She reached down inside her sweater, inside the layers of thermal underwear; she rummaged around and pulled out a chain. Hanging from it was a little gold fish; it glinted in the firelight.

'Pisces,' said Jacquetta. 'Mutability and magic.'

'Your little fish, and her little fish,' said Popsi. 'Separated at birth. Go on, tell us again. It makes me cry.'

Lorna smiled. In the firelight she looked younger. For a moment they could glimpse the resemblance between mother and daughter – the wide cheekbones, the tapering face – though the lines of her pointed chin were heavier now. She threw another log on the fire.

'I was on tour in Greece, playing Juliet, when I found out I was pregnant. At first I just thought my costume had shrunk. Then I realized.'

'Why didn't you tell me?' demanded Buffy.

'Ssh!' said Popsi.

'I knew it was Russell's, of course. But he was older than me. He was married.'

'Sort of,' said Celeste.

Popsi nodded. 'Sort of.'

Lorna felt she was giving a speech. Until Celeste had knocked on her door, ten days ago, she had never even rehearsed it. Now, however, the words had sorted themselves out into some kind of order. This small segment of history had become solid, by repetition; beyond it lay the unknown years that so far belonged only to Celeste. 'When I got back to England I didn't know what to do. It was different in those days, my parents would have been appalled. My father was running the Institute of Statistical Research.' She turned to Celeste. 'That's where you get your head for figures, I forgot to tell you that. He was frightfully old-fashioned. He'd always been against me going on the stage in the first place. And Russell – '

'I adored you!' cried Buffy. 'If I'd known – '

'I knew it wouldn't work, honestly,' she said. 'Even that young, I could tell. You could tell too, I'm sure you could. We'd had the best of each other. Well, I'd certainly had the best of you – '

'All three inches of it,' said Penny.

'For God's sake!' yelled Buffy.

'She's only joking, love,' said Popsi, patting his knee. 'We all know it's three and a half.' She and Penny started giggling.

'Is this the way women talk when they're alone?' asked Buffy.

Celeste turned to Lorna. 'Go on.' She nearly added *Mum*, but she couldn't quite say it, not in front of everyone. She didn't know if she quite *felt* it, yet. *Kidderpore* was something she would have to get used to. She had already practised it in the mirror, *Celeste Kidderpore, Celeste Kidderpore*, like a girl does when she is going to get married.

'Are you sitting comfortably?' asked Lorna.

'Not with this great porpoise hogging all the space,' said Penny. 'I've never known anyone take up so much room.'

'I'm in pain!' Buffy cried. His feet were wedged against the fire grate and his chest was sparkling with glitter from where Popsi had been leaning over him.

'So I didn't tell anyone,' said Lorna. 'When she was born I was offered Electra, in Glasgow. I desperately wanted to do it.' She gazed into the flames. 'I was very ambitious then. I suppose you'd say liberated and independent but it all boiled down to egocentricity. Actors are the most ruthless people in the world. They have to be, to do their job. That's why they make such awful parents.'

'Hear hear,' said somebody.

'Shut up,' said Buffy.

Lorna turned to Celeste. 'So I put you up for adoption. They took you away very quickly. All I gave you was the little fish, my other half, because you were Pisces. And I called you Celeste, just because I loved the name. And that was that.'

There was a silence. Outside, dusk was already falling but nobody had noticed. Lunchtime had long since come and gone.

'Any more of that sherry?' asked Popsi, the tears sliding down her cheeks.

Celeste emptied the bottle into her glass. There was a silence. Even the boys were listening. They sat hunched beside the fire; in their ears, the rings and studs glinted. Bruno had rolled up some newspaper and shoved it into the flames. All that news, all those words, history now, they burned as brightly as the logs. Old wood and old words, they both gave off heat and brought a flush to people's cheeks. What did it matter, the cause of the heat, when it was warming them now?

Celeste had heard this story by now, of course – many times, during the past ten days. She had heard a lot more from this woman she was slowly trying to recognize as her mother. The main events were taking on the glazey feel of a fairy story, a myth for others to repeat during the dark winter evenings. Buffy lay on the floor like a silent radio, waiting to be switched on. He would be telling the story soon, embellished with his own indignant and colourful punctuation. With that honeyed voice he would make it history. His voice was so authoritative, it had such power and resonance and seduction in it. It existed independently from his own muddled life, and soon she was to become part of his repertoire. This gave her a warm, swelling feeling of importance.

She drained her sherry. Melton Mowbray was far away now, back in another life. The girl she was then – she could hardly recognize her. *Celeste*. Her very name had never seemed to fit her, she had never quite fitted in. She has always felt solitary and out of step, though in those days she didn't have the words to voice this, even to herself. Such thoughts would have seemed alarming and ungrateful. Back home you didn't think of your parents as *not your sort*. In London you did, by gosh you did, but not up there. You didn't blame it on *them* if you felt somehow amorphous and undefined, like an out-of-focus photograph. If you felt terribly lonely.

Popsi was talking to Lorna. 'What happened to your career, love?' she asked. 'I saw you on the stage once, you weren't half bad. Course I didn't like to admit it then, because I was a teeny bit jealous.'

'Were you?' asked Buffy hopefully.

'Not for long. I had my own hands full at the time.' She turned to Lorna. 'Course, I might have felt differently if I knew you'd had a *child* with him. But I didn't.'

'Nor did I!' said Buffy.

'I carried on for a while,' said Lorna, 'but something had withered. Oh, I don't know. Something died. Like I was a fire without fuel, know the feeling?'

'I always had too much fuel,' said Buffy. 'That was *my* trouble. So much bloody fuel I couldn't get the flames to start.'

Penny said: 'The trouble with you – '

'Oh, oh, here we go,' said Buffy. 'The trouble with me. Why don't you just record it onto a cassette to save yourself the bother?'

'The trouble with you is that you were so busy making up your own dramas you didn't have any left for your work. Like you played this role – old and cuckolded and broke, poor old Buffy. For a start, you're not even old. You're only sixty-one!'

'Sssh, love,' said Popsi, and turned to Lorna. 'Go on.'

'I was just making empty gestures,' said Lorna. 'I felt it. I knew I was doing it.'

'The women I know, they're always going on about how children ruined their careers,' said Buffy. 'Now you're saying *not* having one ruined yours. You lot want it both ways.'

'Do shut up,' said Penny.

Lorna said: 'I wanted to be doing it for someone else, and there wasn't anyone else to be doing it for. From then on I sort of drifted. In and out of things. Jobs, everything. If you don't have any complications, then you feel quite lost.'

'Or quite free,' said Penny. 'Maybe it's the same thing.' She moved Buffy's leg off her foot. 'You're the most liberated of us all. We just got married.'

'We've just seen ourselves in terms of men,' said Jacquetta.

'And their bank accounts,' said Buffy bitterly.

'Just going to make my camomile tea,' said Jacquetta, drifting out to the kitchen.

'That's what she always did,' said Buffy. 'Make tea.'

'This is such heaven,' said Penny. 'I wish I had my tape recorder.'

'We're not a mini-series, dear,' said Popsi.

'No, we're much better.'

Buffy said: 'You could do us on *Penny For Them. Is your family getting hard and stale? Try adding some Celeste and stirring it up!*'

Popsi wasn't listening; she was staring at Penny. 'You're Penny Warren?'

Penny nodded.

'The journalist? I sent you something and you printed it! About how, if you want to get rid of fish smells, you can boil up coffee beans in the saucepan.'

'Did you?' said Penny. 'I've forgotten.'

'For goodness sake!' said Celeste suddenly. 'This is my life you're talking about! It's not fish smells!' She sat rigid, staring at them all. 'Everything – all my past – I grew up thinking that was the truth! My parents, everything. I trusted them all – when you're a child you trust everyone. Don't you see – all these years, everybody's been lying to me!'

'Join the club,' said Buffy.

Lorna got up. 'I think we all need another drink.' She opened the cupboard. She took out a bottle and peered at the label. 'Madeira. That'll have to do.' She unstoppered the bottle and sniffed it.

Buffy tried to put his arm around Celeste. He fell back, yelping with pain.

'You're so cynical!' Celeste said. 'All of you. If you knew what you sounded like!'

'My dear,' said Buffy. 'If we're talking about lying, what've you been doing to *me* these past two months?'

Celeste reddened. There was a silence. Lorna inched her way around the room, filling glasses.

Celeste said: 'I didn't lie. I was acting.'

'Ah, a chip off the old block,' said Buffy. 'I don't mind. Lucky my overpowering sex drive didn't carry me away.' Penny hooted with laughter; he ignored her. 'Else I might've done something we would all have regretted.'

Jacquetta wandered in with her cup of camomile tea. 'That's what happened with *my* father, I'm sure of it.'

'You still going on about that?' said Buffy. 'Your poor old dad.' He turned to Celeste. 'It's a relief, really. My darling girl. I knew I loved you, but this is better.'

'Why?' asked Celeste.

'Because it need never end. In fact, it's just starting. One can divorce a wife, but one can never divorce a child.'

'No,' said Jacquetta, 'but you can hardly ever see them.'

'Whose fault was that?' he bellowed, twisting round. 'Every Saturday you kept saying they had to go to the dentist, they had to buy clothes for school, every Saturday you were suddenly this diligent mother – '

'Children!' Popsi, put up her hand. 'Water under the bridge, dears.'

Tobias said: 'It's all Mum's fault. We wanted to come and see you.'

'And our stick insects,' said Bruno.

Buffy gazed up at him. 'You remember them?'

Popsi said: 'Quentin always spoke fondly of you.'

Quentin nodded. 'When I was at St Martins I painted an entire "Saint Sebastian Pierced with Arrows" while you were reading *Rogue Herries* on the radio. I said to my friend, that's my father. Your voice was very comforting when I was doing the bloody bits – you know, the punctured flesh. I'll show you the painting one day. It's in my flat.'

'I banged on the window once, but you didn't hear me,' said Buffy.

'At the flat?'

Buffy shook his head. 'At Harrods.'

Popsi put her arm around her son, spilling glitter onto his shoulder. The lurex top slipped lower. 'Now we've broken the ice we can all be friends. Come and have a meal with Quentin. He's a tip-top cook.' She turned to Celeste. 'Your half-brother! My head's reeling.'

Everyone was quiet, trying to work it out. Madeira on top of sherry didn't help. Was India an actual relative? No, but she was about the same age. Nyange was, though. She was a half-sister. She sat in the window seat. She had stuck a

241

sprig of holly in her braids, twining it amongst the shells and coloured threads. She looked as startling and exotic as a votive goddess.

'Tobias and Bruno,' said Buffy, 'they're your half-brothers.'

'Maxine isn't,' said Popsi. 'I had her with Terry. Didn't I?'

Celeste had sorted it all out some time before, when she had first discovered the truth. This lot were experts, but it was still taking them a moment or two. It was like watching a group of crossword-puzzle champions tackling a really difficult one, one of those big-prize ones with cryptic clues.

Suddenly she felt overcome with affection for them all. How her moods see-sawed today! Buffy was right. In a sense, of course, she had lied to them too, or at least concealed the truth, and one always feels responsible towards people one has put at a disadvantage.

Penny, the sharpest of the three, was looking at her. 'All those questions about Buffy, after you'd accidentally-on-purpose bumped into me, you wily girl . . .'

'Oh, ho, the penny's dropped,' said Buffy.

' . . . I sort of wondered why you were so interested.'

'So did I,' said Buffy. 'Poor foolish me, I thought you were jealous.'

It wasn't totally dissimilar to jealousy, was it? The same hot, overpowering hunger for every detail, a similar pain?

Penny was gazing at her, her head tilted. 'You were working out if I could be your mother.'

'And me!' said Popsi. 'Wish I was, you're a real poppet. And I thought you were only interested in telephones.'

'The man never came,' said Celeste.

'Oh well – win some, lose some.'

Jacquetta was cleaning her spectacles with the hem of her shawl. She put them back on, and gazed at Celeste. 'I finished the painting yesterday. I called it *The Lost Child*. I must have had some sort of premonition. Subconsciously, of course. You have his eyebrows, that's what I noticed.'

'I noticed them too,' said Penny. 'Buffy's thick black eyebrows. I remember thinking you ought to pluck them.'

Buffy weakly raised his glass. Celeste refilled it. He looked at Lorna, who sat beside the fire in her darned jumper, woolly skirt and bright red tights. She wore striped socks too, but today they matched. He said: 'This is our child. It's only just sinking in. All last night, after you'd tenderly tucked me in here, under my simple blanket, all last night I lay awake, gazing at the embers of what might-have-been. And yet marvelling that here she is. I didn't sleep a wink.'

In fact both Lorna and Celeste, upstairs in the bedrooms, hadn't been able to sleep a wink themselves. They had been kept awake by the stentorious snores downstairs in the living room. But they didn't like to break the mood.

Lorna looked at her daughter, who sat on the floor next to Buffy's prone body. She herself didn't feel like a mother; not yet. There hadn't been time. It was something she would have to learn from a standing start, like a Berlitz crash course in some foreign language. But maybe neither of them wanted this, by now; maybe it was no longer appropriate. They had missed the mothering years, and were starting out as grown-ups together. Already Celeste felt familiar to her – lovable, even – but they had a long way to go. Oh, it was too compli-cated to think about, with all these people here, and Penny was talking.

Penny was saying, to Celeste: 'What I don't understand, sweetie, is why didn't you just ask Buffy? Why didn't you just ask him how many children he had?'

'Because of the letter,' said Celeste.

'What did the letter say?'

Celeste paused. Everyone was looking at her – even Jac-quetta, who sat huddled on the floor, swathed in a shawl, nursing her tea. *I'm an actor's daughter*, Celeste realized. For twenty-three years I thought my father repaired washing machines. For twenty-three years – oh, I must turn every event around in my hands, lift it painfully and examine it all over again. I've hardly started; it will take for ever.

She turned to her mother. 'Can you pass me my shoulder bag?' Lorna passed it to her. Celeste opened it, unzipped her wallet and took out the letter. She kept it there, between her phone card and her bus pass. She unfolded the paper; the letter was disintegrating at the creases, from re-reading. She cleared her throat, and read to her audience.

'*My dearest Celeste,*' she read, '*This is a difficult letter to write but it must be done. Now that we are both gone I have to tell you something that concerns you. it is a secret that Donald and me have kept from you for all these years past, and you might not agree with that but we did what we thought was best. We have loved you like a daughter, but that is not the whole truth. You were chosen. We chose you because we thought you were the one for us, and God had decided in His wisdom not to give us a child of our own. Except that he did. He gave us you. All these years you have bought us nothing but happiness, and I want to thank you for that. I don't know anything much about your real parents but maybe one day you will be wanting to find out more about yourself. So here is what I know. Your mother gave you this fish, which I leave for you enclosed. I think you are the daughter of a man called Russell Buffery but I am not sure about this. Maybe he would know, were you to find him. Maybe he was married to your mother, but I would think not. Probably he does not know about your existence and in my opinion it is best to let sleeping dogs lie. God bless you, and thank you for being such a joy to us all these years. There is £800 cash for the arrangements in that plastic tub thing with a lid on it, the thing Annie gave us and we never used, that you dry lettuces in. Should you have problems with the plumbing the mains stopcock is in the front garden to the right of the gate, I don't think you ever knew. All my love my darling, Connie.*'

There was a silence, broken by a sob from Popsi. 'Oh, that's so beautiful!' she cried. She sat there like a large fairy, her glitter scattered over the people she had touched – Buffy, Celeste. 'Oh, if only I'd done that. Had my boy adopted. He might be here right now, with us.'

Even Penny was sniffing. She wiped her nose and said, briskly: 'You could have found them out much more easily, you know. You could have gone to Somerset House and asked to see the records. Children's Act, 1975. Adopted children have a right to trace their real parents.'

'I didn't know that,' said Celeste. 'Anyway, I wanted to see what he was like.'

'So you came to London . . .'

Celeste nodded. 'I tracked him down – I just found him in the phone book – and got a job nearby. And by that time it was too late. Each time I found one of you, I found there was another one of you before that.'

'And then another one on the side,' said Penny.

'And by that time it was too late to tell the truth,' said Celeste. 'It had sort of got too complicated.'

'Exactly,' said Buffy. 'One never lies. One just grows up.'

'In her case, pretty fast,' said Penny. 'She'd hardly got her skis on and whoosh! She was off down the Black Run.'

There was a general stirring. It was six o'clock and the three exes were preparing to rejoin their other lives. Back at their homes food was waiting to be cooked, presents to be unwrapped. Their Christmases, stilled by Celeste's urgent phone-call, were waiting to be re-activated. Buffy tried to get to his feet, bellowed with pain, and flopped back on the floor.

'Happy Christmas to you all, my dears,' he said, waving them goodbye. 'My loves, my better halves, my lost delights . . .'

'All right, all right,' said Penny.

One by one they filed into the little hall, and started putting on their coats. Lorna opened the door. Snow blew in and swirled around. She flinched back.

Outside, in the darkness, the garden was deep in snow. A foot, at least. It had fallen while they were busy talking; it must have been falling for hours. There were mounds where the bushes had been; in the distance, larger humps where the cars were parked. It was eerily beautiful, and utterly, utterly silent. No murmur, even, from the main road beyond the hill.

There was no way they could get out. They couldn't possibly drive their cars up the track in these conditions.

They were snowed in.

Thirty-one

They went back into the living room and took off their coats.

'What are we going to do?' asked Lorna.

'This is what Catholics must feel,' said Penny, looking down at Buffy. 'When they want to get divorced. Permanently snowed in. For life.'

'There's hardly anything to eat,' said Lorna. 'There's hardly anything in the larder.'

'We could always cook Buffy,' said Penny. 'There's enough of him.'

'Shut up!' he yelled.

'Char-grill him over the fire,' she said, 'and save one little piece for the doggy bag.'

'Shut up!' He struggled to move. 'This isn't some avant-garde feminist film.'

Penny laughed. '*Lord of the Flies*, divorce style.'

Jacquetta said: 'Can't we phone for help? Leon'll be worried.'

'Oh, no he won't' said India, 'he'll be too busy. Don't you remember? Christmas is so traumatic all his patients phone him up.'

'That's true,' said Jacquetta.

India went on: 'Sometimes they're in such a state he has to open up his consulting rooms for a special session.'

Celeste nudged her. 'Ssh!' she whispered.

Lorna lifted the phone but the line was dead. 'Oh, Lord. The wires must be down.'

The kitchen was crammed with women. They opened cupboards and pulled out drawers.

'There's some fish fingers in the fridge,' said Lorna.

'Have you got a wok?' somebody asked.

'There's some sausages somewhere,' said Lorna. 'I got
them from work, but I think they're date-expired.'

Popsi sighed. 'I know the feeling.'

'There may be some hamburger stuff,' said Lorna.

'I'm a vegetarian,' said Jacquetta.

'You would be,' said Penny. 'Why are difficult people
always vegetarian?'

Popsi had put on an apron. 'Come on girls, its loaves and
fishes time.' She looked in the fridge. 'A bit of cheddar
cheese, one strawberry yoghurt, Lordy, these sausages are
old.' She turned to Penny. 'Penny for Them?'

'Want to add some zip to that tinned cannelloni? Try
mixing it with a little boot polish!'

'Want to stretch that tagliatelle a little bit further? Try
adding kitty litter, for a real family treat!'

'And the left-overs make a super potting-compost!'

Jacquetta peered in the larder. 'Here's some chick peas,
but they take three and a half hours.'

Lorna stood there helplessly. 'I'm afraid I'm not very dom-
esticated.'

'Lucky you,' said Penny, 'you haven't had to be.'

Popsi was rummaging amongst some vegetables. She
pulled out a small, wizened carrot. 'Remind you of anyone,
girls?'

They burst out giggling, even Jacquetta. Nobody had ever
heard her laugh before; they all turned and stared.

At that moment Quentin came in, rolling up his sleeves.
'Leave it to me, dears,' he said.

Outside, the windows shone in the dark. In the garden Bruno
and Tobias were having a snowball fight. They had lost their
teenage languor, they were children again. Whooping and

shrieking, they clawed up the snow, handfuls of it, and flung it at each other.

India opened the cottage door. Light spilled out onto the snow. 'Come in!' she called. 'Mum says you'll freeze!'

But they didn't hear. Suddenly she waded out. 'Nyange!' she called. 'Come out! It's wonderful!'

Buffy and Celeste were alone in the living room. She sat, propped up against his stomach. Outside in the garden they could hear whoops and yells. From the kitchen came bursts of laughter.

'Sounds like Dorm Night in there,' said Buffy.

'They seem to be getting on pretty well,' said Celeste.

'They shouldn't. It's unseemly.'

'They do have something in common.'

'I know.' He paused, listening to a burst of raucous laughter. 'That's what worries me.' He tried to sit up, to listen better, and fell back. 'Pass me my cigarettes, sweetie.'

'You shouldn't smoke.'

'Do you mind? Do you really care?'

She stroked his beard. 'Of course I do, silly.' It was painful, to watch him making this huge readjustment towards her. She had known for months that it lay ahead of him, like a major operation he was unaware that he had to face. She had meant to prepare him for it more gradually – more ceremoniously too, with a gentle talk culminating in a Christmas dinner à trois, back at her flat – but the unexpected events in the wood had thrown the whole thing into disarray. 'Look, I'm awfully sorry.'

'I adore you. You know that.'

'I adore you, too,' she said. 'So is that all right?'

He nodded. He took her hand and kissed the fingers, one by one. He laid her palm against his cheek. In the kitchen the bursts of laughter and the clatter of pans seemed far away. Here there was no sound except the shifting of a log as it settled in the embers of the fire.

'You're got glitter in your beard,' she said.

'You've got some on your jumper.'

'You know I'll never be able to call you Dad. It makes me feel too funny.'

'That's fine by me. Hasn't done me much good up to now.'

She pulled away. 'Listen!' She glared at him. 'You're not a failure! I've seen your boys with Jacquetta, they're just as horrible with her. They're adolescents! I've been in all your lives. I've heard how they all speak about you, your ex-wives, India, everybody, I'm probably the only one who has. I've been like a fly on the wall. Don't you understand? They wouldn't be so rude about you if they weren't fond of you. It's a compliment, in a funny way.' She paused for breath. She had been meaning to say this all day. 'You've not been a failure, Buffy! You've just had more of a past to be a failure *in!* And look – they're all here, aren't they? All your exes. They all rushed down, on Christmas Day too! Listen to them. And your children too.'

They paused. A snowball thudded against the window. Outside, yells echoed over the countryside – all the Christmases he had never had, they were happening here, now. They echoed across the dark, locked countryside.

'You've brought them all together, bless you,' he said. 'You're the only one who could do it.'

'That's not true! I just helped it happen. Don't you see, you silly? I think the reason you can't act anymore is that you're too busy acting out this, this, *scenario*.'

'What scenario?'

'Of poor old Buffy. Poor old battered Buffy, all abandoned and divorced. Penny's right. You've got sort of locked into it and it's not really true! You're not that old. You haven't even got anything wrong with you, not really. It's, like, you've written a part for yourself and those are the only lines you know.'

Just then Jacquetta came into the room. She wore his trilby hat, at a rakish angle, and she had tucked a *Historic Sights of Kent* tea towel into her waistband. She was still giggling.

'Sorry to interrupt,' she said, 'but do you two want baked beans with yours?'

Afterwards they all said, to whoever would listen, that it was certainly the most bizarre Christmas dinner they had ever had, and they should know – they had had some bizarre ones in the past. They ate a concoction of stir-fried tinned ravioli, cabbage, onions, sausages and baked beans with, as Lorna said in her supervisor's voice *your choice of tomato ketchup or piccalilli.* This was washed down with half a bottle of tawny port, a litre bottle of Cinzano somebody had discovered in the back of the larder and three cans of date-expired Budweiser Lorna had bought for some men who came a long time ago to fit her new boiler.

They ate on Buffy. One of his hundred uses, as an ex-husband, was to provide a convenient dining-table. He wasn't allowed to laugh or move, however, or the plates slipped off. Celeste fed him. They sat around on the floor, eating off their laps and off Buffy. They all had Happy Eater napkins, there were plenty of those. Popsi had put a sprig of mistletoe in her hair. Lorna had found, hidden away, a Dizzy Gillespie record. She put it on. Nearly a quarter of a century earlier she had danced to this with Buffy, little knowing that their embraces would lead, after such a long hiatus, such a long, waking sleep, to the presence of this flushed young woman tenderly lifting his grizzled head and shovelling food in. A daughter, popped up from nowhere! As they all became drunker this fact struck them as both wonderfully strange and utterly inevitable.

Even Jacquetta had drunk a tumblerful of Cinzano. She looked down at Buffy. 'Remember those picnics in Provence, when Bruno and Tobias were babies? Remember the smell of lavender and camembert?'

'I remember everything,' said Buffy.

'Even when you were too drunk to remember,' said Penny.

He tapped his head. 'It's all in here. In my as yet unwritten

251

memoirs. Even as you sit here, like hyenas around the carcass of an old water buffalo.'

Celeste looked at the three ex-wives. 'Say it was worth it! You can't just switch it off, can you? Say it was all worth while!' She drained her glass; her brain buzzed. 'Say you miss him.'

Penny raised her hand. 'Only if we don't have to have him back.'

'I just want to know,' said Celeste. She had such a long, laborious past to recover, it had to mean something. All of it. Otherwise what was the point?

'I miss you.' Penny looked down at Buffy. 'I miss you when I want to go to the theatre. Thingy never goes to the theatre. I miss you when I've got something to say that only you'll understand. Something about tennis balls, for instance; I was thinking about rich people's tennis balls the other day. There are things I'll never have a reply to, now.' She munched, thoughtfully. 'I don't miss your dog, though.'

Popsi said: 'I was thinking about you only last week, pet. They'd pinned up this sign saying *More Stalls Upstairs*. You once said to me that there were two signs that always made you feel depressed, though you didn't know why. One was *More Stalls Upstairs* and the other was *Light Refreshments will be Served*.'

'You remember that?' asked Buffy.

She nodded.

'I don't,' he said.

'You weren't even that bad in bed,' said Penny. 'We were only joking, about the carrot.'

'What carrot?' demanded Buffy.

'We had our moments, didn't we?' she said. 'At least you *talked* afterwards. And during. Sometimes you talked so much we had to stop.'

'Ssh!' said Popsi, 'not in front of the children.'

Jacquetta gazed at a piece of ravioli, stuck on the end of her fork. 'I miss the person I was, with you. When somebody goes, the person you were, with them, that person disappears too. Nobody else can bring that person back. When a marriage breaks up, it's two people you've lost.'

There was a silence. 'That's deep,' said Popsi. The mistletoe had slid below her ear.

'It doesn't end, does it?' asked Celeste. 'Look, we're here! We're here now!'

They sat there, in tipsy contemplation. The meal was finished. They screwed up their napkins and threw them into the fire; the flames flared. They lifted their plates off Buffy's stomach. Celeste turned to her mother. 'Did you miss him?'

Lorna stood up, holding a handful of plates. Behind her, a piece of holly slipped beneath the picture frame and fell to the floor. She shook her head. 'Not really.' She stepped over Buffy, on her way to the kitchen. 'But I missed you.' She turned to Celeste. 'I missed you all the time. When I worked in Selfridges I thought you'd come in to try on a jumper. Then I moved to Dover and started a little flower shop. Weddings and christenings, we made up these bouquets. I thought – who knows? One day? Silly really, but I always hoped. Then they knocked us down to build a car park and the only job I could get round here was in catering. Not my thing really, but I thought – all those people passing through, surely one of them might be you? All those years, feeding other people . . . I thought you'd walk in the door and somehow I'd recognize you. I thought you'd be wearing the same sort of clothes I liked wearing, even the shoes. Which was ridiculous. I just thought I'd know who you were.' She paused, at the door. 'Oh, I missed you all right.'

Outside stood a snowman. Large and shapeless, it stood in the middle of the lawn. It wore Buffy's trilby hat and his overcoat. It stood facing the glowing curtains of the cottage. The conker eyes gazed sightlessly as the snowman stood facing the music. Dizzy Gillespie played, echoing down the years. Music to dance to, to fall in love to; music for sex and for love. The snowman stood there, freezing hard. Around it, the ground was scuffed and muddied by the children's feet.

The Dizzy Gillespie record finished with a click. They sat there in the silence. After a moment they realized it wasn't completely quiet; there was a low humming sound. Maybe it was the record-player motor.

They sat very still. Popsi belched. 'Whoops,' she said, 'pardon.'

They listened. There was a far rumbling sound, the sound of an engine. They held their breath; they felt like castaways, hearing the drone of an approaching airplane.

It was getting louder. Suddenly they jumped up and hurried to the window. Crowding around it, jostling each other, they pulled open the curtains. A sheep's skull fell to the floor.

They pressed their faces against the glass. Outside, a pair of headlights shone in the darkness.

'It's Leon,' said Jacquetta. 'Just when I was starting to enjoy myself.' She turned round and said to Buffy. 'He's always been jealous of you.'

'He hasn't!' said Buffy, from the floor. 'Has he?'

'Why do you think he writes all those books?'

Penny stared into the dark. Torchlight was approaching, bobbing across the garden. 'It's Colin, being all manly,' she said. 'do you know, he's never said he loves me. This is his inarticulate way of showing it.'

'I used to say I loved you!' said Buffy. 'All the time.'

Quentin nudged Penny aside and pressed his nose against the glass. The torchlight was closer now, dazzling him. 'Maybe it's Talbot,' he said. 'But I don't think so somehow. Anyway he can't drive.'

The doorbell rang. Lorna went out to answer it. The other women waited. For some reason they looked sheepish, as if they had been caught *in flagrante*. They heard a man's voice, in the hall. They heard the rumble of motors and more men's voices, out in the garden. They smelt exhaust fumes.

Lorna came back in. She spoke to Celeste. 'It's that man we met in the wood last night.'

Celeste stared at her. 'What?'

'That man who took such a fancy to you. The man with the awful wife.'

'He's here?'

'What an angel,' said Lorna. 'He's come to resuce us. He's got them to bring the snowplough down the lane.' She turned. 'Celeste?'

But Celeste had gone. She had stumbled over Buffy and rushed out into the hall.

Thirty-two

The next day the snow melted. In the wood the trees dripped; secret sighs and creaks. A soft thud as the snow loosened and fell from a bough. In Lorna's garden the snowman was melting. Gradually, Buffy thawed. The burly shape dwindled, perspiring in the sunshine. The overcoat sagged; the hat sank into its shoulders. As the hours passed it subsided gently into its own pool of water.

The next day, all that remained was a bundle of empty clothes on the scuffed and muddy grass. A puddle, surrounded by the skiddy footmarks of its children.

Thirty-three

Later, months later, when Celeste and Miles were living together, he said to her: 'Just think. A little tin of fishes led me to you, my gorgeous. Pilchards! I don't even like them. Do you?'

She shook her head. A little gold fish had led her, too – back into the past and forward into the future. Sometimes, when she looked back to the events of that winter it all seemed like a fairy story. If she went back to the antiques arcade Popsi's booth would be shuttered up with a metal grid. *Who? Nobody of that name here. Who has a name like that anyway?* If she opened the paper and read a travel piece by Penny who could believe it? Had Penny really sipped a daiquiri in Barbados or was she lying on somebody's floor spinning her own dreams? The recycling book was never published; the Leisure Experience was never built.

Waxie and the other squatters had long since moved into her flat and changed the locks. In fact she had never gone back at all. The rabbits and telephones and colanders; they had never really belonged to her. They were just props that had helped her form this new character, Celeste; props that seemed to mean something at the time, if only she had understood.

What did it all mean, and did it matter anymore? Everyone she loved, she had them now, and they had her. She had joined them. She had even helped create an ex-wife of her own – Brenda, languishing in Swindon. She felt so guilty about this that she had started to read Leon's book. She had joined them all right, her tumultuous new family.

And that afternoon she was meeting Buffy for tea. They were going to plan his delayed sixtieth birthday party, to which everyone was invited. They had to meet early because he was working that night. He was playing Mr Hardcastle in *She Stoops to Conquer* and, what with the wig and whatnot, the make-up took ages.